Lightning in my Wires

CAITLIN AVERY

*Andrea —
Everyone has stories to tell...
Some of ours crisscross :)
Hope you enjoy it
("Mike" sure did)
xo Caitlin*

For Mom and Dad:

Who taught me my very first lessons in love.

"If the Reader prefers,
this book may be regarded as fiction."

~ Earnest Hemingway
"A Moveable Feast"

"Your vision will become clear only when you look into your heart. Who looks outside dreams; who looks inside awakens." ~ Carl Jung

Saturday, February 2, 2002

A Special News Report interrupted the Oprah show yesterday to cut to a press conference with the President. It's been five months since the terrorist attack on the World Trade Center. Now the President has announced plans for an attack on certain Arab states. I'm saddened by our current policy on foreign affairs. America is suffering from post-traumatic stress, and like everyone, I yearn for assurance. But the thought of a pre-emptive strike does nothing to reassure me. Nor do the government recommendations to buy duct tape and a gas mask. In the midst of my anxiety about the impending threat of violence, I realize that I might achieve a sense of security if Max and I get engaged. So I waltz into his office to address the state our union. He balks, says he's balancing the budget.

"Max," I implore, "if you want to learn to communicate you need to practice, and there's no time like the present." He just sits there, speechless.

Max is happy to discuss the plot to kill Bin Laden, but he'd rather run away or hide in a cave than talk about love. So I take the helm and enumerate the reasons why it's time for us to talk about marriage. I remind him that I broached the subject last summer and he said he needed more time to think about it, so I generously gave him six-months. I also point out that the one-year anniversary of the day we moved in together is right around the corner. On Valentine's Day last year he'd presented two little boxes to me. One of them contained a heart-shaped charm from Tiffany's and the other held a key to the new house he'd bought; a proposition for me to move in with him. I hope to get another proposition from Tiffany's this year to make it all official. It doesn't have to be Tiffany's; any two-carat, three-stone, square-cut diamond ring will do, but now is not the time to talk about details. Instead I emphasize my point with a mild dose of sarcasm. "Times a wasting—and you're no spring chicken, you know." Max says he feels like an old man lately, at the tender age of thirty-three.

With a faraway look in his eyes, he says, "Give me a minute to finish this." I retreat to the living room, to give him space and time. I have butterflies. This could be an important moment in our relationship! Maybe I should get my camera. I want to remember exactly how it happens. Too late, he's in the hallway. I grab a seat on the couch, cross my legs, and act as relaxed as possible. Max enters the room and sits down next to me. "You're the first woman I've ever wanted to marry," he says with a smile. I soak in his wonderful words. He takes a deep breath, I hold mine, and with a whale of an exhale he explains, "But the way I feel these days, I don't know what the future holds. I'm sorry. I need to focus on myself right now. Which is why [big sigh]...I think you should move out."

Max was recently diagnosed Manic-Depressive. I've learned to accept the dark declarations on his down days, but I also know that manic Max might whisk me away to get married in Paris. It's not always clear which end of the spectrum he's on. This is not what I expected.

"Max," I whine, "breaking up won't solve your problems..."

"I'm suffocating. I don't know what else to do."

My first thought is: You've got to be kidding. I just spent the entire year decorating this place! I try counting to ten (my shrink's latest suggestion for anger management) but it's a weak attempt, and temper gets the best of me. "You want me to leave?" I seethe. "After all I've put up with? I stuck around through your depression, your secrecy, and all your other malfunctions. I can wait to get married, but I refuse to move out in the meantime. We need to work on this together."

Why can't Max see that 'we' will be fine as soon as he applies the lessons he's learned in therapy? I've seen a shrink off and on for ten years, and know all too well about the healing power of psychiatry. The right balance of meds and a good analysis is all he really needs, that, and maybe a dose or two of Viagra.

I'm about to delve into another diatribe when the doorbell rings. Nice timing. I head for the door and put an end to this nonsense. "Obviously you need more time to think about it."

"Fine," he sighs. "I'm going for a ride." He slinks out to the driveway as I swing open the front door. The postman hands me a large box. Mom has sent me a care package. Ha! At least somebody appreciates me. This gift could not have come at a better time. I sign on the dotted line then head to the kitchen to grab a sharp knife and a stiff drink. I'm about to unveil the contents of the package when Max tears down the street on his motorcycle.

An hour later I'm nestled on the couch, salting my second margarita with a bunch of tears, when Max calls to apologize. He asks me to bear with him. He's in the Marina, gassing up the boat to go lobster hunting. "Don't wait up" he insists. "I'll be home after midnight." I blow my nose, wipe my eyes, and go into caretaker mode. "I hate it when you go diving alone." He promises to double check the anchor, says 'I love you', and goodbye. Satisfied with our reconciliation, I pour myself a celebratory drink and plunk back down on the couch to open the box again.

A note from my mother says she's sent the entire collection of my scholastic history: stories, poems, paintings, and every report card I ever received. "Now that you're good and settled in your own house," she writes, "it's time for you to take over the storage of this childhood memorabilia." I lift the stack of manila folders to find a navy blue electric blanket. Shortly after we moved into our four-bedroom abode I convinced Max to move our bed outdoors, to the open-air gazebo that takes up half the back yard. Inside the gazebo is a fountain that runs out of a rock wall and into a blue-green pool filled with Japanese goldfish. The water empties into a moat that runs around the gazebo. This, combined with the massive stone fireplace, creates an incredible atmosphere for sleep. The electric blanket is a perfect addition to this scenario.

Wrapped inside the blanket are two worn-out diaries and a stack of withered poems. How appropriate. The diaries were tucked between my mattress and box spring for more than a decade; they probably feel right at home in bedding. Skimming through them, I'm reminded that Max isn't the only one with problems. I've been in therapy long enough to know I have my own row to hoe when it comes to mental health. A teacher once told me, "When you point your finger at somebody else, there are three fingers pointing back at you". I realize I was a little hard on him. Max feels bad enough about himself. He doesn't need me to berate him. I'm such an idiot. No wonder he won't marry me! To ease the pain of the guilt, I mix another cocktail. A bubble bath seems like a good place to ponder my disgrace, so I stumble to the tub and run the hottest water I can stand. My head starts to pound. I scrounge around in the linen closet for the Ibuprofen. The bottle is wedged behind the birth control pills I've abandoned, a sad reminder of our abstinence. There's also a balled up tissue that hides a razor blade.

Cutting is a vice that's gripped me since I was a kid. It's the easiest way for me to absolve my sins. Max doesn't understand it. The last time I cut myself he made me promise never again, but that was before I found his secret stash of cocaine and decided he had no right to dictate rules for good behavior. Besides, I'll be in bed by the time he gets home, so he'll never know. I realize I'll have to tell my shrink about it next week, but that'll be an impetus to discuss the bigger issues.

I strip down and stand naked in front of the vanity. Tying my shoulder length blond hair back with a rubber band, I note that it needs some fresh highlights. My reflection stares back at me. It likes what it sees. My addiction to exercise helps me look like I'm twenty. Ten years out of high school and I still have the six pack of abs I developed as a Varsity gymnast. Closing the bathroom door to reduce the chill in the air, I pinch my nipples and relish their wrinkled erection. Then I cup my breasts, give them a tender squeeze, and decide that's where I'll cut this time. Given our lack of intimacy, it's the one place Max will never notice. With margarita in hand and razor in the other, I step carefully into the tub.

The effect is cinematic. Red droplets mix with the steam of the bath and run like tributaries into the jasmine scented foam. Unfortunately, I'm too drunk to feel anything. I do enjoy the precision of the blade though. Smooth and sharp, I bleed without going deep, which prevents any permanent scaring. After a bunch of superficial incisions I'm done. Calm washes over me. I take one last sip of my drink, admire my penance, and then slip into sleep. I don't even sober up when Max coaxes me out of the tub shortly after midnight.

When I wake up at noon, Max has been up for hours. He washes the salt water from his scuba equipment as I stumble into the shower to wash away the salt water from my tears. The hot water burns my damaged breasts as sickness churns in my empty stomach. I squat because it's difficult to stand. Moments later, I'm huddled on a chair in the bedroom bundled up in my yellow robe, when Max enters. It takes a while for him to speak. Finally, without eye contact, he mutters, "I need you to move out. I can't live like this."

    The fog from my hangover lifts as the midday sun shines on the damage I've done. *I can't live like this either.* Overwhelmed by remorse, I retreat to the bathroom, crumple on the floor next to the toilet and rest my heavy head against the cool white porcelain. Time stops, despite the clock's incessant ticking. Through a liquid haze I gaze up at the stained glass window above the sink, and wonder: how will I survive without this opulence? I listen to the sound of the water as it splashes down the fountain outside. Doves coo on the live wire above the house. Our German shepherd barks at a passerby. Fresh tears sting my swollen eyes as I run my hand across the mosaic tiles of the table I made for Max last year. I'm crouched at the edge of my own personal ground zero. The world as I know it is ending. All hope for homeland security is gone.

"We act as though comfort and luxury were the chief requirements of life, when all that we need to make us really happy is something to be enthusiastic about."

~ Charles Kingsley

Monday, February 4

I'm having another bad day. I just got off the phone with my folks and I can't believe it; the special delivery from Mom last week was meant to deliver me an angry little message. If it weren't for her knack for subtle sarcasm, the package would've had "fuck you" written all over it. "Fuck you" is more my father's style. He's not afraid to say what's on his mind, especially when he feels slighted. So it shouldn't surprise me that Dad had to explain Mom's disdain after she handed the phone to him in the middle of our conversation, citing irreconcilable differences. In the end, I was not able defend myself. My mother refused to talk and I didn't have the energy to duke it out with Dad. Guess I'll have to bitch to you instead.

Max and I stayed with my folks at Thanksgiving when I brought him to Boston for my high school reunion. During his initial tour of their place I mentioned how great some of their furnishings would look in our house. We've been trying to figure out how we could jazz up our budding abode. My parents have this blue and white checkered, antique wash bin they brought back from Munich in 1975. It resides in my earliest memories as a toddler in Germany, and I've always assumed I'll wind up with it someday. According to my mom, it was some comment along those lines that made her feel like I had one hand on her will and the other one on the lid of her casket. My mother is 56. What did she think I meant? Hurry up and die, so I can get my hands on that amazing wash bin? Give me a break. It'd be one thing if she was pushing ninety and I'm tip-toeing around placing nametags on all the valuables. I just wanted to get in touch with my own interior design sense. God forbid I've inherited the same taste as my mother.

Evidently that's not the only thing I did that pissed her off. A few days later I came across some old records in a drawer where my schoolwork and diaries were stored. With jubilation I exclaimed: "Hey, these are mine!" What Mom heard was: "What are you creeps doing with all my stuff?" I certainly understand why she'd be offended if that's what I said. Anyway, according to Dad, she thinks I'm unbearably selfish, so she rid her drawers of everything she's graciously stored for me all these years.

After my father shared that tidbit I didn't have the strength to admit that Max is about to toss my stuff out of his house too. I also haven't the strength to call the antique store to cancel the untimely order I placed with them two weeks ago. After three months of contemplation, I purchased an eighteenth century Italian armoire for the living room, and requested some custom adjustments before they delivered it, this morning. Grandma passed away last year and I inherited a little money. I wanted to spend it on something I'd own forever; a special memento, to honor my grandparents and pass on to my grandkids someday—so long as they didn't mention they wanted it while I was still alive.

I went back to the antique store five times before I committed. So here I sit, sneering at my gorgeous contribution to a house I must vacate as soon as possible. This armoire is proof purchase that "nesting" has been my defense against reality since the day I moved in here, and my buyer's remorse is amplified by one simple fact—I totally saw this breakup coming.

By the end of the six-day stay with my folks I was ready to end things with Max. During our visit he went from charismatic to despondent. For the first few days he couldn't talk enough about cameras with my photographer father. By the end of the week he was monosyllabic, hardly uttering a word to me, let alone my family. The night of my reunion he was so disengaged, and pissed for no apparent reason, that I was embarrassed to introduce him. When I pressed him to act a little more civil towards my friends, he stormed out of the hotel and wandered around Boston until five o'clock in the morning. Then he scaled the wall of my parent's condo, climbed in the three story window, and snuck into bed like nothing had happened. My parents were surprised to see him the next morning, since they knew I'd come home solo, but I'd warned them about his mental diagnosis, so we all just chalked it up as appropriate behavior for a guy who was certifiably crazy. It was a far cry from the way I described him in the months leading up to our trip. Family and friends had heard all about our amazing love affair. Come show time, Max would not support the façade. The problem was that he was supposed to be perfect: charming, devilish, witty and playful, wealthy, well dressed, and undeniably handsome.

When we first started dating I thought I'd won the boyfriend lottery, especially after our trip to France. I'd known him for four days when he invited me to St. Tropez. Three weeks of topless tanning on the Cote D'Azur was an instant cure for the depression I'd wrestled with before we met. Max confessed that he'd been depressed as well. On the flight back to L.A., he dutifully tried to describe the severity of his mood swings to me. "Consider your self forewarned," he said. I didn't believe him. I mean, how bad could his attitude be when he had the money to flee whenever he needed to? I decided as long as I caught a regular glimpse of his bright side, I could accept the shady side too.

Thanksgiving was the first time he got depressed during a vacation. It was the first indication I had that my maniacal superman was being medicated into submission. "Balanced" meant he was no longer tempted to drive his motorcycle head first into a wall, but he didn't have the I-can-do-anything zest for adventure either. It also translated as "celibate", because none of his nine medications made any improvement to his mysterious—and complete—lack of testosterone. So the rollercoaster ride that was our love affair acquired the monotony of a Ferris wheel in the short time it took two psychiatrists and a physician to squeeze Max into a test tube of experimental drug therapy. As I began to realize there would be no firecracker state anymore, I no longer felt like a winner. Instead I wondered how bad it would have to get for me to leave him. The line was drawn right in front of where we stood when we left Boston.

I changed my tune when he swept me away for another amazing rendezvous right after Christmas. A month ago we returned home in a Gulf Stream jet after six days of skiing in Sun Valley, Idaho. Max is an attorney and the private flight was courtesy of one of his biggest clients, Mr. Robert Marshall, who owns a casino in Vegas. We headed home to recover for a day before cruising to Catalina Island on Max's 38-foot speed boat, for a black tie New Year's Eve event. This exciting getaway rekindled the romance, and convinced me to give it one last chance. How can I walk away from the glamour of it all? I thought. I'd rather stay and slit my wrists every once in awhile.

Unfortunately, we're both miserable human beings and exorbitant excursions can no longer eradicate our pathetic perspectives. Buying the armoire wasn't nearly as stupid as asking Max to discuss marriage last week. Maybe I should pick up the phone and call my shrink right now. I could fax over the diaries Mom sent, and tell her they're Cliff's Notes for the tragedy that is the history of my love life. And all this regret is exacerbated by the fact that the antique store cannot accept returns on purchases that have been altered at the customer's request. That's a loose translation of what the Mexican delivery guy said when I tried to refuse the armoire. I really want to take a hammer to the beveled mirrors, the misery they reflect is so ugly—oh, that's just me.

Maybe I should try packing again. The original plan for today, it was a fantastic outlet for my anger. As I yanked the picture frames off the freshly painted walls the holes they left behind expressed exactly how I feel. I really hate to leave this incredible home. Saying goodbye to Max isn't as painful as saying goodbye to his possessions. I decorated this house like the one that resides in my dreams and thought the perfect surroundings would create a perfect existence. I really believed the periwinkle walls would make Max happy again. When I consider all the pills he has to pop each day, I see I was a little off base.

I don't have much faith that those pills will solve his problems. I've spent a pretty penny on anti-depressants over the years and they haven't fixed me. The good news is: if money can't buy happiness, I can quit crying about the fact that my economic status is about to nose-dive. Ugh—back to apartment living, with a roommate. I don't even own a car right now. Max has been loaning me his. I have a motorcycle and a bike, but a car is so much more comfortable. So who cares? For the last year I've lived in the lap of luxury, and where did that get me? Maybe comfort has little to do with satisfaction.

There are a couple of things in this house that make me truly happy and I refuse to leave without them. Sandy and Pebbles are the kittens I adopted last year. They don't need much, and they provide me with endless hours of entertainment. As long as I have them to get me through the next few months I won't need much either. You know what? Forget this easy living. If the cats can live without the koi pond, so can I. Better to leave behind a legacy of happiness then a dumb old armoire anyway. That settles it. From here on out, I'm going for broke—and contentment.

Saturday, February 9

Its official: I'm out of here. I'll move out on Valentine's Day, which bookends our co-habitation quite nicely. This time last year I was celebrating what I thought was the precursor to a future engagement. Now I'm debating whether or not to gift wrap Max's house key in a Tiffany's box before I return it to him on Thursday. Better watch the sarcasm, he might take offense and refuse to loan me his truck to carry my stuff to the new place. He's acting like a real gentleman, all too happy to assist me with my move. He even bought me a new computer today, as a going away gift. Great, he gets to keep the dream house and I get a stupid computer. Smells like a consolation prize, and I'm responding to it the same way I did one Christmas when I was three.

In 1976 I asked Santa for an airplane. I wound up with a model version that was small enough for my parents to fit into the overhead compartment on the flight to my

Grandparent's house in Ohio. I'd clearly specified in my letter to Santa that I wanted a plane I could climb into, one that would be capable of soaring to great heights as well. In short, I wanted a plane I could fly. I was hugely disappointed by the toy substitute I unwrapped on Christmas morning, and had a little tantrum. Earlier today when Max presented the computer to me, I wanted to throw that sucker like I'd thrown the plane. But I'm an adult, so I counted to ten instead. That didn't work to cool me down either, so I grabbed my bicycle and headed off at breakneck speed towards the beach. I rode fifty miles before I felt tranquil enough to return.

 I just got back from Palos Verdes. It feels great to go out and sweat when I'm stuck in a sour disposition; physical work beats the anger right out of me. Peace by shear exhaustion is better than no peace at all. On the way back I collected a little extra serenity when I passed several signs along the bike path that advertised a "Peace Parade" next month. The organization that posted the flyers is practicing a Season of Nonviolence in response to the terrorists attack six months ago. Peace must be exactly what I need to practice right now, since I actually had the notion to stop and grab a flyer. Normally nothing can slow me down during a workout. Just the other day some cute guy asked for directions while I was in the middle of a great run and instead of pausing to talk to him like a normal person, I made him drive along side me while I huffed out the information. This time, some greater good got me to stop. Although in the time it took to cram the flyer into a pocket stuffed with a patch kit, Power Bar and Goo, my heart rate never dropped below 160. So it can hardly be considered resting.

    I put the Peace Parade on my list of things to do as soon as I got home. I've been making a lot of lists lately, but they have nothing to do with the move. They have to do with which direction I'm headed from here. I think I'm finally ready to end the battle for sanity that's raged inside me since I was a teen. I spent the last week perusing my old journals and I'm tired of all the dissatisfaction. I need a new MO. Maybe I should check out the center that's sponsoring this 'Season of Nonviolence'. I'll put that down as number four on the list of things I'm willing to try to control my mind. The first three are: yoga, meditation, and a complete frontal lobotomy. Yoga has been part of my exercise life for the last year and I notice a distinct improvement in my attitude for about thirty minutes after the class. Unfortunately, I only do yoga once a week and the serenity doesn't stick.

    Come to think of it, writing seems to calm me too. I should add that to the list. Long before I started smoking pot, I wrote poetry to defuse the lightning in my wires. When I was a kid, my parents gave me an option to read for a half an hour past bedtime. I don't know if the stories kept me awake or what, but my mind continued to fire despite my parents command to put it all to rest. And counting sheep seemed like an incredible waste of time.

So under the inauspicious glow of a flashlight, I transformed insomnia into reverie. Afraid to get caught with the light on, I worked with incredible efficiency. I'd construct the entire verse in my head before I grabbed the pen. Granted, I tossed and turned a bit first, but when I was ready to write the words came to me like an immaculate conception. By the last line I'd be drifting off, as if the pen had been dipped in sleeping potion.

I wonder if the Zoloft has numbed my need for poetic escapism. Chemical warfare on the brain has been known to kill the creativity in artists and geniuses alike. Or perhaps it's the pot and the vodka that put me to sleep these days. Maybe I should try conquering my demons through writing again. Some guy named Edward Lytton once said, "The pen is mightier than the sword". Maybe it's time to lay the razorblades down and put that computer to good use. Guess I should thank Max for it after all.

Wednesday, February 13

I'm restless after a futile hour with my shrink this afternoon. Dr Brown acted like my tale was stale this time. I guess she's bored with hearing about the same old shit. I know I'm sick of wallowing in it. As she drifted off, I wondered: what's the point of all this yapping? Week after week she asks the questions and I give the answers—shouldn't it be the other way around? The only direction she offered me today was, "You can't continue to do the same thing and expect different results." Duh, I know I need to change my ways, but I don't know how. Unfortunately Dr. Brown frowns on offering specific instructions. It'll probably take many more sessions for me to figure it out on my own. Lucky her, how else could she afford her Beverly Hills home?

I left her office in a funk today, only to return to the house of pain. I hate this place, since it's no longer mine. I'm sure Max can't wait to lock the door behind me tomorrow. That's right: V-day is the day our breakup becomes official. I haven't had time to contemplate this rejection because I've been preoccupied with my move. Now there's nothing left to do. Everything is boxed, except my sorrow. I'm tempted to drop into the void and get wasted, but—a la the advice of Dr. Brown—I know I need to find new ways to deal with frustration. Better to remove myself from this space, and steer clear of Max and medicinal temptation. I'm trying to decide between yoga and a movie when I notice the "Peace Parade" flyer I got in Venice last week. Upon closer inspection I see the event is sponsored by an organization called "Agape". In addition to parade information, the flyer says, "Join us on Wednesday nights from 7-9". I decide to give it a try—just in the nick of time. At a quarter to seven Max pulls in as I back out of the driveway.

    Twenty minutes later I steer my motorcycle into the industrial park that houses Agape, in Culver City. It's ten past the hour, so I hurry past a bunch of dread-locked folks and push my way through the double doors of a nondescript warehouse. Muffled acoustic music seeps out of second set of doors at the end of a long hallway. I quietly slip through entrance number two into a massive room filled with a few thousand chairs. A bald man in a paisley shirt sits on the stage strumming a guitar while hundreds of audience members sit silent and still with their eyes closed. It looks like a sanctuary. Great, I wanted something to distract me from the voices in my head, now I hope the same voices entertain me during the inevitable sermon. I imagine this is how my shrink feels each time she dutifully prepares to listen to a bunch of bull. I'm tempted to make a run for it but then a sweet-faced lady hands me a program and ushers me to my seat.

I glance at the people beside me. The young woman on my left looks like she hasn't had a hair cut, ever. The woman next to her is polar opposite; sassy and sixty, she wears giant gold loops in her ears; they compete for attention with her bouffant do. Her outfit screams Knot's Landing. As a matter of fact, I think she *is* one of the actresses from Knot's Landing! I sneak a second peak as the guitarist pockets his pick and a chubby cheeked black man approaches the pulpit. I prepare to grin and bear it, but the guy breaks into song instead. At least they have good music. No sooner do I relax in my seat when the preacher arrives and begins his speech. My skin starts to crawl. The word "God" gives me hives, and this guy won't talk about anything else. I'm about to climb inside my head and ignore him when the Reverend mentions unconditional love. He says that's what "Agape" means. Then he adds that it's

Greek, for LOVE FEAST. Suddenly I'm hungry to hear more.

Unfortunately, this quick side note offers brief relief from a whole lot more talk about God. Rather then stress about allergenic message in the microphone, I focus my attention on the paintings that adorn the purple walls. Each picture features a woman in flowing garb, encircling a luminous sphere. Magenta, lavender, and blue, the sweeping strokes in oil and watercolor, enrapture me. The colorful fairies lead me down memory lane, as I recall a similar maiden I created as a kid. Suddenly the Reverend's words are drowned out by a sea of nostalgia...

Sunday morning: 1985. I'm combing the beach during a church retreat on the coast of Maine. Sand dollars rise to the top of my bucket filled with ocean jewels. Gulls hover above, waiting for a handout. They smell seaweed and think I have treats for them, but these shells are ornaments for my mermaid, and I protect them as if they're offspring of the Hope diamond. My hope is that I win top prize in the sandcastle contest. Even at age twelve I aggressively pursue the sweet smell of success called "first place".

This is the Sunday school of my childhood. Our congregation has convened on the beach and stragglers are being summoned for the sunrise service. It's hard to tear myself away from the task at hand. I need to collect the best decorations before the other kids descend; the early bird catches the pearl. But then Guitar Man strikes up a cord and Mom waves me over for the ceremony. We open with the song "Puff the Magic Dragon". In a church filled with hippies, some of the elders have already puffed the magic dragon. We all have our agendas, although it's scarcely six a.m.

Surrounded by the scenery of an infinite ocean, how can I be expected to pay attention to the Minister's remarks? The Sand Pipers tease me, I want to bob and weave in the waves as well. Their dance entrances me—I love the element of danger. The little birds risk life and limb to catch crabs that scurry under the surf. The white water must seem like a tidal wave to a four-inch piper; and they run with neurosis, as if braving the break for the very last time. I am mesmerized. Eventually my attention gets drawn back to the circle by the James Taylor tune, "How sweet it is to be loved by you".

This I can jive with, since my experiences at summer camp include many a James Taylor song sung around the campfire. This particular song refers to God, I think, although I never really notice any mention of God in our Unitarian services. We never read The Bible anyway. I can't recall any theological expressions from church, although I do remember planting daisy's on Easter Sunday, and making hand-dipped candles at the autumn festival, and singing carols on the front steps of our Puritan tabernacle on Christmas Eve. I also remember the sound of the bell as it rang out from our 18th century steeple to announce the hundredth birthday of our eldest member. "Older than God", he declared, with his mouth full of cake, and I believed him. So the only image of God I had etched upon my mind as a child was of Clayton McKinnon, who owned a liquor store in Lincoln, and talked with his mouth full.

Tonight, at the age of twenty-nine, I gaze up at the collection of painted pixies and see a new and improved version: Goddesses—who happen to look a lot like me. I'm strangely comforted by this scene, as I remember the Unitarian church as wild and free, a place that shaped me into who I am today. And I still enjoy a good sing-along, which is why I return to the present tense when the paisley guitar guy breaks into a soulful rendition of, "You've got a Friend," by James Taylor—one of my all-time favorites. I jubilantly join the Agape crowd in harmony.

When the song ends I look around at the vast room of people as they celebrate what they've received. Like the good old days, I haven't paid attention to what's been said, but I still feel like spirit has found me. I get the sense it has something important to say to me, so I listen with intent. The Reverend asks the newcomers to stand. I rise slowly and join twenty others who look as apprehensive as me. The congregation blesses us, and then the ushers hand out love notes that welcome us to Agape. It's the first love note I've received in a very long time. As I sit back down to listen to the benediction I hear one thing loud and clear: "God is love—a love that's there no matter what."

When the service ends, I clutch my love note and file out of the sanctuary. I feel much better then I did when I arrived. Floating through the parking lot, I zip and snap my jacket to prepare for the breeze of the freeway. Suddenly, I realize what was wrong with my therapy today. All I did was talk, but I don't need to learn to talk. I need to learn to listen. The thought of that makes me snicker as I wedge the love note behind the windshield of my bike. Swinging my leg over the saddle, I secure my helmet, and turn the key. "Happy Valentine's Day," I say, out loud. And my engagement to myself is under way.

"The important thing is this: to be able at any moment to sacrifice what we are for what we could become."

~ Charles Dubois

Sunday, February 17

I woke up in a black hole this morning. The white walls of my new room should feel like clean slate, but right now they seem like a sad contrast to the colorful existence I left behind at Max's. This is the fifth place I've moved to in the last five years. Looks like I'm a serial nomad. And with no man, no career, and no car, there's really no reason for me to call this place home either, so what's the point of unpacking? Maybe I should leave the walls blank and redecorate the interior of my soul instead—it hasn't felt livable in a long time. Or I could just embrace the vacancy, pull the covers over my head and sleep for the rest of the day.

Fuck, no such luck. The kittens heard me stir and now they insist that I feed them, the little buggers don't pay any heed to my melancholy. I shuffle to the kitchen to fill their bowls. If only these fish flavored nuggets could please me so, I'd spend the rest of the day on a Friskies binge. Aside from their munching, the apartment is saturated in silence. My roommate's bedroom door is shut and I don't know if she's asleep or gone; we're strangers still and I'm unfamiliar with her tendencies. Max has probably been up for hours. He used to wake me up on Sunday mornings with a tray that held coffee, the newspaper, and a Gardenia in a tiny vase. It's so lonely here. I hate it when my day starts out like this! Nine o'clock in the morning and already I need an attitude adjustment, or perhaps a bullet in the head.

    I plop on the couch to figure out what I should do today. In order to climb out of this abyss I need to find some sort of community. I phone my friends to see if they'll hang out with me. After two calls I've exhausted all possibilities. What a loser I am, and it's my own fault for abandoning my comrades in exchange for Max's social scene. I was so involved with high society parties and excursions on Max's boat last year that I failed to maintain my friendships. So Max gets the house, the boat, and all the playmates too, while I am left with nothing. Calamity is out to get me, so I return to my room for a wake and bake bong hit, where I find the flyer for the Peace Parade has slid to the floor in the night. I stick it to the tack board propped against my desk. Agape's schedule of services is listed at the bottom of the page, there's a sermon at eleven o'clock today. I'm not quite sure why their service made me feel so good the other night, but I could use another taste of whatever it was. Luckily I have just enough time to get dressed and zoom down there.

The extra time it takes to get stoned makes me late and I arrive to a standing room only. I wonder if discomfort will be worth the insight I hope to collect as I dodge all the God talk. To sneak out now would be rude so I accept my position as great vantage point to check out the crowd. Ganja-awareness helps sweeten the eye-candy as I absorb the spectrum of color that radiates through the room. There's a huge variation in skin tone, and the cultural menagerie is outfitted in an even grander variety of couture: I see Birkenstocks, high heels, bellbottoms, silk suits, skull caps and African head wraps.

After gawking for a half an hour my attention eventually turns to the words of the sermon. "We all have the ability to create an ideal existence through prayer and meditation," the Reverend says. "When it comes to change, you must plant the seed. Then feed it every day, until the universe receives what you want to achieve. And when life gets tough," he adds, "a positive perspective provides us with the power to survive less-than- perfect circumstances." I'm completely psyched about what he says until God enters the picture, and suddenly my interest returns to the visual stimuli. Glancing around the room, I notice a woman with her eyes closed and her hands placed palm up on her thighs. She has her thumbs and index fingers pressed together in a ring. Ten seats down from her is a man in the same position. These people are peppered all along the back wall. I think to myself, how rude to be so zoned out! At least I have the decency to pretend like I want to listen. But at the end of the benediction the Reverend thanks them for their meditation. Then he says they're here to offer spiritual mind treatments to anyone in need. I know I need something but a mind treatment sounds a little wacky. I opt to adopt his positive perspective instead. In an attempt to look on the bright side of life for the rest of this day, I slip out of the warehouse and into the light, wearing peaches and cream colored shades.

 Unfortunately, optimism fades when I return to the apartment to find my roommate is gone for the day. This tidbit of info is part of the message she left about someone named Adrian, who called me at ten. But I was here at ten, why didn't she tell me then? I didn't hear the phone ring. Guess she was on the other line. Oh well, I wish I knew if it was Adrianna who called. Adrianna lives in North Carolina and I haven't talked to her since our high school reunion last year. Seems like a good enough reason to give her a buzz. I really want to connect with someone.

I grab the phone. Lo and behold she did call this morning, to tell me she's pregnant—with twins! This is huge news. Adrianna's the first of my friends to get pregnant and it blows my mind. Talk about seeds of change. I can't even comprehend all the change she's about to face in the name of motherhood. I also can't seem to stir up any genuine congratulations because the contrast between her situation and mine totally depresses me. The only aspect of the conversation I can appreciate is the fact that it's over the phone, so she can't see me cry as I lie about how thrilled I am. The more she exudes joy, the more impossible the concept becomes, and sadness swells with every fake felicitation I offer her. By the end of the call I feel horrible. The Rev. said the trick to a satisfied life is to not let bad news wreck your perspective. So what do you do when good news ruins you? I go back to bed.

At a quarter to four my feet hit the floor in a meager attempt to face the light of day again. I might have dismissed the afternoon altogether if it hadn't been for the ring of my cell phone calling me to enter the land of the living—room. I missed the call, but received an important message: to give this forgettable day a second thought.

Party pal Danielle called to say she was headed to the Westside for an impromptu Bar-B-Q in my neighborhood and thought I'd want to join her. Seems like a perfect plan, so I hop in the shower to cleanse my negative attitude and prepare for a fun-filled drunken evening.

    I begin my trek to the party at six. The sun has sunk and I feel bad that I spent the most of the weekend in a funk. I still feel moody and need to psyche myself up for the social scene. Barrington Liquor is the first stop on my five block stomp. I purchase a liter of Stoli, a quart of cranberry, and thank god for the strong Cape Cod that's about to cap off this crappy day. I recognize that my enormous urge to catch a buzz may mean trouble. Nothing good ever comes out of my decision to get shit faced, and tonight the temptation to overindulge is undeniable. As I haul ass up the gradual hill towards San Vicente, wild energy pulses through me. An elevated pulse pumps blood to my broken heart and makes me feel alive again. But then something I heard at the service this morning pops into my brain and tells me to slow down, and take some responsibility for my destiny.

    I downshift into second gear, wait for the coast to clear and cut across busy Barrington to enter the quieter part of the neighborhood instead. As I wind around the block I breathe the cool air of this crisp February night and remember the relaxed look of the people as they meditated at Agape this morning. I decide to meditate for the rest of my route, but unfortunately, I'm not quite sure what that means. Closing my eyes is not an option and I don't know what else to do. So I stare at the ground, continue to place one foot in front of the other and try to will some sort of spiritual intuition. What am I supposed to do? I wonder. Should I ask the universe a question? I look to the sky for guidance—and there it is, right before my very eyes. Pasted to a second-story apartment window for the entire world to see is a sign painted in large block letters that reads: LOVE IS THE ANSWER. I'm still not sure what the question is, but at least I've got the answer.

Ten minutes later I arrive at the bar-B and present the host with a gift of Stoli. Then I tell him I'd like a cranberry juice on the rocks. After two hours of idle chitchat I head back home. Now I'm sitting here all alone again but I feel so much better than I did before. Although I am a little stir crazy from too much sleep. Sure wish I knew how to meditate—guess I'll have to ruminate instead. As far as that sign goes, I don't know exactly where I'm supposed find the love that is the answer for me, but developing some self-respect seems like a good place to start. Hey, I showed some impressive restraint tonight when it came to getting hammered. I think I'll smoke a little pot now as my reward. What can I say? I'm looking for love, not perfection.

Friday, February 22

Package number two arrived from my mother just now—I'm afraid to open it, could be a whole new can of worms. Is this one meant to sting or to comfort me? She didn't mention anything about it when we spoke last week, perhaps she was preoccupied with the news of my breakup. I hate to discuss failure with my folks so they became privy to the news of the move a few days before it happened. They were empathetic, but not at all surprised. After Max's depressive display in Boston they had the notion that our relationship was on the rocks. The fact that Max and I quit speaking at the end of the week was a good indication that our days were numbered. I can't believe that I chose a man who fights like my mother—a la incommunicado. Unfortunately for me, and for the powers that be, communication breakdowns often result in a hostility that leads to war.

And war is what I will declare if this package contains another passive-aggressive message from Mom; with all that I've been through in the last month I could use a knock down, drag out fight. I guess I should leave it sealed for a while. I'm still a little shell shocked from the revelations her last package produced, and the contents disturb me more than the context under which they were sent. I was surprised by my mother's spite, but I'm stupefied to find how much the thoughts in my juvenile diaries resemble contemplations today. Twenty-nine, and I still whine daily about the lack of control and joy in my life.

Is it human nature to focus on the injustice in our lives? The leaders of the free world sure seem to gravitate towards constant contention. Shuffling through my old poems last night I found one I wrote when I was ten, called "War". Today I worry about a terrorist attack on LA, back then I worried about Gorbachev and his Russian Brigade. The year was 1983 and our nemesis was the Soviet Union. I was in the fifth grade when "The Morning After" premiered on national television. The film examined what would happen if a nuclear bomb was dropped on American soil. My younger brother and I were not allowed to watch it. My parents wanted to shelter us from propaganda about nuclear war, but that didn't stop me from being consumed by concern. I spent a lot of time wondering when we were going to be obliterated by the almighty A-bomb.

My anxiety climaxed the morning after "The Morning After" debuted. During my daily dog walk before school the voice inside my head said I might not make it to middle school if Russia dropped The Bomb. A fear-filled conception drove me to hurry home, where I showered my mind with remedial rhyme as I conditioned my hair. With only ten minutes to prep before breakfast I forfeited getting dressed so I could pen my elegy instead. In the end, it was a powerful purge that swept those fears away. I can remember it clear as day. Hastily wrapped in a towel, my hair dripped down my back and onto my cherry red carpet as I wrote the entire verse in ten minutes. Inspired by the war in the Middle East at the time, it went like this:

> War is nothing you say young man?
> Ahhh, but it is, just look at Iran.
> Everybody's fighting, no love is there,
> People are dying and nobody cares.
> When it comes to us we will be ready,
> To fight back and kill, just as many.
> So we are safe until about,
> All the bombs go off in a mushroom cloud.
> So now what's happened?
> It's like we've been knifed,
> No flowers, no animals, not a single life.
> That's what war is, it's horrible and dumb.
> One day there's lots, the next day there's none.

The clearer the fear became on paper, the softer it was on my psyche. I shared the poem with my friends on the playground later that day, but I never showed it to my parents. It was the early stage of the information breakdown we've suffered ever since.

I generally avoid discussing sensitive topics with my folks. My father's temperamental tendency towards dictation makes it difficult to have any sort of diplomatic discussion with him. As far as Mom is concerned, any real concerns should be addressed by a professional. She sent me off to a psychiatrist when she discovered my self-abuse. She sent me to a gynecologist when she found out I was having sex. And I asked my friend Jenn if I could have one of her training bras so I wouldn't have to face the lingerie lady at Macy's if Mom tried to pawn me off on her professional opinion. Oddly enough, Mom never mentioned the bra in the laundry, and it took her two months to realize I was depleting her stash of tampons after I secretly got my period. I wouldn't have been embarrassed if she'd tried to talk to me about these developments, but I didn't want to initiate the dialogue. The more situations that came and went in silence, the more self-conscious I became about talking to my mom. I followed her lead, but I never felt the safety behind the silence.

As I got older I realized her reticence was a huge advantage when it came to mischief. Mom expressed disappointment via the cold shoulder, a technique that essentially let me off the hook from expressing remorse. There are two occasions that stand out in my mind. The first one happened when I was about eleven and she found a cigarette butt I'd thrown in the trash. It was sitting on my bed when I got home from school. No comment from Mom, she just acted pissed off at me for the rest of the day. The exact same thing happened when she discovered I was on birth control at the age of sixteen. She'd gone to the pharmacy to pick up her prescription and they gave her mine instead. Once again, the evidence was sitting on my bed when I arrived home from school. But rather than talking to me about it she gave me the cold shoulder. Hey, I wanted to say, you're the one who sent me to the gynecologist!

As a rebellious teen, I saw her as a pushover, and it made me want to challenge her authority. I wonder what my mother would say if I told her how lonely it felt not to have anyone to talk to at that age. At one point she decided that she needed to know what was going on with me—so she read my diaries! I wonder if she read all the desperate poems too. Maybe that's why she sent them back to me, to shut them up, and shut them out. I wonder what would happen if told her about all the times I've wanted to kill myself. That might get her yapping. If I thought it would put an end to the guessing game we've created I might try, but it would probably drive an even bigger wedge between us. Besides, I've learned to read her silent messages fairly well. Lately they're being delivered by the United States Postal Service. Speaking of which, I guess it's time to open that box.

Wow, it's a bona fides care package! She sent me a bedspread, and a new feather pillow! There's also a mirror, two strings of dragonfly Christmas lights, and a book called "The Path to Tranquility". So what does it mean? Is she sorry for my recent loss? Does she want to make up for the angry conversation we most recently never had? Does it simply mean she loves me? There's a note at the bottom of the box that reads: "The book is filled with quotes from the Dalai Llama. A friend of mine recommended it. She said it might help get through these tough times. Hope you feel better soon, love, Mom." Now the Dalai Llama is the professional she recommends to get me through this latest development. Fine with me, after sixteen years I'm fed up with psychiatry.

So what's with the female notion that home decoration is the fast track to feeling better? Who am I kidding? I can't wait to see how the bedspread goes with the drapes I bought yesterday! I better go, my roommate just got home and I want to show her all this cool stuff, and then I have a thank you note to write. Actually, make that a phone number to dial. I should try talking to mom. Stranger things have happened, after all, I've lived to see the fall of Russia as a superpower. Despite the recurring war in the Middle East, the world has changed quite a bit since 1983, so why can't I? "Wars will end when men refuse to fight," is one of my favorite quotes. Could it apply to mothers and daughters as well? Only time will tell.

Sunday, February 24

My roommate headed off to mass this morning at the ungodly hour of six a.m. I happened to be stumbling out of bed to use the bathroom, or I never would have known. After a few more hours of sleep I decide to use her cathedral commitment as an example and start my day with a dose of spirituality as well. I head off to the eleven a.m. service at Agape with one major goal in mind: to pay attention the entire time.

I pay relentless attention for about twenty minutes; from the opening song to the end of the announcements. Impressed with the long list of upcoming events I decide to attend the new member class scheduled this afternoon. When the sermon begins, I drift into la-la land until the music kicks in at the end. I suffer from a mental deficit when it comes to the sermons, but I always seem to leave feeling refreshed. After the service I hang around the bookstore for a while, and then examine the display tables outside in the parking lot. In addition to food and trinkets for sale there are tables filled with information about charitable organizations, spiritual retreats and vacations, and numerous projects promoting Agape's "Season of Nonviolence". After indulging in fried catfish and corn fritters, I sign up to serve food to homeless folks on Easter Sunday. Next I gather details about the Peace Walk next weekend. A Native American group that does "peace walks" year round will lead us in a ceremonial blessing followed by a procession down the boardwalk from the Santa Monica Pier to Venice Beach and back. Participants are to wear all white and walk in silence. I don't understand how onlookers will know it's a Peace Parade if we're not allowed to speak, but I'm a newcomer to the language of peace, so what do I know?

An hour later the new member class begins and I join fifty other people inside the sanctuary. We introduce ourselves and give a quick statement about to why we're here. A number of people say they were raised in a rigid religion and want to find freedom in their spiritual practice. "I'm searching for a new groove," I say, "I'd like to learn how to pray." As it turns out, I don't learn anything about prayer today, but I do get a lesson in meditation. The orientation begins with a condensed explanation of the Science of Mind philosophy. The basic purpose of this religion is to become one with God, love, and the universe. Agape holds the theory that God is love, and meditation can help you achieve a sense of oneness with this omnipresent devotion. There are some basic tricks to meditation—each designed to help you think about nothing. It begins with a focus on the breath. Then you can zone in on counting, or a mantra, or music to help quiet the brain. The technique they suggested we start with involves counting each breath until you get to ten and then starting over at number one.

The minute I get home I decide to hop in the tub and try it, but random thoughts redirect me until I'm at fifty and considering what to eat for dinner. So I try another version where I whisper "Allah" with every exhalation. Allah means "the one". For me it means the one that doesn't work. I wonder if my ability to multi-task negates my ability to meditate. Oh well, I do get an "A" for effort, since I gave it a whirl until the water got cold and the cats began to meow for their dinner. Practice makes perfect, I'll just have to try and try again. I think I may acquire a taste for Zen eventually, until then I'm happy to rely on writing for clarity. I started to write "Dear God," at the top of the page this time, but I got self-conscious and erased it. Come to think of it, all the entries I wrote as a child are directed at someone too. I've written volumes of one-way conversations that address some sort of entity. I wonder if I've been talking to God all these years and didn't even know it. That would mean I've been encompassed by love the entire time and loneliness is a figment of my imagination. Holy Cow! I can't believe what 60 seconds of meditation has done for my thinking already. At this rate, I could have my entire life figured out by the end of the week. Look out universe, you're about to become one with me. Now where was I? One…two…three…

Saturday, March 2

I just spent the last couple of hours in a temper tantrum after this brand new computer froze up and I lost three pages of text! The fact that I forgot to hit "save" during ninety minutes of writing fueled my fury and I swore at myself as I punched the keys, until I gave up on restoration and went for a punishing run instead. I took off at an uncomfortably fast pace and after a few miles got a cramp in my side and had to walk. Sulking all the way home, I decided if I couldn't recover it I should rewrite what I'd written while it was fresh in my mind.

With sweat on my brow I hammered the keyboard in a last ditch effort to find the lost pages, frantically searching for a doc. called "Peace Be Still". Humbled by the hypocrisy, I turned the computer off and meditated. I can't say for sure if I reached Zen, but ten minutes of deep breathing got my heart rate down at least. I think I'm relaxed enough now to quit dwelling on my ineptitude and focus on gratitude instead.

This morning I took part in a Peace Parade to protest the war in Iraq. One hundred Agape members joined a group of Native-American "peace keepers" and together we marched along the beach boardwalk from Santa Monica to Venice and back. We held no banners and made no statement to indicate our purpose. The fact that we were dressed from head to toe in white and walked in a silent single file was left up to the interpretation of the onlookers. Surprisingly, many of them got the message.

The entire round trip took less than an hour, after which we collected our thoughts in a circle of retrospect. I shared my observation of a young girl and her mother who we passed going both directions. As we slipped by them a second time the little girl said, "Look mommy. Here are all the polite people." The montage of other stories painted a much more elaborate picture than the one I'd experienced. The homeless man that prayed in Islamic as we passed had apparently been hurling obscenities and shaking his fist at the sky when we first approached, but then he dropped his arms, began to chant, and gave thanks for our presence. Someone else told of a yuppie-looking man reading a newspaper, who started to chant, "NO more war, NO more war", as we wound around him on the way back to our starting point.

    The minute I returned to my apartment I sat down at my computer to express how incredible it felt to be part of the Peace Parade. But I lost those thoughts when my computer froze. Now I'm beginning to think that my feelings are not the notable aspects of this day. When it comes to trying to make the world a better place it's a little ridiculous to look at the effect my actions have had on me. Maybe the fact that I lost the original details is a sign from God telling me I need to try again. Perhaps this is also God's way of presenting me with options when things go wrong. So here is my attempt to make up for all the angry energy I expressed after the Peace Parade today. It's also an opportunity to make up for all the negative stuff I've said about my mom lately, by giving her credit where credit is due. Mom is the one who taught me that feeling good about projects that improve people's lives does not, and should not, come from recognition for your contribution. The real reward comes from the knowledge that you stood up for what you believe in, and had the courage to go beyond the average call of human duty.

    Our family lived a bohemian lifestyle compared to the average Massachusetts' residents. My parents were the only people who drove a VW bus in our town, and I guarantee my Dad was the only heterosexual man in the entire North East to wear a Speedo at the beach. My parents' colorful style must be attributed to our experience of living in Europe and California before settling outside of Boston. I'm just glad Mom didn't have the inane notion to go Euro at the beach. Although I can't help but wonder: if the cops had been summoned for the indecent exposure of my topless Mom, would my brother and I have been able to convince them to haul away Speedo-clad Dad in the name of child abuse? Unlikely I'm sure. Nevertheless, Mom was sensational in other ways, especially when it came to political and social activism. Always involved in a new project, she was a member of the Sudbury town counsel, a trustee for our church, and frequently volunteered for projects and field trips at school, all while maintaining a part time job. She often involved my younger brother and me in extracurricular missions. I remember when I was nine she entered the family room early one Saturday morning and said, "Turn off the TV, we need to furnish an apartment for a homeless man."

"Aw Mom," my seven year old brother moaned. "Is he gonna smell worse than the hitchhiker lady last week?"

"Maybe, but that's why we need to hang him a shower curtain. That nice young woman needed a ride last week.

This man needs a home. And you two watch entirely too much TV—so turn it off, NOW."

We begrudgingly climbed into the V-dub and headed to Boston to help Mom and her coworker move a bunch of Salvation Army furniture into a tiny apartment. Mom's coworker had befriended the man after passing by his makeshift enclave every day on her way to work. When she discovered he was on the street because he'd lost his job and had no family to turn to, she and my mother decided that he needed a shove in the right direction. The guy was kind of old and unable to carry anything heavy, but he offered many thanks. I was surprised to see how such a disheveled man could be a real sweet pea after he received a shower and second chance.

My mother has the innate belief that everyone deserves to be treated with respect and equality. She was firm about her rule that no word should ever be used in vain if it targeted and belittled certain types of people, so the popular schoolyard insults, like "Retard" and "Fag", were strictly prohibited. Homosexuality became a hot topic for us in the early 80's after my cousin Ned admitted he was gay. Ten years later he died from AIDS, on Thanksgiving, during my sophomore year at the University of Colorado. My mom had returned from a visit with Ned, at his family's home, one week before he passed and warned me that his days were numbered. She asked that I send him a card, but with no idea how to approach the issue of his death I struggled for days about what to write. I eventually chose a Kahlil Gibran quote as the message and sent Ned a hand-painted card to wish him well and on his way. He died before it arrived. My sadness was enhanced because I knew the fear of words kept the note from getting to him on time. A few months later I found myself tongue-tied on the topic once again. In the midst of a class discussion about the effect that AIDS had on the sexual practice of my generation, some bozo interjected to say that his sexual practices hadn't changed because "AIDS is a gay boys' disease, and God's way of getting rid of them." I was absolutely dumbfounded, but couldn't find the words or the courage to say a thing. I've owed Ned my eternal blessing ever since.

So in the tradition of my Mother's philanthropic ways, I participated in the California AIDS ride from San Francisco to Los Angeles three years ago. As one of the minority heterosexuals in a flamboyant group of costume clad homosexual and bi-cyclists, it was a way for me to enjoy a taste of Ned's flaming lifestyle. 3,000 of us blazed a brilliant trail of awareness down the California coast and raised 11 million dollars for AIDS research. My mom may have taught me that quiet contributions can send a powerful message, but on the ride I discovered that making a bunch of noise can be quite effective too.

Over the last twenty years I have participated in my own silent protest by never using the word "fag" to describe someone. There have also been times when I spoke out and called attention to other people's use of that term. Each approach has its merit. Whether big and loud or small and proud, my mother showed me that the influence of a single person can rearrange the world. So who cares how I felt after the Peace walk this morning? The important thing is that I followed my mother's footsteps and lent myself to an important cause. Thanks Mom, for giving me the perspective that breeds super heroines. I hope to become one of them someday.

Sunday, March 3

When the phone rings at 9 o'clock this morning I reach over to shut the sound off, but I see "Mom" on the caller ID and instinctively believe she's received my telepathic "thank you". So I grab the phone, give a cheery 'hello', and wait for her loving response. "I've been thinking about you lately", she says. I smile and thank God for sending her my blessing. "And you know what?" She continues, "I'm fed up with your crap."

I give God the finger and frown. "Why are you mad at me?"

"Your father and I are seeing a marriage counselor."

I snicker. "You've bickered for years? Why quit now?"

"I really don't need the sarcasm."

What does she expect? Mom advocates psychiatry for everyone. She's battled depression for years and thinks therapy is the "Be all to end all" problems. I dig deep to find a tone of sincerity. "Congratulations, I can't believe you got Dad to go to therapy."

"Well, he agrees we've reached an impasse and need some pointers. Anyway, counseling has shown me that you're a lot like your father, and it affects the way you and I relate. I think we need to talk about it."

"Can't hurt," I say.

"You are so fucking bullheaded."

Okay, that hurts a little. "Yeah, just like Dad. So whose fault is that?" I ask.

"I married a monster and gave birth to another—it must be mine." She chimes.

Holding my breath I count to ten, and hope the reversal of our silence and rage will turn the tides and help us to get along better. Besides I'm too sleepy to scream, so I hit snooze and let her rip into me. Locked in a defensive gaze at the white walls that cradle me, I appreciate the distance between us, and the fact the phone can't expose my withdrawal. In the end, I get through the entire call without a rebuttal, but only because her comments are thwarted by the initial insult, and I'm consumed by one terrible thought: if I am just like my father, then how will I ever learn to live with myself? Eighteen years and I never learned to live with him.

Growing up, the power struggle between my father and I resembled that between lion and cub: fighting to near death until one of them slinks away to become king of her domain elsewhere. Now the 3,000 miles between us gives me some perspective, and I can actually say the traits my father passed on to me have made me strong in many ways. Dad's determination genes helped me achieve the highest batting average in the state as a high school softball player. His intellectual genes got me on the Dean's list in college. And the genes of his independence allowed me to move clear across the country to start my life as Lioness.

No doubt about it, I am who I am as a result of all the guidance he gave me, including lessons on how to raise my voice. Of course, his tempestuous supervision drove me crazy during adolescence, and was downright impossible to deal with as I became a self-assertive teen. By the time I left for college I could hardly utter a word to him without feeling like it was a precursor to the next fight.

Our tendency towards embroilment started very early on, which makes me wonder if I was bred, or actually born, to be bullheaded. By middle school my father and I yelled at each other regularly in escalated frustration. The classic scenario for an argument was Dad helping me with my math homework. I shutter at the mere mention of the word Algebra. My mathematician father insisted on showing me new and improved ways to find the solutions because the text book definitions weren't good enough for him. I'd get pissed because he offered too much information; he'd get pissed because I refused to pay attention, and the scene would explode into rage. The most potent instruction I got during those sessions was how to lose my temper. The only factor that didn't add up was his response to my imitation. When lessons with decimals lead to lessons in decibels I was sent to my room, and the number of tears shed in the after-math is incalculable. I did not appreciate his efforts, since his help felt like the third degree when I didn't understand the numbers.

Of course there were plenty of instances where Dad's attention was appreciated. He worked full time and still found time to coach my softball team. He also attended every one of the plays I was ever in, beginning at the age of five. Both my parents were on a relentless pursuit for enrichment in our lives. Weekdays were filled to the brim with piano, flute, and swim lessons, gymnastics practice, and art class. Our Sunday family outings were quite diverse as well. My parents introduced us to the witches of Salem, Plymouth Plantation, endless museums, and the term "Carpe Diem". On warm weather days we hiked, biked, and canoed our way around the wooded suburbs. During cooler months we'd head to the city for dim sum in China Town, or the All Saints parade in Little Italy.

I was definitely raised with the mentality that boredom is not an option. Unfortunately, my gravitation towards kinetic energy hinders my ability to relax these days. There are two basic tools I use when I need to calm down; I spin into a tizzy until I'm tired enough to sit still or I welcome depression and let it kill my will. Both traits have kept me from finding a healthy mate. Max and I dated because we related to each others insanity. Even at our best we were a couple of roosting Dodo's. One thing's for sure, my parents didn't raise me to be a flightless bird. A little cuckoo maybe, but I think I'm ready to migrate away from that idiosyncrasy.

Saturday, March 9

It's four a.m. I can't sleep. For the last hour I've been flipping through the box of stuff my mom sent me and now all my report cards—dating back to second grade—are sprawled across my bed. The general consensus is that I was a talented and enthusiastic student. Yeah, I was enthusiastic, about getting everyone to like me. I've always been good at doing what I need to do to be popular. It's a habit I established in 1980, when my family moved to Massachusetts.

At the age of seven I entered a new school, second grade, and an ugly stage. As one of the shortest kids in my class, I had huge feet, buckteeth, and 20/200 vision. Eager beaver describes my physical and scholastic characteristics. To make up for my vertical and visual shortcomings, I acted like a big wig, sat in the front row, and raised my hand like a game show contestant after every question. I quickly won my teacher's admiration, but my classmates labeled me "Geek".

Luckily we moved in next door to another second grade girl named Sharon. Our proximity encouraged a fast friendship and she helped me get admitted into her gang. None of them were in the same class as me, but they accepted me with open arms on the playground. They were a tough crew, and I knew as long as I had their friendship no one would mess with me. From that point on, I used my goody-two-shoes attitude to stay out of trouble. Not to avoid it, but to avoid getting caught. By the end of elementary school I'd learned that 'good girls' have a great chance of getting away with mischief.

In middle school I figured out how to get accepted by the popular kids. Contacts, braces and a curling iron fixed my flaws, learning how to French kiss got me into the cool parties, good grades kept my parents at bay, and getting involved in student council, the school band, and the "Catalyst Program" for gifted kids, allowed me to push the envelope when it came to misbehaving. My eighth grade Catalyst teacher wrote on my report card that intuition and creativity allowed me to think fast on my feet. Around the same time the teacher wrote that note, I got caught twice for shoplifting. She was right, my quick-witted fast talk allowed me to walk away before the shop owner called the cops. This type of behavior impressed my delinquent friends, but I wanted to impress everyone. So I learned to save my wild side for the hell raisers and pull my smarty-pants on when I wanted to impress the snobs. As difficult as it is to please all the people all the time, I embraced the challenge and entered high school as a first class chameleon.

Freshman year I quit playing the flute, band didn't fit in with my agenda. I became an all around athlete and played with the "jocks" instead. I still hung out with "punks" on weekends, smoking pot, doing shots and having sex with my upper class boyfriend. All while maintaining the grade in the advanced classes, where I hob knobbed with the "snobs". I went to enough keg parties for the jocks to forgive me for hanging with the punks. I got in enough mischief for the punks to forgive me for hanging out with the snobs. And the snobs were so preoccupied with their own insecurities they were unaware of my indiscretions. Being a member of multiple groups got me the recognition I wanted; I was voted 'Big Woman on Campus' senior year. Inside, I felt like a loser on the verge of total rejection—guess I fooled everyone.

Today I have a Masters in the art of Le Masquerade. It was put to good use when Max took me to St. Tropez. We'd known each other for all of four days when he invited me to go away with him. Despite my annual income of twenty-five grand, I put on an air of affluence and plunked down a full months wage for the business class ticket to France. Max covered all the other expenses, and after our first shopping spree I had everything I needed to blend in at the chateau of his oil tycoon friend. We had an incredible time; never mind that I returned home with a busted lip and a broken tooth after a night of smoking opium in Monte Carlo. On my last night there I fell down a flight of stairs during a hallucination—I thought I was an eagle and stepped off the cliff. C'est la vie. Scars are par for the course when it comes to rubbing arms with the right peeps. Usually they're self-inflicted, because I can't stand the fundamental me. But each time I switch characters to connect I lose a little more self respect, and it's gotten to the point where I have no idea how to be me anymore.

Case in point: tonight I decided to make friends with my roommate. I need to find some healthy playmates. Amy seems like the perfect candidate; she's into fitness, she's motivated when it comes to work, and she goes to Mass every Sunday. I went dancing with her tonight, and we hit it off magically; grooving on the dance floor, getting free rounds of drinks from the men at the bar, squeezing into the handicapped stall to do line after line of coke together. It's amazing how much we have in common. So now I'm wrestling with the temptation to cut myself. Cocaine and razor blades are like honey and tea—they enhance each others quality. I feel like I need to get under my skin and dig deep to find the person I was born to be. It says right here on my report cards that I'm a good girl at heart. I guess the drug-snorting, butt-kissing, cheap talking bitch is just a glitch in a game, that I'm really tired of playing.

8:00 am:

Sharon has set me straight. I called her at six—nine, Virginia time—and she was up having coffee. I was up because I hadn't come down from my amphetamine-induced anxiety. Feeling out of control, I turned to my life-long lifeline. I've known Sharon for twenty-two years now, and even though she's lived faraway from me for the last ten, she's the closest thing I have to a best friend. I decided to call her after I found a poem called "Treasure Island" at the bottom of my box. I wrote it for her after we left for college; it details our childhood stomping ground.

The day we moved into our new house Sharon came knocking, with an invite to show me Clay Mountain. Clay Mountain was a mound of dirt excavated during construction of my house. It lay halfway between her house and mine and offered us tons of dirt-filled fun. With no window visibility from either of our homes it was the epicenter of the area in which we built our secret forts. A stream lay two hundred yards back, and was the borderline for the swamp. Throughout the years we rowed down it, waded through it, fell in it, and even ice skated on it from time to time. Deep in the woods beyond the swamp was a retired railroad track that served to guide us during our many expeditions. As long as we maintained a reasonable distance between our trek and the tracks, we could always find our way back to the Island.

Treasure Island

On the mossy side of the trees,
Just opposite Clay Mountain, lay the swamp;
A juxtapositious gold mine, that hid waterfalls and
Roses, minks and mussels, and little girls when need be.

By the banks of the stream, gum vines and skunk
Cabbage sunk their veins in the slime that was known
To swallow cat's whole, during experiments testing the
Probability of them landing on their feet, every time.

The shady canopy blanketed secret forts, and sacred
Rites, and the noise about training bras and boys.

It was a safe place to go when you didn't really want to
Run away from home.
It was a great place to sleep when you weren't old
Enough to go camping alone.
It was the best place to be when you felt like exploring
the universe, but had to be back in time for dinner.

And Sharon and I owned that space

That lay between Newton and Whispering Pines.

We could sing and dance that space.
We could laugh and cry that space.
We could live and die that place.
It was ours.

The seemingly infinite acreage behind our homes offered endless play, but when it came to a serious escape, the railroad track was the best place. That's where we ran away to when times got tough. I remember one time Sharon and I sat on the tracks for hours, debating the issue of training bras. At ten years old Sharon's mom told her she wasn't allowed to wear white T-shirt's without a bra anymore. Anyone who has seen the movie "The Outsiders" knows that blue jeans and a plain white Tee's have been the staple outfit for boys since Jimmy Dean hit the scene. As tomboys Sharon and I emulated that look, and we weren't about to let a little puberty cramp our style. Her mom didn't understand that everyone would be able to see the bra through the Tee, or how embarrassing that would be. So we ran away to the tracks to rebel against her mother's lack of sensitivity. Unfortunately, as I worked to console Sharon and convince her boobs were cool I tapped into my own concern that I might never get mine! Together we sat, lamenting the fact that we had no control over our development. I told Sharon that wearing a bra wasn't that big a deal, and certainly not worth the right to wear white t-shirts.

"Wait till you have to wear one." She whined, "I bet you come crying to me!" Her comment made me feel better. Not from the promise that I'd ever grow boobs, but from the promise that we'd always have each other's shoulder to cry on. And that promise rang true as I shared my coke invoked doo-doo with her this morning. "I did a bunch of blow last night and I feel like shit. I need to get my act together and be a better person."

"I wish I could find some cool trouble to get into," she replied. "I got drunk last week and stumbled face first into a deer carcass hanging outside our front door. That's way worse than being a drug-whore at a night club." Sharon's a biologist and lives in the Appalachian Mountains with her hunter boyfriend. She has a love/hate relationship with the woods. She won't live anywhere else, but I think she gets bored there. I know where she's coming from; when we were young we had all the adventure we wanted right outside our back door, until we'd finally had our fill of climbing trees. We yearned for new and exciting places, but our small town didn't offer many options. So we never made it out of the woods in our quest for a great escape. Instead, new horizons were crossed at keg parties under the forest canopy, and nighttime hikes through the trees on psychedelics.

Sharon and I did all the same drugs in high school, but somewhere along the way I started to feel lost in an exploration that had no boundaries. For all the times I saw her lose control, I never saw her suffer the same remorse as me. Come to think of it, none of my party pals ever expressed regret for acting drunk or stupid. I'm the only person I know who considers suicide a cure for the common hangover. When I told Sharon I felt bad about last night she said, "You're a little hard on yourself sometimes."

"I like being dramatic," I told her.

"Then go get an acting gig and quit apologizing for yourself."

Satisfied with her recommendation, I joined her in reminiscing about the good old days. She reminded me about the time we ran away after I got into a screaming fight with my father. We sat on the tracks while I tried to decide if I would *ever* go home. It felt good to think I had a choice—made it easier to face the trouble I was in, including the threat of being grounded.

"Consider last night your runaway trip to the tracks." Sharon said, at the end of the call. "Now go back and face reality. You can ground yourself if it makes you feel better."

Grounded is exactly how I needed to feel.

Monday, March 25

I just got back from a trip to the neighborhood coffee shop, where I ran into my long lost buddy Rick. He's one of the first friends I met when I moved here, and we've been in and out of touch ever since. As I sat in the sun sipping a honey spiced latte I spotted him a block and a half away. There was no mistaking him: bright orange and white Hawaiian shirt, black notebook in hand, big smirk on his face. Rick tells a joke every five minutes and I think that continues when he's alone. The endless notes of hilarity he jots down in that little book, fuel a sly smile. Rick is one of my favorite people. A comedy writer and closet inventor, his unique interpretation of life's machinations make him an electrified conversationalist, although he rarely shares any of the details of his inventions with me. "I swear I'm not crazy," is all he ever says about them.

Rick isn't crazy—quirky, but not crazy. His collection of Colonel Sander's paraphernalia makes him eccentric. The mystery and humility behind his concepts makes me think he's some kind of genius. When I asked him what he's been up to he said, "My greatest work of all time."

"Grab a seat and tell me about it."

Fat chance, as usual, he danced around the answer then boomeranged the question back at me. Never afraid to share the details of my own inventions, otherwise known as theatrics, I launched into a tirade. First I gave Rick a rundown of all the extravagance I enjoyed while living with Max. Then I turned up the drama and exaggerated the financial collapse I've suffered ever since the breakup. Only after I'd milked the 'woe is me' out of my eviction from easy street, did I admit the relationship was love-less, sex-less, and left me totally uninspired. At the end of my spiel, Rick poignantly pointed out that the only thing I lost, that was of any value, was my inspiration. His comment took me right back to the day we met; when inspiration was all I had, and was the one thing we had in common.

Rick and I established a friendship when I was fresh out of college and shoving off the shore of parental dependence into the sea of starving artistry. By contrast, Rick was already a bona fide success. At the age of thirty he'd just finished a four year stint as staff writer on two different sitcoms. He had the pay stubs to prove it, and the fancy accoutrements. The signs of his success that impressed me the most were his '71 convertible Jaguar, and the fact that he had a personal shopper. The jaguar ranked pretty high on the gauge of celebrity, but the personal shopper sounded like a piece of material blue yonder; it was just the kind of prosperity I hoped to find when I agreed to go with my roommate to an alumni dinner for her film school. She said it would be the perfect place to meet some aggressive young writer/actor/producer types. As luck would have it, her school's biggest triumph sat down right next to me.

When Rick arrived at our table in his olive green suit he stood out against the field of black that peppered the room. A committed fan of color, I cheerily exclaimed, "Nice suit!"

"I'm the garnish for your martini tonight. Sorry I'm late, looks like you need another." He waived the waiter over. "I'll have what she's having."

"Double Stoli, up, with a twist." I announced.

"Make mine a single." The waiter reversed his steps and Rick confessed, "I'm a light weight, and I'd hate to wind up face first in your lap…I mean, my glass."

"Well I'd hate to see you ruin that suit." I concurred.

"I'll take that as a compliment, and pass it on to my ragman at Macy's."

"What's a ragman?" I asked, feeling green.

"My personal shopper," he said. "If it were up to me, I'd wear Hawaiian's all the time."

By the end of the night I knew Rick would be the perfect mentor. He was down to earth, funny, and hungry. I needed guidance on how to break into the acting business as quickly as possible and Rick was Speed Racer when it came to the fast track. He'd landed his first gig as a sit-com writer at the age of twenty-six, and although he'd recently been "released" when his show went off the air, he was hardly fazed by the uncertainty of the next step. He told me he was very excited to develop his own projects, even if it meant being unemployed for a while. Seven years later Rick's still unemployed, and nearly penniless. This tidbit slipped out as he exposed a few of the details behind his "greatest work of all time." A few months ago Rick received a call from a former sit-com colleague named Andy, who had read Rick's latest show proposal. Andy thought it was brilliant and told Rick he wanted to help get the show developed. Then he gallantly offered to quit his job at Disney and work on Rick's project for free. A month later Rick and Andy started a company. They're not making any money yet but Rick says success isn't measured in dollars and cents. He believes his show will change the role that television plays in people's lives, and the invention he plans to expose on the show will change the way people drive.

"What do you mean?" I asked.

"I reinvented the wheel." He said.

"Can I see it?"

"It's a secret."

I grinned. "Will it fit on the rims of your Jaguar?"

"I sold the Jag to pay for the patents." His eyes filled with pride.

"How can you be so positive when you're broke?" I sighed.

"My dedication determines my outlook."

"Wouldn't it be nice to get paid?"

"Sure," he said, "but money's never been the force that fueled me."

"There's nothing you want in exchange for your work?"

"A Nobel would be nice."

I let that one simmer as I slurped the last of my drink. During my relationship with Max I devoted all my time and energy to building a life that would appear successful by American standards. Moving in with my rich boyfriend landed me in a situation of wealth and apparent achievement. Until that point, I had little to show for five years of living in L.A. I went from being a struggling artist to living in the lap of luxury. Max didn't support my desire to be an actress, but it didn't matter. Acting wasn't giving me the validation I needed. Max offered me plenty of validation: a trip to France, a pearl strand, a rabbit bag, leather pants; these were the rewards I received from him. They made me feel rich and appreciated.

There was a pregnant pause as I watched Rick furiously write something in his notebook. Suddenly I felt the gestation of my dreams again. With all the conviction I could muster under the shadow of my resignation, I said. "I want to get back into acting again."

Channeling Groucho Marx he said, "Call the union. Tell them you want a re-union."

"I think I want to be a writer too." I said, out of the blue.

"Then start writing."

"I've been writing. Can you help me get better at it?"

He thought about it. "Let's exchange expertise. I need to get in shape."

"What kind of shape?"

"I want to get down to my original birth weight."

I laughed. "We better jog at least a couple times a week then."

We shook on it and I offered to buy him a latte to-go. He was much obliged—said he needed the extra fuel for the long walk home. I gave him another dollar to catch the bus. Four bucks later I had myself a guru; one of the best investments I've made in a very long time. I'm beginning to feel rich again.

Thursday, March 28

Rick and I have run together twice since Monday. Both times he wore a Hawaiian shirt and brought his notebook with him, and both times he stopped mid-jaunt to write something down. When it happened for the third time in twenty minutes today, I jogged in place until he was ready to go, although I wanted to grab the book and chuck it onto the ninth hole of the golf course we circled. How can I get him in shape at this rate? I wondered with exasperation. Then I remembered it wasn't a race, it was Rick's chance to exercise while I asked him about writing. So I gave up on burning calories, and focused on the burning question instead: "Do you have to carry that book when we run?"

"Yes," he said.

"Why?" I cried.

"Because writing is fed by all the little observations you make throughout
your day."

"Can't it wait 'til we're done?"

"No. I have to write them down now, or I'll have to fish for them later."

"Why can't you just remember them?"

"Takes up too much space in my brain; I write them down so my mind can move on to the next thought in the series."

"Fine," I said, "give me that thing." I snatched the book from him and scrawled "HEART RATE" at the top of the page.

"What's that?" he asked.

"I'm putting my thought down on paper, so I can move on, and welcome my next conception."

"Drum roll, please…"

"I need to be more flexible." Grinning at my own profundity, I hooked my fingers through the fence and grabbed my foot to stretch my quad.

Following my lead, he grabbed his foot in hand, and asked. "Hey how's Kelly?"

"I don't know." I said. A pang of guilt rang through my head.

"When was the last time you spoke?"

"I don't know." *Yes you do*, the voice in my head sang.

"You still friends?" He pried.

"I guess." I lied. *And you digress*, the voice sighed. *Care to expand?* "We just don't have much in common since she moved to back to Boston."

Rick sneered. "You guys were like Oscar and Felix when she lived here." He was right, and I was left with an interesting thought: why do opposites attract? In the case of Kelly and me, dissimilarity was the key to our connection.

Ironically, we shared the common ground of growing up in the same small town. Shortly after I moved to LA I heard through the grape vine that Kelly was a California transplant too. A grade apart in school, we were never really friend's back then, but as young adults our hearts pulsed with the exciting prospect of making it in the movies, which gave us plenty of reason to commiserate. The high cost of living initially convinced us to share a place, but we developed a fast friendship, based on our contrasts.

Kelly's desire for financial security landed her at a full time job in sales. My desire for a flexible schedule—to accommodate the auditions I planned to finagle—forced me into waiting tables. I wound up with access to people our age, while she had access to really good pay. I found the parties and she paid for drinks. She inspired me to work, I reminded her to play. Along the way we became each other's confidantes. Our differences helped us defeat our weaknesses. A successful saleswoman, Kelly taught me how to promote myself as an actress. A committed athlete, I taught her how to use the gym as stress relief from her sixty-hour work week. As time wore on I worried that the demands of her job were distracting, and encouraged her to find work that would give her the time to write her screenplays. She agreed, and quit her sales job to move on to a career in the "industry". Unfortunately, that job was even more involved, and kept her way too busy to write. Kelly's inability to do what she came here to do was the first indication that it wasn't meant to be. I also couldn't help but notice how much she missed her family. I can't say I was terribly surprised when she decided to flee after she got fired from her job as personal assistant to a V.I.P. at NBC (who was a narcissistic prick, if you ask me). I was, however, incredibly disappointed. I couldn't believe that after two and a half years together she was going to leave me to fend for my self. Disgusted, I called her a quitter, but it was fear that made me lash out at her. I wondered how I would stay motivated without her. A few years later I threw in the towel too.

Perhaps it was my own disgrace that led to our final meltdown. All I can say is the contrast between our lives was hard for me to take the last time I saw her. When Kelly came here on business last year I felt like a failure. She was working at a job she loved, living in a condo she owned, and was engaged to a man she dated for less than a year. I was working at a gym, living in a studio apartment, and dating the manic-depressive mess named Max. Max's connections were the most impressive thing I had, so I asked him to score tickets for Kelly and me to attend an exclusive party at Hugh Hefner's mansion. When Kelly confessed that she could care less about attending, it cracked our fragile friendship. Then the night before she returned home, we had an argument about where to go to dinner that escalated into a full-blown fight. We were no longer speaking when she left town. The barrier between us was solidified when I visited Boston at Thanksgiving and decided not to call her while I was there; a slight that Kelly's sister likely brought to light after she saw me at our high school reunion.

The entire situation settled itself in the recess of my mind, until today. It may have been an ineffective run, but Rick provided me with a ton of tips on how, and what, to write—quite a productive lesson. On the way home I thought about all the fun times Kelly and I shared during our two and a half years together. The minute I walked in the door I dug through my albums to search for proof of our meaningful friendship. There were vacation photos of us in Catalina, San Diego, and San Francisco, along with endless pictures of us at parties, including a very exciting night at the Grammy's. Every shot was highlighted by smiles, and no evidence of discontent. On the other hand, as I flipped through the photos of Max and me, I was immediately reminded of how often we fought. Max and I had many problems during our year and a half together, yet I did everything I could to keep that relationship afloat. Kelly and I had one minor argument and I abandoned the friendship.

Makes me think I need to learn how to choose my battles better. Strong bonds are worth fighting for, not the bonds where fighting is the common denominator. Contemplating the absurdity of my actions, I closed the album and picked up the phone. I had no idea what to say, but dialed Kelly's number anyway. The minute she heard my voice she said, "It's been way too long."

"There's no time like the present."

"Well this is an amazing present. I can't believe you remembered my birthday."

Stunned by my dumb luck I announced with cheer, "Happy Birthday!!"

We spoke for a few minutes before she had to go meet some friends for dinner. I told her to call me when she has more time to talk. The ease of the short conversation gave me the encouragement I needed to email her a real apology. I hit send and was just about to open up my journal to document today's 'observations' when a thought interrupted me. I grabbed a post-it and wrote a note to buy a pocket-sized tape recorder to carry the next time Rick and I go for a run. I don't want to screw up his formula for cataloging ideas, but he needs to pick up the pace if he wants to become a lean writing machine. As for me, I didn't get much of a workout this morning, but making up with Kelly made my heart beat a little stronger. Running may keep me in shape, but it doesn't do much to heal my soul; finding out who my real friends are might.

Monday, April 1

When my cell phone rings at 6:15 this morning, I'm right in the middle of devouring a crumpet with lemon curd. Sticky fingers prevent me from digging through my bag, so I let the call go to voice mail. Having just returned home from my first and only personal training appointment for the day, I'm contemplating whether or not I should go back to bed. The answer will be determined by whether or not I brew a fresh cup of coffee, since the cup I swallowed at the crack of dawn has worn thin. After a rinse in the sink I rummage through my bag, snag the phone, and stare through my smudged spectacles at the "private number" listed on my caller ID. The pull from the slow rise of the daylight savings sun inspires me to make the most of my day. So I grab the can of Don Francisco's Hawaiian Blend and check the message. It's from Max. "I need you to pick up the armoire," he says in his brisk British tone. "Call me when you get the message." I am bewildered.

The armoire was delivered to Max's house two days after he asked me to move out, and he said I could leave it there as long as I needed. While it fits wonderfully alongside all the other antiques in Max's high-ceilinged living room, he suddenly decided he wanted nothing to do it. Since there was no way to squeeze it inside my new apartment, we agreed to sell it; although 'we' became 'me' as soon as I moved out, and we quit speaking to each other. It was on my credit card so it was my responsibility, if I wanted to recoup any of the $1700 I'd spent. I'm still in the planning phase of this seemingly enormous undertaking, and now he has the audacity to ask me to deal with it immediately?

My internal temperature rises as I habitually shirk my shrink's suggestion to count to ten before my temper flares. The only number I can think of is Max's as I maniacally dial it on my cell. He answers and I blurt out, "Why do I have to move the armoire?"

"Because I'm renovating, and it's in the way."

Flabbergasted I ask, "What am I supposed to do with it? Strap it to the back my bike? You know it won't fit in my apartment!"

"Not my problem," he says. "It's in the driveway and there's rain on the way, so I suggest you come get it today. But it's up to you." Then, *click*—he hangs up on me.

I am livid at the thought of having to move with this monstrous piece of furniture. Moments later I speed off towards his house on my motorcycle. I have no idea what I'll do when I get there but I've got my combat boots on, and I'm ready for a fight.

Upon arrival I walk right in the front door without so much as a quick 'hello' to Max's dog in the driveway. The house is empty. I mean absolutely empty: there's no furniture, the walls and the ceiling are gone, and there are signs he's about to tear up the hardwood floors. I peek in the kitchen. Outside the bay window I see the garage is filled to the brim with furnishings. The armoire sits alone in the driveway. Suddenly I see Max slip through the gate from behind the house. I grind my teeth and prepare to pounce. He opens the door to the kitchen and is clearly surprised to see me. Avoiding any semblance of social grace, I blurt out. "What are you doing to your house? It looks like freaking a war zone in here."

"Adding on," he says.

"Looks more like subtracting." He grabs a smoke from a pack on the counter and steps outside. I grab one too and follow him out, snatching the lighter from the top of the bar-b before he has a chance to. After a couple of intense drags, I hand him the lighter and say, "the armoire's going to have to stay here a while longer."

"Fine," he says with the arrogance of the upper hand. "There's a tarp in the garage if you want to cover it. Construction starts next week and I want the armoire gone by the time it's finished. I'll give it away if I have to."

"FINE," I growl. "Can I borrow your camera so I can post it on ebay?"

"Sure." He says. Then he stubs out his cigarette and heads inside.

Riley, the German shepherd, nuzzles my hand with her snout, but I'm too pissed off to pet her. With smoke coming out of my lungs and my ears, I can't help but wonder what's up with Max and his spontaneous renovations. By the time he returns with the digital camera I'm bubbling with sarcastic curiosity. "So what's with the remodel?" I prod. "I thought you were stressed about money."

"Life's too short to worry about money." He says with a smirk.

"How are you going pay for all your medications, and therapy? You're still going to therapy, aren't you?" I ask, testing the waters of our strained familiarity.

"No." He says and slinks away again.

The reflection in the mirror of the armoire captures my indignation. He shredded my heart and now he's tearing up the house? I guess he needs another project in destruction to absorb his non-medicated manic energy. Oh well—not my problem. I'll just take my pictures and leave him to spin out of control, by himself this time. I take a dozen shots of the armoire from different angles and then hunt him down again. He's sitting in his empty office looking distant and distracted. I ask him if he'll email the pictures to me while I go outside and cover the armoire. He nods without looking up. When I return for the second time he's staring at the keyboard, fingers still. Fully aware that I'm at his mercy to store the armoire, I speak in as friendly a tone as I can muster. "It's all set out there, thanks for letting me leave it here." His non response pisses me off but I remain civil. "You need to think about going back to your shrink Max. Cutting out your meds and therapy cold turkey is a bad idea."

He gazes at me with a blank stare. "I don't need them anymore."

"Who told you that?" I ask.

"My Doctor," he says.

"Which Doctor...your *witch* Doctor?" We smile in spite of our spite.

"No, the one I go to for hormones."

"So what does he think it is—a nasty case of P.M.S?" I jab.

"No, a nasty case of M.S," he says.

"I don't get it."

"Don't worry you won't. It's not contagious."

"What do you mean?"

"I have Multiple Sclerosis."

Snappy comebacks are swallowed by shock. I am speechless. My first thought goes to the remodel; is this about wheelchair access? All I can say is: "Oh."

In the name of evasion, he switches gear. "I emailed the pictures to you."

"Thanks." I mutter humbly.

Sensing it's time to go I stumble through an excuse about having to meet my next client. After a clumsy "good luck," I slip silently through the front door. It's a long and solemn walk to my bike. For the first time I feel sorry about losing him. Ever since the breakup I've been more upset about losing Max's house then his love, but seeing it torn apart today made it easier. The painful part, the crack in my heart, has been caulked with anger, but that too is beginning to disintegrate; the same way Max is beginning to disintegrate. As I settle into my saddle a contorted image of him invades my mind. I drive away feeling lucky, and guilty, and pray for him all the way home.

Only after I sit down to write do I realize its April Fools Day. It reminds me of an April Fools joke I played when I was eighteen. I pulled a stupid prank and called my boyfriend, my best friend and my dad, to tell them I'd been in a car wreck. I let them live with it for a minute before I broke into laughter and said, 'April Fools'. But none of them found it to be funny. Now I know how they felt. I wonder if Max is pulling my leg. I'll kill him if he's kidding. No matter what, he's a dead man. And I feel like a fool.

Sunday, April 7

Allergies put me in a sour mood this morning. The congestion they bring feels like some sort of treason; there's no rhyme or reason why the particulates I lived peacefully with for years, are suddenly the enemy. I blow my nose for the twentieth time, knowing I need to do something to improve my snotty attitude. Meditation is the first thought that wades through the mucus in my head, but that requires guidance. So I shift into fifth gear, gobble down an egg sandwich and hop in the shower. One Claritin, two nasal sprays and three puffs on my inhaler later, I'm off to Agape's early service. Unfortunately, the energy I have to generate to get there on time, combined with the rush of epinephrine, ruins my ability to engage in the meditation at all. As the reverend begins his speech my hyperactivity peaks and his fancy words about God make me antsy-er than usual. I feel like I'm ten again, desperate to be excused so I can cruise outside and blow off some steam. I still need a chill pill, but church is clearly not what the doctor ordered. Halfway through the opening statement I become overly conscious of the whistling sound coming from my nostrils. Apology seeps from me as I sneak out of the sanctuary with an air of someone headed for the bathroom. As I step out into the bright Sunday morning light, I know I've made the right decision.

High energy often morphs into nervous energy for me, which often leads to twisted and depressive thoughts. Determined to have a good day, I wonder how I might transcend that tendency. As I contemplate an extended ride in the canyons of Malibu, the word "Yoga" flashes across my brain. Satisfied with this suggestion, I hop on my bike, zoom home, change clothes, and grab my mat before continuing on towards Santa Monica.

I take two stairs at a time on the three-floor climb towards the class; it feels like I have enough amperage in my veins to fuel a train. The first thing I see when I enter the room is a substitute teacher. My face warms with frustration and consternation pulls my brows down. Is this punishment for ducking out of church? I chuck my mat on the floor. I knew this was going to be a bad day. Glancing around the room I can't help but notice how thin the crowd is in the normally packed studio. "Don't get pissed" is the mantra I think as I slink towards the bathroom in search of a tissue. Behind the confines of the stall walls I blow my nose with enough conviction to clear my nose and stuff my discontent. On the way out I peer at my reflection in the mirror above the sink and think, "Please help me God." Back on the mat I make a pointed effort to smile at the teacher as I remind myself I can sneak out if he sucks.

Moments later "Zach" introduces himself. Then he initiates the class with a song he plays on this piano / accordion-looking thing. He calls it his harmonium and after a few minutes of very mellow music he begins to sing. The words repeat and his mantra is a good bit more upbeat than the one I construed as I pooh pooh-ed his presence. Eventually he encourages us to join him in his chant, and each round helps me unwind a little more. I'm well on my way to serenity by the time he finishes and exhale a sigh of relief as he asks us to focus on our breathing. Despite my concerted efforts to clear my nostrils, they're still stuffed up and I'm distracted once again by the whistling wind coming from them. When Zach asks us to expel hefty consecutive breaths I am finally feel free to toot my horn, and low and behold, a hundred rapid-fire huffs later my sinuses are clear! After what seems like an eternity of forced exhalation, we move from ventilation into meditation as Zach explains a technique called "Ujjayi" breathing. I cross my legs and focus on the sound of the air as it passes the back of my throat. Then, per Zach's instruction, I silently state my intentions: for class, the rest of the day, and the life I have left ahead of me.

Closing my eyes I try to drill the intentions into my head, but Zach interrupts my determination when he says, "Now let them go." Not sure what he means, I wait for clarification. "Perfection is a good direction to head in," he says. "But the minor steps we take on the way to our destination are worth noting as well." Maybe twenty minutes of church was good enough, I think to myself. Zach continues. "You have your entire life ahead of you. There's no rush." I exhale a sigh of relief as I return to my focus to my breathing. "Don't worry about the big picture," he concludes. "You have plenty of time to succeed. So right now, just breathe."

I've been practicing yoga for a year now and never knew about the power of slow and controlled breathing. My regular teacher teaches Power Yoga. His class is physically intense, and his bust-a-move workouts have plenty of merit when it comes to strength and endurance. But they have very little effect on the strength of my spirit. Today I am on a totally different plain. Zach's class allows me to forget all about all the other people around me. It feels like I'm by myself, yet surrounded by love and support and inspiration. My mind becomes clear and my body still.

My chest rises and falls with the wake of the Ujjayi. The ever steady breath carves a line of truth into my frenetic energy, to reveal serenity, deep down inside of me.

Zach strikes a cord on the harmonium during the resting pose at the end of class; it brings tears to my eyes. They slip down my face and pool in the bottom of my ears as he offers his benediction: "Stay focused, committed, and healthy, and life will give you everything you need." He finishes by placing his hands in front of his heart in the prayer position as he ushers the word, "Namaste." All I can do is lay there as the lights come back on and Zach makes some announcement. I return to earth when he mentions there are a few spots left for his yoga retreat in Ojai next week. My heart swells—I've got to be there! Seems like a great idea, until I realize that I'm really not prepared to finance such a retreat. Luckily, a second thought obliterates the first: I do believe that Yoga will help me find sanity and resolution. Moments later I step outside, float across the street towards an ATM and withdraw the two hundred dollar deposit. I fill my cells with the crystal clear April air and surreptitiously thank God for the order of my priorities.

Friday, April 12

I'm sitting on a rock by the banks of a creek where succulents surround me. They're illuminated by the full moon rising, its brilliant tender light makes them the most welcoming cacti I've ever seen. Maybe it's my relaxed mood that makes them seem sweet. Or the luscious scent of Jasmine that's been occupying my olfactory's for the last eight hours. The bouquet of pink Jasmine was the first impression I got as I cruised down the dirt driveway towards the Matilija Hot Springs. Now I can taste it, at least I wish I could—it smells so good. The rush of water at my feet exacerbates the chill in the air but I'm plenty warm; thanks to the hand-woven sweater I wear, the thrill of being on vacation, and the intense beauty of the midnight sky in Ojai.

I left L.A. at noon today, pumped full of rushed exhilaration. Up at five, I trained four clients in three hours, made last minute arrangements for the care of my cats, and dropped my duffle off at the yoga studio, to be carted up by the instructor so I wouldn't have to balance it on my bike. Pressed by an overactive morning I decided to take the long and winding way to Ojai, and from the moment I headed out of town the world slowed down. Rather than follow the coastal road, I crisscrossed the mountains that rise from the sea between Malibu and Santa Barbara. The first solo excursion on my motorcycle, I was a little nervous, so I took the backcountry route away from traffic and high-speed travel. Slaloming between cars on the freeway is nowhere near as fun as negotiating the twisty mountain roads. Leaning side-to-side into the sweeping turns makes me feel like a pelican soaring swiftly above the ocean. By the time I drive past the Rock Store on Mulholland Highway I'm surfing Cloud Nine—enjoying each breath of fresh air that inflates my lungs and lightens the load from the busy week drifting behind me. Note to self: I want to learn everything I can about breathing this weekend.

During three and a half hours of virtual silence I indulge in a gluttonous amount of positive thought. Max's M.S. news has affected me. Our separation has become my salvation; it inspires my declaration to live a long and healthy life, and have as many different experiences as possible. As far as this weekend goes, I have very specific goals: I want to meet cool people, learn more about Yoga, and forgive myself for the part I played in the destruction of Max's and my relationship. I'm ready to accept this latest failure as an inevitable part of the learning process, and to stop holding such a grudge about it. Every step I've taken so far has gotten me to where I am right now, which—for a few slippery seconds—feels like Nirvana. As I roll past the orange groves above and beyond Santa Barbara I strain to recall the last time I felt so satisfied, when summer camp pops up in my mind.

Some of the best times of my life were spent at Camp Coniston, in New Hampshire. I spent two weeks there every summer from age eleven to thirteen, and in my fourth year was there for an entire month, as a Counselor-in-Training. Every summer those two weeks at camp provided me with more novel experiences than I had during the entire school year. By the end of each session I had new friends, new hobbies, new confidence, and a greater appreciation for that place called home. Sometimes I even walked away with a new boyfriend, a pre-teen love affair that invariably ended on the last day, but was completely heartfelt nonetheless. Most of my friendships at camp faded away after the last day, but that didn't make them any less important, because the pace at which we got to know each other was based on openness, not emptiness. That we all came from different background didn't prejudice us the way it might have if we had the time to pick and choose.

During my last year at Camp Coniston the bond that forged between me and the other Counselor's in Training was made strong by all the incredible 'firsts' we shared. We became empowered as certified life savers. We collectively spent a night scattered individually around the lake, and slept "alone" in the woods and learned to face our teenage fears of isolation. The final phase of our initiation involved a three-day hike up Mount Washington. The most ferocious peak on the East Coast, it gave us an opportunity to conquer the demons behind weakness, giving us a taste of I-can-do-anything. On the evening before the final ascent we stayed above tree line, at a cabin called Lakes in the Clouds. After dinner that night we hiked up to a high point to catch a glimpse of a meteor shower; in one hour I counted forty-five shooting stars.

I return to the present tense when a lone car shoots past me in the other lane, redirecting my attention to the whistling wind inside my helmet. There's an obvious drop in temperature at this higher altitude, on the first stretch of the Maricopa highway that heads North above Ojai. I can't wait to get to my final destination and jump into the hot springs. I also can't wait to stretch out in the first Yoga class this evening. I'm getting a little ahead of myself, and realize I need to stay focused on the ride. That reminds me of another expectation I have for this weekend: to learn to stay in the moment. Motorcycling certainly requires that kind of focus, that's why it's so exhausting to do for hours on end. Oddly enough, I feel fresh when I pull into the dusty lot of the retreat center and park my chariot at the base of the path that will guide me to my cabin. Speaking of which, I need to go to bed—it's late. I better get some sleep if I want to make the most of tomorrow.

Wow…a dragonfly just landed on the rock beside me. Someone once told me that crossing paths with a dragonfly is a sign of imminent fortune, but I don't need this iridescent bug to tell me there are some amazing things heading my way. Like vibration on the tracks sent by an impending train, I can feel them coming.

Saturday, April 13

I don't have much time—the next yoga class starts in forty-five minutes, but I have to write about this guy I've been hanging out with all day. I'm ready to turn the page in regards to my breakup, and I think this guy Mitch is the ticket to getting ole' what's-his-name out of my head. He's so cute: six' five", sandy blond hair, and shoulders that fill the door when he walks in the room. He's a screenwriter, who volunteers at the Los Angeles Animal Rescue in his free time. He says he's been "up to his knees in bunnies" lately, while he helps find foster care for the three hundred rabbits that recently arrived at the animal shelter where he works. He and I arrived here at precisely the same time yesterday. I pulled up on my powder blue motorcycle and parked right next to his navy blue Bronco. "Nice bike," he said as he grabbed a beat up backpack from the passenger seat and turned his baseball cap backwards. With the lid no longer shading his eyes I could see they were a crystal green, like tourmaline. "Thanks," I said, sensing a connection. Sure enough, when we sat together at dinner last night I felt the tickle of libidinous butterflies in my belly; something told me we'd be spending a lot of time together. That ticklish tension moved towards the region below my belly when I saw him naked in the hot springs this morning—I've been tingling ever since.

I've actually been in multiple states of appreciation since I woke up this morning. It started in the seven am yoga class. I was very excited when Mitch arrived and plopped down behind me. I sensed he wanted to get a good look at my ass, so I opted to do a little stretching before class. I offered him a quick hello then casually bent down to grab my ankles. As I gazed up between my knees I could see he was pleased. After a minute passed I eased my way down to my mat, spread my legs and lay my chest flat on the floor. Satisfied with my subtle vex of flexibility, I lifted my trunk and crossed my legs in preparation for the meditation. I was already in the zone when instructor Zach asked us to focus our attention on the fire at the front of the room.

After five minutes of total silence, he asked us to begin the "Breath of Fire." The vigorous heavy breathing lit one inside me, or maybe it was Mitch's enormous feet that got me so hot. What can I say—my ex's teeny weenie

English feet left much to be desired. With twenty of us packed like a matchbook in the relatively small room, our "breath of fire" warmed the entire space, but it wasn't overly crowded. I welcomed the bodacious souls that surrounded me, the rationed atmosphere connected me to their heartbeats and helped me appreciate our shared struggle—each of us stuffing our blood cells with oxygen. Zach completed the breath lesson by transitioning us into ujayii breathing. He reminded us that when done properly, ujayii sounds like a wave rolling up the shore. He said that if we learn to breathe with strength and serenity we can endure the most intense challenges. Breath was the only aspect of my being that I noticed during class. By the end of the workout I was soaked in sweat, and completely invigorated.

 Afterwards I had a breakfast of scrambled tofu and heavy bread, the kind that looks like a seed garden and tastes like gerbil food. Vegan fair makes me carnivorous, and when Mitch pulled up beside me, I suddenly craved Bratwurst. By the time he mentioned he was going to catch a soak in the hot springs I was ravenous. Tagging along seemed like a good way to see what he looked like in a bathing suit. That is, until I arrived, and found the hot springs overflowing with naked people. I've never been one to baulk at the idea of getting naked. Usually I'm happy to show off my hard body, but this time was different. I was worried about the fading scars on my breasts from the cutting episode I had the night Max said he didn't want to marry me. No one has seen my naked body since and I wasn't sure if the wounds were still visible. Facing my back to the crowd, I slowly untied my bikini top. A quick glimpse reassured me that I was clean—scar free. I knew that giving Mitch a glimpse of my naked body would seal the deal, so I climbed into the tub next to him. I felt calm and excited at the same time. There's nothing wrong with me, I thought to myself. Then I hugged my body tight, embracing everything I was hiding under the bubbly surface.

I've been wandering around naked ever since. I did put some clothes on to attend the slightly more satisfying, yet excessively grainy lunch. Mitch and I talked the entire time. He's such a good guy. I heard more about his volunteer work at the animal shelter. He told me the sad yet oddly entertaining tale, about raiding a farm in Calabasas last weekend, where he and several other volunteers confiscated hundreds of rabbits from a breeder who had let them multiply out of control. My eyes swelled as he told me about the horrible living conditions they'd found them in; the image of this California cowboy rounding up bunnies, six at a time, made me madly attracted to him. Immediately after lunch a few of us decided to sunbathe by the creek. Once again, clothing was not an option. I don't know which is worse: the tacky tan lines of summer, or the alabaster white that highlights Caucasians in early spring. A fair number of us had butts that shone brighter than the sun. Luckily there were a handful of black beauties in the group to even out the tones. I kept staring at the Black women, to see how their bodies differed from mine and was surprised they were no more voluptuous. I assumed the rumors about large sexual body parts applied to black men and woman alike. Of course, they all had bodacious booties, but I have a pretty round butt for a white girl so they had no advantage there. Hands down, I had the most manicured muff in the group. I take pride in grooming my petunia. Mine was like a bonsai tree compared to some of the nappier bushes I saw.

    I love being able to stare freely at people. There are very few times when it's okay to gawk, but this was one of them. When a punk kid walks down the street with blue hair and a pierced face, he's asking to be noticed. When a buck-naked woman scrambles across slippery river rocks on all fours, she's asking to be ogled. And when a handsome young thing named Mitch hands me his bratwurst in the middle of a vegetarian weekend, he's asking to be devoured. That's exactly what happened when we found ourselves alone at last. Down river, where a waterfall splashed into a sparkling pool, we dove right into each other. Surprise, surprise—beans and rice are not the only source of protein around here, and the Japanese aren't the only folks who appreciate the beauty of a bonsai. Anyway, I'm thrilled to say I've moved on from old what's-his-name to MUCH bigger things.

I'm writing for the second time today because I desperately need to chill out. Maybe the full moon is making my heart pound. Or perhaps I'm just excited about the possibility of a little make out session with Mitch later. He asked me if I want to join him down by the river to share a bottle of vino he has stashed in his truck. We've been told by the yoga instructor and the folks who run this place that there are absolutely no drugs or alcohol allowed on the property. Rebel minds think alike—I've got a couple of joints back in the cabin. It's nice to have a partner in crime, and besides, as long as we walk off the property we won't be breaking any rules. I need to find something to bring my heart rate down, or I won't be able to sleep. I'm totally wired from everything that happened today.

The second yoga class was even more rewarding than the first. With Mitch having gone his separate way, there were no distractions. I spent the entire class totally unaware of anyone around me, which was difficult at first, because the class was outside on the lawn in front of the dining hall. During the initial meditation I kept thinking about the birds and the rustling trees. The breeze negotiated its way around my body, while the flow of the creek negotiated its way around the rocks below, where Mitch and I had gotten our rocks off a few hours earlier. Thoughts kept returning to my orgasm, that delightful moment when the sun beating down on my bare skin was no match for the warmth exuded by my groin, as Mitch's hot breath steamed my inner thighs. Smiling during meditation is proof purchase that the mind is not where it's supposed to be, but I didn't care. I even opened my eyes a couple of times to gaze in wonderment at the incredible atmosphere. When Zach took us into downward dog, I knew the only way I would stay focused is if I reverted to my old version of yoga and made it as physically challenging as possible. I managed to exhaust myself so much that I wanted to take a nap at the end of class. Instead, I had to rush back to the cabin and prepare for the next scheduled event—the Sweat Lodge.

Last night when Zach described the Sweat Lodge ceremony to us, I eagerly committed to what he described as a "rebirth". But dragging my weary self back to the cabin after yoga, I no longer cared about it. All I wanted to do was lie down. So I chugged a bunch of water, gobbled a power bar and took a two-minute shower to reinvigorate. Then I wrapped my body in a turquoise sarong, slipped my feet into matching blue thongs, and headed off towards the massive fire that had been burning since this morning. As I approached the fire ring, I saw a bunch of filthy people strewn across the lawn. The Sweat Lodge held only twenty at a time, so we'd been divided into two groups. The last of the participants from the first group were now exiting the tent: covered in mud, vapor rising off of their sweaty bodies, the majority lay lifeless on the ground. A few of them walked around, fanning themselves. They looked completely cooked.

I spot Mitch sitting on the lawn and am about to lie down next to him when Zach walks up and gathers group number two. We circle around the fire. The Shaman introduces himself and his assistant, who's been managing the fire all day. He speaks briefly about the significance of the ceremony and encourages us to establish a specific intention for the experience. Then he hands each of us a small bunch of sage tied with a red string and we file into the blanketed fort. Mitch enters directly in front of me. At six foot five, he practically has to crawl in the cramped space. I'm shocked by how small it is. I'd list the total capacity at six; we manage to squeeze in sixteen. I settled my butt into the dirt and arrange myself in a cross-legged position. My knees are pressed against Mitch and the woman on my left and inches away from a deep pit in the center of the space. At five foot three, I'm one of the few people whose head does not touch the thick army green blankets that cover the fort. The thought of sharing this experience with Mitch initially excited me, but the confined space makes me wish I weren't sitting next to the biggest person in the tent. I scoot as close as I can to the woman by my side; with her petite frame and shy disposition, I figure I can beat her in the battle for oxygen.

The Shaman is the last one to enter. He informs us that the sage and dirt contain cooling qualities, and rubbing them on our skin will bring relief during the hottest moments. Then he begins to pray in his Native American language while his assistant, the fire keeper, drops hot rocks into the pit. The Shaman blesses the rocks and throws a handful of aromatic seeds on top of them. The assistant closes the flap and the space goes black. It's so incredibly hot I can't believe it. When the Shaman sprinkles water onto the hot rocks; it evaporates into thick steam and increases the temperature by at least twenty degrees. I feel like my lungs might melt, and pray for distraction as my eyes try to adjust to the dark. My attention moves from the heat to the incredible glow coming from inside the rocks. The fire has illuminated their cores—they're transparent.

I've never seen anything like it, molten granite the color of amber. I wonder if the heat will make me see-through too.

One thing's for sure, I'm totally overdressed. Careful not to elbow my neighbors in the ribs, I shed my sarong and settle my bare butt into the cool dirt. My cross-legged position doesn't last long, since the only way to get my face close enough to the 'cooling' dirt is from my knees. Right about the time I shift my position, the seemingly reserved woman on my left starts to whisper 'mother fucker.' I can hear her hushed profanity throughout the rest of the ceremony.

The ritual consists of us sharing our prayers, one by one, around the circle. The Shaman instructs that the first round of prayer is for 'someone else.' On my turn, I wish for a cure for M.S. When the last person in the circle has spoken, the tent flap is re-opened. We collectively suck in molecules of fresh air and I imagine from the outside, the tent must look like a giant lung, inflating as we exhale. The man outside delivers more hot rocks. One person evacuates. I contemplate whether or not I can handle the next round, but then the flap is closed and my fate is sealed. The Shaman announces the second round of prayer is for our selves.

I've contemplated my intention for this ceremony all day long. Earlier this morning when I worried that nudity might expose hidden scars from self abuse, I was struck by the absurdity of how much damage I've done to myself throughout the years. So I decided an apology was in order, and I would use the Sweat Lodge to say, "I'm sorry." Now that I'm sweating enough to dissolve, it's hard to concentrate on that resolve. My body temperature seems unnaturally high. My thoughts fluctuate between clawing my way out of this tent and sucking it up. I'm usually pretty good at dealing with physical stress, but when the stupid Shaman sprinkles more water on the rocks, it takes everything I have to focus my humid mind on my commitment.

As a kid I was always able to grin and bear it when it came to physical stress. Facing it head on made me feel strong. But the tiniest amount of emotional stress demolished me every time. Nothing made me feel worse than crying. Around age twelve I started to punish myself for tears. I can still recall the first time I beat myself up for being a crybaby. A fight with my Dad had crescendo-ed into screaming; shrill and hateful. Anger begot tears, which begot more anger; I was furious at myself for crying in front of him. My fury got me confined to my bedroom, where I paced back and forth and muttered, "Shut up, you idiot. Quit crying." The more disgusted I became, the harder the tears fell. My fury continued to escalate until I couldn't handle it. The rage in my heart made my head spin. In an effort to quit reeling, I grabbed the rotary phone from my desk and slammed the receiver against the side of my head. The tears stopped as endorphins kicked in. I slammed myself again. Suddenly, the pounding in my head was replaced by throbbing; superficial and manageable. My hostility was contained. I ran my fingers along the goose egg on my scalp. My hair no longer stood on end like it did when we were yelling.

I'm abruptly brought back to the tent when Mitch squirms beside me. I want to yell, "Stop fucking touching me!" All day long I couldn't get enough of him. Now I'm ready to scratch his eyes out if his sweaty arm so much as grazes mine one more time. It's amazing what a hundred and forty degrees will do to your patience. The two of us sit smack dab in the middle of the group—number seven and eight, in the circle of sixteen. I'm extremely thankful when another frantic body rushes out during the fifth of sixteen prayers we have to sit through. I have five minutes to figure out what my prayer will be, how I should say I'm sorry. I take a mental inventory of the brutality I've suffered at my own hands: I've taken blades to my ankles, wrists, breasts and thighs. I've banged my head against a wall, burned myself with a lighter, rubbed my skin raw with the edge of a quarter, and bruised my feet with barefoot kicks to a metal pole. Each time my anger would be immediately put to rest, but I'd spend weeks covering up the damage. I remember sneaking into the locker room during high school gymnastics practice to change the blood stained sweat guards that cushioned the "grips" on my wrists, the one time my escapade with the blade had gone too far.

This is exactly what I'm thinking about when it's my turn to pray. Editing the extraneous information, I blurt out, "I'm going to love myself from this day forward." There is a pause as my words are absorbed, then Mitch jumps in to begin his prayer. He talks about giving his life more meaning. He says he's going to quit his job and work full time at the animal shelter, so he can "save the rabbits." I burst out laughing. I don't mean to belittle his bunny love, but the heat has made me hysterical. Luckily, his comments are short and sweet—only eight more prayers to go. Sweat pours down my back. I fold forward to get my face as close to the dirt as possible and catch a cool breath from the tiny bit of air as it seeps from underneath the tent. Rolling my forehead temple-to-temple across the dirt, I whisper, "I'm sorry…I'm sorry…I'm sorry."

By the end of the round, the energy in the tent is frantic. People are on the verge of screaming, or crying, or ripping the tent to shreds. I almost flee during the second to last prayer, as the temperature spikes to an unbearable high. When the flap is finally lifted, two people instantly beg to be excused. I'm also tempted to tuck my tail between my legs and bail, but I cling to the voice of reason that carries me to the finish line every time: I think I can, I think I can, I think I can. As the rock man starts to furnish the tent with another collection of inferno granite, I realize I have nothing to prove. The final round feels like punishment, so I let myself off the hook, and decide to be kind and gentle to my body. The assistant's about to close the flap when I lunge forward on all fours and announce, "I've had enough."

Never have I felt such relief as I did when I stepped outside that tent. My legs were about to give; they'd fallen asleep from sitting on my knees the entire time. I lay down in the crisp grass as tears welled up in my eyes. Instinct would have me to stuff the frog back down my throat, but then I relaxed, and let them roll. Tugging at the lawn under my palm, this afternoon, I realized there are many ways to feel grounded. Lying under the blue sky, inhaling the scent of jasmine, and listening to the trees seemed like a great place to start.

That's why I'm out here alone tonight. Everyone else is in the dining hall, singing along with an acoustic guitar and a bunch of bongos. I was having a blast until my heart started to race. So I stepped outside to practice the art of feeling grounded. I need to learn how to distinguish the different types of arrhythmia. Anxiety and fear tend to drive my heart to a place that makes me want to shock it into submission. Right now my heart's skipping because I'm happy to be alive. Maybe I should stop trying to subdue the thumping. Maybe I should just bridle it, and enjoy the bumpy ride.

Sunday, April 14

I did it! I managed to get through a meditation without any assistance. No guide, no music, no candles, and no counting to make the time fly. For four minutes and forty-three seconds my mind lay perfectly still. I set the timer on my watch for five minutes, but right at the end I involuntarily opened my eyes, looked down at my wrist, and saw there were seventeen seconds left. It was a knee jerk reaction. Spontaneous restlessness pulled me out of the void, but I still count it as a successful attempt at stringing multiple minutes of meditation together in one solitary session. I really hope this unmapped exploration helps me stop feeling so damn lost all the time.

So far, so good—that new-fangled instinct brought me all the way home from the Hot Springs this morning. As I pulled out of the dirt driveway of the retreat center and headed back down Highway 33, I figured I had two options: I could return to LA on the same back roads I'd taken on Friday, or I could hop on the interstate and take the fast track home. I contemplated the best plan while I pumped gas at a filling station in Ojai. My first thought was that I really missed my cats. My second thought was that I was a worn out from the weekend and wanted to hurry home and enjoy a leisurely afternoon. I knew taking the freeway would give me time to lounge around on the couch and catch up on some of the zzzz's I missed last night. The problem with the direct route is that it's a lot less beautiful and a lot more stressful, which seemed dangerous considering my sleep deprived mind. So I asked the gas station guy if he knew an alternative. Turns out he's a biker too and was looking for an excuse to show me his custom Harley Soft Tail with ape hanger handlebars. He told me to go back the way I'd come, beyond the Hot Springs, to find "the sweetest ride this side of the I5". When he said he'd be surprised if I saw more than a couple of cars during the first seventy-five miles, I was sold. The cats and the couch could wait. This sacred Chumash Indian land had more to offer me. Slugging down a bottle of Gatorade, I prepared for yet another journey. I thanked the man for his recommendation, threw my leg over the seat and settled into the saddle. "Speed safely," he hollered as I slipped my helmet on and fastened the chinstrap.

I was just leaning into the third turn on my way back up the Mountain, when Mitch came around the corner in his Bronco. He honked and waved, and looked confused about why I was driving back up the Maricopa Highway. Afraid to let go in the turn, I gave him a cool nod and indulged in the decadent memory of our twenty-four hour love affair. After an unforgettable day, Mitch and I spent last night together too. We had sex on the wet grass, and spent hours talking and rocking under the full moon—swinging side-by-side in our sleeping bags, on a hammock strung between two trees above the river. Lying with my head against his chest I felt warm, but when Mitch drifted off to sleep, I shivered with insecurity. Too preoccupied to rest my weary head, I wrestled with paranoid presumption: I wonder if he still loves his ex-girlfriend? He mentioned her tonight. He wants to quit his lucrative job as a writer and volunteer his time to save a bunch of bunnies. Do I want to date an unemployed rabbit fanatic? He's probably not going to ask for my number anyway. Damn, I shouldn't have slept with him!

I was slipping into the habit of berating myself, when a déjà vu flashed before my eyes like a firefly. Back at summer camp, I'm sitting in a field with a twelve-year old boy. We've managed to sneak away together on the way back to our cabins, after the closing campfire ceremony.

Aside from the wildlife, we're finally alone. Framed by tufts of whistling wheat, and sage, our flirtation is harmonized by the sounds of cricket and crow. Tomorrow is the last day of our two-week stay and now it's time to say goodbye. We kiss. I watch my breath disappear into the frosty night air; it's a breath to remember.

Last night in the hammock that breath came back to me, and I started to appreciate our time together, for what it had already offered me. In the end, all the worry was absurd; Mitch asked me for my phone number this morning. So when he drives by I'm tempted to berate myself for being an idiot and doubting his good intentions. Recognizing the nastiness of that thought before it escapes my mouth, I stifle it, and it dies. Winding my way up the juniper-lined, sun-streaked highway, I realize I need a complete revamp of my silent dialogue. I need to quit referring to myself as an idiot. If I'm going to end this era of abuse, I've got to stop cutting on myself with blades and words.

The hum of a bunch of motorcycles coming from the other direction brings my focus back to the road. The buzz of their engines has the unique sound of a dry clutch, the subtle 'ping' tells me it's a crew of Ducati's. One by one they throw me a low wave. One woman, riding "bitch" on the back, gives me the thumbs up. Smiling, I think to myself, yeah…I'm cool. After they pass I get the sudden urge to smell the atmosphere, so I balance the bike with my knees in the straightaway, slow down to thirty-five, and use both hands to unlock and flip the lower half of my helmet up, so I can feel the dew and hear the roar of the river that runs along the road. I've only seen one car so far: a VW bus, parked askew, its passengers spilling out of the side door and scrambling downhill towards the river. There were four young men, wearing shaggy surfer hair and colorful board shorts; each carrying an inner tube around their waist like a fat, black, tutu. It reminded me of a circus. I've also passed a dozen campsites, and twice as many bikers. I'm leaning into another swooping turn when five crotch rockets barrel past me. The riders are all wearing leather race gear and their kneepads scrape the ground as they scream around the corner. Within seconds they fade away, and the silence is bliss. The trees thin out as I approach the summit. At the top I spot the intersection, way down in the valley where the gas station guy told me to bang a right. He said that would take me east towards the I5. Coasting down the switchbacks I inhale the last of the clean air before I hit the exhaust filled freeway. A hawk circles high above the valley. Spotted cows are off in the distance. Ninety miles outside of L.A; I may as well be in Iowa.

Thirty minutes later I enter the freeway, where I shift into fifth and accelerate to ninety. I slalom between the cars to get in front where they can see me. Glancing down at the speedometer I notice the clock. The day is young—I have no reason to hurry. I back off the throttle and slip into a slower gear. At cruising speed it's safer to think about things. At sixty-five my mind returns to camp again. I spent seventy-five days there in total throughout the years. Flipping through the Rolodex of that experience, I'm awestruck by how much I achieved, and became, during a mere two and a half months. Time well spent—chock full of lessons. Not unlike this weekend.

When I finally get home at three-thirty, the first thing I want to do is take a bath. The cats are thrilled to see me. Sandy curls up on the bathroom rug while I soak. Pebbles—his frisky sister—jumps up on the rim of the tub and carefully maneuvers her way around the perimeter. I block her path with a rubber ducky, to see what she'll do. She immediately knocks it in the water with a swipe of her paw and keeps on walking. When she jumps back down to the floor, I put the duck on the rim again to antagonize her. She takes the bait, balances on her back feet and bats it back into the brink. This goes on for five or six rounds. Tired of getting splashed, I place the duck on the rim one last time and then knock it towards her. She runs off in a flurry, with Sandy trailing behind her. Laughing, I slide down and get everything but my head under the water. That's when I decide to meditate.

    I set the timer on my watch for five minutes. Closing my eyes, I focus on the slow and steady pace of my inhalation. Images float across my mind, like clouds. But rather than attach a reaction to them, I let them blow by, and simply focus on my breathing. When I come out of the trance, seventeen seconds early, I'm not disappointed. On the contrary—I have a complete sense of satisfaction. Feeling prune-ish, I decide it's time to get out of the bath. As I twist my hair in a towel, Sandy comes strolling back in and does a figure eight around my legs—kitty hugs, I like to call it. Tapping me with his tail, he tells me it's time for dinner. Meditation is great, but feeding my cats is still the most important thing I do each day. That's exactly how I feel as I fill their bowls with love and tender vittles.

Monday, April 15

Back to the grind! I was up at 4:30 this morning and trained five clients by 9:00 a.m. Luckily Rick was last—his perpetual comedy routine makes the time fly. He was in a particularly cheery mood today, which made him all the more fun to be around.

"We had two great meetings for the show last week," he announced, as we rounded the first corner of our jog around the Brentwood Country Club. "At the first one my creative advisor convinced a very important person to join our company as a board member."

"Who," I asked.

"I can't tell you his name. But he's the president of marketing for one of the biggest car companies, and they spend a *ton* of money on advertising. Which reminds me…" he abruptly stopped, grabbed a mini notebook from his breast pocket, and scrawled something down. As soon as we started to run again he continued. "The second meeting was with two of my fraternity brothers from University of Miami. They're successful entrepreneurs, and…drum role please…they wrote me a huge check on Friday! Now I have more money in the bank than I ever did as a studio writer."

"I don't believe it." I said.

"What? That I have money?"

"No, that you were a frat boy!" I jetted out ahead of him and announced with faux repulsion, "I cannot be friends with you, *ever again*."

Refusing to fall for my cheap trick to lengthen his stride, he lagged behind. "It's not what you think," he hollered behind me. "Our frat was filled with freaks, geeks, and rejects. We even had a couple of gay guys in our house."

"Is that why you started to wear gaudy shirts all the time, to ward them off?"

"You don't like my attire?" He inquired.

I looked back at his magnolia-print, pink and lime green polyester button-down. "Rick," I said, without the slightest slant of whimsy. "Those flowers give me asthma. You should really consider a material that breathes."

Not about to let his floral fashion sense hold him back, he hurried to catch up with me. "Sneer all you want. Six months from now I'll be in the best shape of my life, I'll be back in TV, and women will beg me for dates. This shirt will come in handy then, I tell ya." I raised an eyebrow and prepared for his punch line. "You know…camo?" Noting my confusion he clarified, "It'll hide me from the overzealous ones." Then he crouched behind the Bougainvillea vine that clung to the fence around the golf course. "Ouch!" He yelped, as a thorn stuck him in the butt.

"The best shape of your life?" I ribbed. "What's your heart rate?"

He ignored me. "I'll just have to find a woman who loves Hawaiians as much as I do…the shirts, not the islanders."

"What are you going to do about camouflaging that 1970 Datsun you drive?"

"It won't matter. I'm going to find a girlfriend who loves me for who I am—now that my streak of bad luck has ended."

"I like that nothing's-gonna-stop-me-now attitude. Let's tap into it on the next lap." He guffawed and I changed the subject. "So how long was your run of bad luck?"

"Seven years" he said, tripping on the root of a Eucalyptus tree.

"Did you break a mirror?"

"No, I quit my job."

"Seven years is a long time to be unemployed. What finally broke the spell?"

"I quit believing in God."

"Rick, you need to lighten up a little..."

"Don't tell me..." he retorted in defense.

"I mean *on your feet*" I said. "You're pounding."

He added a prance to his step and went on, "For seven years God has had it out for me. I've always said: 'if you don't like being punished, get rid of the punisher.' So I took God out of the equation and suddenly my luck turned around."

"What did you do differently?" I asked.

"I told him to go to hell, quit praying for a miracle, and put my trust in myself."

"I need to do that too." I concurred. Then I subtly implied my budding belief in the need for existential assistance. "But *I* need all the help I can get."

"Here's the best piece of advice I can give you," he said. "You have to be your own number one fan, especially when it comes to your acting career."

"I don't have an acting career." I reminded him.

"You will soon. There's a role in my show for you."

"I'll believe it when I see it," I said.

"That's exactly what I told God the last time we spoke. He hasn't shown."

We ran in silence for a few and I started to think about my long lost aspirations, and the acting ambitions that drew me to L.A. in the first place. At the industry dinner where Rick and I met, I had a strong premonition we'd become fast friends, and he'd play a pivotal role on my path to acting success. At the time I thought it would happen on the 'fast track', not seven years later on the dirt track that runs around the Country Club. Nonetheless, I was excited about the prospect of being on Rick's show.

"You think I should join the union again?" I asked.

"It's not about what I think, or what I can promise. What did you promise yourself?"

"I said I'd pursue acting for ten years; but I threw in the towel at five."

"There's your answer. You're committed to another five at least. But there's one thing you should know," he said with a stern look on his face.

"What?" I asked.

"If you get back into acting—it's over between us. I mean its bad enough that you're chasing me around this golf course all googley-eyed. But I promised myself I'd never get involved with an actress, especially one I have to work with every day. So you better to come to terms with *that* before you make any brash decisions."

"Done," I said.

"We can fool around *before* the show gets off the ground," he offered.

"Nice try, Rick. Now come on—pick up the pace. You run like a wuss. I want you to run like a guy who has the gall to produce his own TV show."

He immediately stopped running and announced with indignation, "That guy can afford to pay someone else to run for him." Then he pulled a twenty from his pocket and said, "Go on, give me your best shot. I'll meet you at the end of the block in a half hour."

"Anything for a joke," I said with a snicker.

"No. But I will do anything to get a good look at your ass. Now, come on—pick up the pace. You run like a wuss. I want you to run like a woman who's…trying to escape a serial killer." With that he made the screeching noise from the movie "Psycho", and started to chase me.

Comedy is a lot more fun than running—but don't tell Rick that.

Tuesday, April 16

I'm working on my computer when it rings a cheerful "ding", and announces, "You've got mail". It's only been a few months since I established my first email address. I'm an infant when it comes to the world of electronic correspondence; family and friends are the only folks who are privy to my new address, so I'm delighted by the prospect of a midday "hello" from one of them. I hit 'save', close Word, and open my mailbox. There sits a message from Nina Darlington, a high school classmate who I haven't spoken to since our reunion last year. I'm trying to figure out how she found me when I realize she has written to me and a whole slew of other people, on behalf of our good friend Adriana. The subject reads: Bad news about Adriana and the boys.

Frantic thoughts rush my brain in the split second it takes to double click on the envelope. The last time Adriana and I spoke, she informed me she was pregnant with twins.

My first concern is that she's been in an accident. I scan the page to find the pertinent details. Nina writes that Adriana gave birth to her babies almost six weeks ago—four and a half months early. The boys weighed 1.5 pounds each and had health problems too numerous to list. One of them had surgery on his lungs yesterday. He died on the operating table.

When I spoke to Adriana two months ago she was completely elated. Almost four months pregnant, she had waited to share the news since the chance of miscarriage is highest during the first trimester. By early February everything was fine, the babies were developing normally, and plans for the nursery were well under way. She joyously shared with me her process of motherly discovery. Adriana has been looking forward to motherhood for as long as I've known her. She was the only person I knew who loved babysitting, not for the money, but for the chance to be around kids. She studied child development in college and went on to work in a nursery. Since the day she got married, Adriana has wanted to get pregnant. But after three years of failed attempts, she and her husband Brian were tired of putting sex on their list of things to do; the by-the-book approach took the fun right out of it. So they decided to up the ante with fertility drugs. After multiple trips to the doctor's office and months of daily hormone injections, the process took. Two months ago Adriana was the happiest I've ever known her to be, her life appeared to be perfect.

Now I can't fathom the depth of her sorrow. She must be absolutely devastated. I'm sure that's why I haven't heard anything about this from her. I have no idea what I'm supposed to do in response. Maybe she doesn't even want a response. After all, she's not the one who sent the e-mail. Speaking of which, I really do not appreciate the cyber-convenience of email when it comes to the announcement of someone's death—seems a tad impersonal. What was Nina thinking when she wrote that flippant subject heading anyway? Which folder should I file it under, the "bad news" basket? I can't believe I just received a "carbon copy" message, from an acquaintance, to tell me one of my best friend's babies has died. Should I hit reply and send condolences to Nina? Maybe I should send her an electronic card that she can forward to Adriana. Right now email is making me feel totally *dis*connected. I have the notion to pick up the phone and call Adriana directly. But what would I say? I don't know what to do.

Meditation seems like the key, so I cross my legs and pray for peace for the second time today. Since I returned from the Yoga retreat last week, I've meditated for five minutes each morning. Starting the day from a place of serenity seems like a good plan. Today the scale has been tipped by this calamity, and I need to get centered again. I begin the meditation with the intention of finding acceptance. Acceptance became the theme of this day when I opened my book on Daily Meditations this morning, and read an entire paragraph about it. The Dalai Llama says situations are not inherently good or bad, and even the most painful experiences offer valuable lessons. I'd hate to disagree with a man whose decree is peace, but that viewpoint seems ludicrous right now. What sort of lesson is Adriana supposed to take away from this? What's the optimistic angle here, "things can't get any worse?" Bullshit. It can always get worse, her other son still clings to his life. What if he dies too? Or will the yin and yang factor of the universe save him? No, because balance, just like justice, is something we can work towards, but never really achieve. Screw Buddha and the idea that life is perfect at every given moment. Losing a child is the worst tragedy someone can face. What's the lesson in that?

Life's not fair. That's the lesson that resonates for me. Come on, this tiny baby spends six weeks, his entire life, fighting to survive, while stupid me has spent *at least* six weeks throughout the years contemplating suicide. Would it have been different if I'd been forced to fight for my life? If Adriana's other twin hangs in, will he appreciate his luck, and live life to its fullest? Or will he feel the same eternal loss as his mom?

I need to focus on the positive, so I can come up with something to say to Adriana. I guess one positive thought is that her infant son probably received love from everyone around him. The doctors and nurses, all the people who knew him, must have hoped for his survival. Imagine that. I wish I were so lucky. Woe is me—I must shut up! That's not the kind of comment you write on a sympathy card. Adriana is mourning while I sit here wallowing, posing cockamamie questions about the meaning of life and death. Guess I should leave the suitable words of solace to Hallmark.

Saturday, April 27

I should have known Mitch and I were in different zones from the minute he phoned. It was the first time I'd heard from him since we returned to L.A. He called me last Saturday night to say that he really wanted to see me again.

"I thought I'd be hearing from you," I said. About five days ago, I thought.

"Sorry I didn't call sooner. I've been working really long hours all week."

"Writing?" I asked, intrigued by the idea of dating a fellow artiste.

"No, working at the animal shelter. Remember the rabbits?" He asked, with a slighted intonation.

"Oh yeah, how's that going?"

"I'm exhausted. But I feel like I'm starting to find meaning for my life."

"That's how I feel too."

"So," he said, none too eager to ask about me, "you want to come over and watch a movie or something?"

"When," I questioned.

"Now," he replied.

"Oh," I said, surprised by this last minute proposal. "I haven't had dinner yet. Would you want to grab a bite to eat?"

"Um, sure, we could do that."

Ignoring his lack of enthusiasm, I made up for it with my own. "Great! Why don't you pick me up in forty-five minutes?" I offered. I knew it would take me at least that long to shower, get dressed, and put on just enough make-up to make loveliness look effortless.

"O.k., I'll be there at 6:30 sharp", he said.

I gave him directions, then hung up the phone and began my race to get ready.

At a quarter past seven my phone rang. "I'm here," he said, without so much as 'hello'.

"I'll be right out," I said. Then I waited a couple of minutes to give him a dose of his own medicine. I didn't want him to know I'd been ready and waiting by the door for almost an hour.

When I found him standing in the courtyard I was pleased that he had made the effort to park and meet me halfway. Although I must say I was a tad disappointed to see him in the same worn-out baseball hat and jeans he'd worn at the yoga retreat. My opened-toed heels, opal earrings and Kenneth Cole handbag, created quite a contrast. When he opened his mouth to speak, I was sure he was going to compliment my attire so I smiled and looked humble, knowing he was probably impressed by how well I cleaned up.

Instead he said, "Wow, I didn't think you'd be into leather. I thought you were an animal lover."

"Its imitation," I lied.

"Oh, that's good," he said. Then he added, "You sure you don't want to change shoes—your feet might get cold."

I had already compromised myself once by not complaining about his lack of punctuality, I didn't want to be manipulated any further. I did, however, have the sudden urge to run inside and exchange my leather bag for an even more magnificent rabbit fur purse Max had given me, but I was hungry and didn't have the energy to be so antagonistic. Besides, I am a lover, not a fighter. So I said, in the sweetest manner I could muster, "No thanks, I'll be fine."

Unfortunately I forgot that his Bronco was essentially topless. Thirty seconds into the drive my hair was mussed, my feet were frozen, and I was beginning to have second thoughts about this date. The saving grace was when Mitch asked if I like sushi, which happens to be one of my favorite indulgences.

"I eat fish." He said. "I just don't eat mammals."

"The definitive factor being…mammary glands," I asked.

He didn't laugh. So I told him that my favorite sushi bar was right around the corner. I knew I could walk home from there if the date got any worse.

A half an hour later, no longer suffering from starvation, I actually started to enjoy myself. It felt good to be out on the town with a handsome guy. We flirted quite a lot, and he spared no expense when it came to ordering. I couldn't help but notice that he was as comfortable dropping a pretty penny on dinner as he was at dropping names, although most of the people he said he worked with were directors and writers whose names I didn't recognize. I did, however, recognize the films. After he mentioned a major blockbuster movie he'd been hired to "punch up", I wanted to ask him if he was pulling my leg, but then he admitted the secret to his success.

"My stepfather is Michael Mancetti, he's the executive producer for those movies."

The actress in me suddenly perked up. I was one degree of separation away from a major Hollywood producer! Mitch could help jump-start my career! The possibility, however far fetched, allowed me to stay interested in Mitch's continuous monologue. His banter about "the business" continued through the last bite of mochi, at which point I was satiated by sushi, sake, and Japanese ice cream. That's when I recognized that he hadn't asked a single question about me.

As the valet drove the car up, I mentioned there was a video store around the corner. Mitch told me he had a huge selection of movies back at his house, so we headed there directly. The first thing I noticed when I entered his living room, besides the fact that he had expensive taste, was the enormous area sectioned off for rabbits. In addition to seven bunnies, there were five heads of lettuce and a whole mess of hay. It somehow compromised the lovely décor.

"These are the ones I've adopted so far. Once they're litter trained, I'll bring home more."

"They're so cute," I said, reaching down to pet one.

"Don't touch!" he yelled. "They haven't been around people much—they bite."

"Oh," I said, retracting, "at least they're fun to look at."

Right then one of the rabbits started humping another. "They'll settle down and start acting normal soon."

The catch phrase, 'fuck like rabbits' came to mind; this behavior seemed normal to me. But maybe it was my libido and the sake talking. I decided to let it go, and changed the subject. "So where's this amazing movie collection you were talking about?"

He directed me over to a bookcase that lined the hallway. From afar it looked impressive. There must've been three hundred videos. I scanned over them, looking for something along the lines of "Sex and Lucia" or "9 1/2 Weeks". The conversation at dinner may have been one-sided, but I knew from experience that Mitch gave me plenty of attention when it came to sex. At this point I was more interested in getting him in the sack than sitting through a two-hour movie, while the rabbits got all the action.

Unfortunately, "action" seemed to be the only genre that Mitch was interested in when it came to the cinema. The only movie that featured a female lead was "Showgirls". After I saw that, I decided to forget the movie and chalk this "date" up to an extended booty call. Dinner and an orgasm would be good enough for me.

"What do you want to watch?" Mitch asked, as he entered the hallway from the kitchen and handed me a 22-ounce Budweiser.

"There's so many of them. It's hard to decide."

He grabbed "Wild Wild West" off the shelf. I panicked, knowing I couldn't sit through ten minutes of such atrocity. We spoke at the very same time:

"I heard that movie sucks," I said. "My dad produced this one", he said.

We stood in silence. Our union wasn't meant to go beyond the bedroom, so I cut to the chase.

"I don't care much about seeing a movie. Want to give me a tour of the rest of your house?" I asked, knowing his bedroom was the only place I hadn't seen.

He took the hint and minutes later we were making out on his king sized crib. The sex was good, but not good enough to make up for the rest of the evening. I knew as I drifted off to sleep that this would be the last time I saw him.

That was one week ago today. Needless to say, I'm hanging out at home alone tonight. A few months ago the prospect of being by myself on a Saturday night would've depressed me. But I'm fine right now, especially when I think about the bullshit I put up with last week in exchange for ten seconds of coital satisfaction. Booty calls are fine—a girl's got to do what a girl's got to do. I'm just not sure I'm ready to start dating. If Mitch and I had had an amazing time I might be singing a different tune, but I'm once bitten, twice shy. Speaking of which, I definitely prefer the company of pets that don't bite. Mitch's preference for rabbits and "Rambo" popped into my mind earlier while I lay on the couch with my cats watching a movie. As if to reinforce my decision to stay home tonight, Pebbles curled up on my lap while Sandy lay on the couch beside us with his motor running. Together we watched one of my all-time favorite films, "Life is Beautiful". Indeed it is; especially when you cuddle up with a couple of warm and fuzzy friends who never complain about the subtitles.

"Solitude is a silent storm that breaks down all our dead branches. Yet it sends our living roots deeper into the living heart of the living earth. Man struggles to find life outside himself, unaware that the life he is seeking is within him."

~ Kahlil Gibran

Sunday, April 28

Pulling out of the Agape parking lot this morning, I feel forlorn. I took part in a new member meeting a few months back, but I've been anonymous at church ever since. Today I wanted to be different, so I made an effort to introduce myself to some of the other members after the service. Unfortunately none of the conversations went beyond the "nice to meet you" stage. The older I get, the harder it is for me to engage in casual social conversation. Maybe I'm tired of the clichés that crop up in the initial dialogue. No doubt about it, when it comes to congregations, I have a harder time relating; must have something to do with the fact that "God" still gives me the heebie jeebies. That fact makes me an imposter inside a sanctuary. I'm afraid I'll be chastised for atheism. That's why I rushed for the parking lot after two feeble attempts at bonding with bona fide devotionals.

As I weave my motorcycle in and out of Sunday traffic on the 405, isolation bears down on me. I itch to find someone to talk to. As soon as I get home I call Rick and invite him to lunch. He's not home. Neither is my roommate. Bummer, we've had some good conversations lately. She's toying with the idea of breaking up with her boyfriend and has bounced her thoughts off me almost every day. It's my turn to bend her ear. But things must be better between them—she headed over to his place yesterday and still hasn't made it back. Two strikes down. In one final act of desperation, I call one of my party-girl pals. She claims she can't talk, or listen, because she's hung over from a night of raving on ecstasy. Two more calls and its over, there's no one left to dial. Fed up with good intention, I opt to get high and rearrange my closet.

An hour later I'm sitting cross-legged on the rug, pulling tubes from my bong and up to my neck in boxes. I grab the largest box and drag it towards me. It's the collection of scholastic history that my mom sent me right before I moved out of Max's. The folder sitting on top of the pile overflows with poetry. There are a hundred pages. I decide to file them, and begin the process by making piles, according to theme. When I'm done there are four piles:

Nature, Friends, Family, Angst and Love. "Angst" and "Love" started out as separate themes, until I realized the poems in those piles each contain a bit of both. So I combine them. In the end, that stack contains about thirty poems. Flipping through them this afternoon, I am painfully aware of the egregious amount of time I've spent contemplating love that's ultimately been lost. I'm also aware that, historically, being "single" is detrimental to both my confidence and my psyche.

The earliest poem from the stack called 'Angst and Love,' is a piece I wrote when I was twelve. It's titled "Nightmare", and tells the story of a king who has everything he wants in the material world, yet no one to adore. In the end, he decides he'd "rather be poor and unhealthy, than have no one who wanted to care." I wrote this poem in sixth grade, during my first year of middle school. I remember it was a good year for me scholastically, and socially, but it happened to be one of just two school years that I didn't have a boyfriend. By seventh grade things went back to normal and I wound up in my first "relationship". I say "relationship" because Danny was the first boy I ever fooled around with beyond first base. There are a number of different poems about Danny under the category of "Angst and Love"; most of them pertain to my never-ending question "Does he *really* love me?"

Apparently he didn't, because shortly after we passed second base, he broke up with me.

I was devastated. I know that for a fact, because it's documented by another poem that describes suicidal contemplations. It wasn't just 'food for thought.' I actually popped six children's aspirin in my desperation to end it all. Granted, I didn't even scratch the surface of mortality *that* time. A week later I wrote about going off the deep end, from a seventh-grade point of view. That appears to be the running theme in the love poem pile: love fades and I threaten to jump off a cliff. Boyfriends are not the cure for insecurity. I've had plenty of them, and I'm still lonely and insecure.

I wish I'd devoted my energy towards working on myself, rather than working on my relationships. Seems like such a waste of time. Max was everything to me last year—now we're not even talking. Yeah I feel lonely today, but I felt lonely most of the time I lived with Max. Whenever he got depressed I thought it was my duty to hang out with him and try to cheer him up. He was so despondent during those times that I may as well have been alone, based on the lack of interaction between us.

The problem is, after 20 years of boyfriends, I haven't found either half of the duo that could make up a great relationship. Maybe I should find Mrs. Right before I look for her partner. After all, I'm the only person I have to live with for the rest of my life. I can always run away from relationships, but I can't run away from myself. That's what I need to remember the next time I go searching for someone to unite with—I may be passing up an opportunity to finally unite with me.

Monday, April 29

I can't stop reading through my collection of old love poems. I always thought my problems with relationships came from making the same mistake over and over again. But reading about them now, I see my errors evolved, and I went on to make new bloopers when it came to choosing a beau. All of my relationships have had unique malfunctions, and each time I get a clearer understanding about what not to do. But will I ever figure out what to do?

Five major relationships, and yet I'm still a bumbling fool when it comes to love. The string of poor choices clearly started out with the two losers I dated back in high school. My first true love was Alex: a suburban skate punk with a quasi Mohawk. He was an Eagle Scout and a member of the church youth group that was two years ahead of mine. He was also the boy I lost my virginity to, and for that he holds an exclusive place in my heart. Alex was cute, sweet, and funny—especially when we were high.

Unfortunately, he had the I.Q. of a kumquat, which made him really endearing, like "Lenny", from "Of Mice and Men". He was as loveable as he was dumb, and I fell head over heals for him one weekend during a church sponsored ski retreat. The seed of puppy love was planted on a chairlift in Burlington Vermont; back at home in Boston it blossomed into, "I never want to live without you".

That's one of tacky line from one of many cheesy poems I wrote to Alex. They're laid out on my bedroom floor right now. Scrawled at the top of one of them is a quote by Richard Brautigan that reads: "The petals of the vagina unfold like Christopher Columbus taking off his shoes. Is there anything as beautiful as the bow of a ship touching a new world?"

That's still one of my favorite quotes, but I can't say I can relate to it. I was barely 15 when Alex popped my cherry and anyone who's lost their virginity as a teen knows it's not exactly the most beautiful thing in the world. Of course, when it finally happened after four months of heavy petting, I was plenty ready. I'd been curious about sex since I started to masturbate at the age of eight. At fifteen I no longer knew why I was supposed to say, "No," so I said, "Yes," and we went at it with gusto. In the car, at the park, the school gym, whatever our whim, we did it all the time. And it was fun, as long as we didn't have to talk about it. I had zero interest in telling him what I needed, so I accepted his version of a good time, and gave myself orgasms as need be.

I also had zero interest in discussing birth control, so Alex brought the condoms and I suffered through the lackluster sensation of latex. I didn't know how to get my hands on the pill, until my mother took me to a gynecologist for my first feminine check-up at the age of 16. Fortunately, the doctor wrote the prescription without my mother's knowledge. Unfortunately, she found out about it about six months later when she went to CVS to grab a refill for her medication and they gave her mine instead. Damn the single-pharmacy small town. In classic form she presented silent castigation and left the package on my bed. I offered to pay for them, thinking that might get her talking. The conversation that ensued was short, and not so sweet. "You're too young to be doing it," she said.

"I'm old enough for the pill," I retorted, "but I can 'do it' without, if you prefer."

Sarcasm shut her right up, until I wound up with a yeast infection six months later. My second trip to the gynecologist instigated a nasty comment from my mother, where she blamed my filthy infection on dirty behavior. I suppose she wanted to shame me. When shame is attached to sex it creates pungent self-loathing. Lucky for me, the gynecologist kindly straightened her out; he said using panty-liners plucked from the bottom of my locker probably caused the infection. He told me to be more sanitary with my sanitary napkins, but mentioned nothing about cutting back on sex.

The only embarrassing thing that ever happened during sex was when Alex accidentally came in my eyebrow at the end of a blowjob. In order to keep humiliation to a bare minimum, I never spoke about sex with my mom and never gave Alex another hummer. Despite a couple awkward stumbles, I do believe I handled my introduction to sex with a good bit of grace and maturity.

For the most part Alex and I had a great time together, both in and out of the backseat of his car. It didn't matter that he was dumb; I loved how dedicated he was to me. He placed me on a pedestal, and since he was intellectually inferior, I felt at home there. Besides, I went out with him because he was cool, not smart, and the fact that he was two years older made me pretty cool too. As a sophomore I dated a guy old enough to drive, who could take me to prom and bring me to all the upper-class parties. For my first two years of high school I was completely in love with Alex. And then he went to college.

I know—I couldn't believe he got in anywhere. I guess Scouts have clout when it comes to admissions. Alex's experience as an Eagle Scout and triple varsity letterman earned him a slot at a mediocre college in Rhode Island. From that point on our relationship was defined by long distance and long letters, but not much else. My ability to outshine him when it came to conversation was heightened by his binge drinking. It was difficult to find interesting things to talk about during nightly phone calls; he was often in a drunken stupor. Dutifully, I continued to honor my commitment to him the first year we were apart.

Despite being tied to a long distance boyfriend, junior year of high school was all about freedom for me. I was now licensed to drive and personally invited to all the cool parties. High times went into high gear. But when Alex returned home at the end of the year, hey had the audacity to tell me I should tone it down before I got myself in trouble. Feeling defensive I told him I didn't know how I felt about him anymore. I said I wanted to keep my options open and broke it off with him. For the rest of the summer I celebrated single-hood by getting hammered with my best friend Rebecca. For the first time in my life I didn't care about finding a boyfriend. I was waiting with baited breath to go to college; in the meantime pot, acid, mushrooms and booze provided an excellent escape from my otherwise dullish small town existence. The search for the eternal keg party became our quest, and Rebecca and I found our selves at all the wildest wing dings.

One night during the middle of our junior summer, Rebecca and I went to a party thrown by the older brother of a classmate. Towards the end of the night, Rebecca told me the older guy I had been dancing with was an urban legend when it came to street fights and D.U.I's. It was a warning to steer clear. I took it as a dare and opted to increase his infamy. I offered him what I thought was a one-night stand, but the subsequent romp was "the best sex" Mike ever had, and I wound up with a part time boyfriend. Part time, because his girlfriend was away at college and I didn't want to be tied down, unless it involved long socks and bed posts. So my second relationship was with a twenty-two year old high school dropout, who offered me booty calls in the name of love. I didn't care. I was out to have a good time and Mike was one hunk of a bad boy.

Mike and I continued our secret affair into my senior year. Neither of us wanted to advertise it, since his girlfriend and my parents would be very displeased. But when Rebecca and I heard about a huge party, a few towns over from where we lived, it seemed like the perfect opportunity to rendezvous with Mike. The party was being thrown by my co-worker from the video store. He was an older guy, already done with college, so I didn't think many people we knew would be there. Mike was supposed to meet me at the party but he got lost and never made it. In my over-zealous party form, I was shit faced by nine. Pissed and insulted that Mike didn't show, I decided to have a good time without him. At midnight I stepped out to the porch to smoke a cigarette. I shot the breeze with some unexceptional guy for five minutes, but thought he was boring. As I stubbed out the butt, I spotted a dead bird a few feet from the porch in the back yard. With drunken sentiment I said something childish about giving it a proper burial. The next thing I knew the two of us had stumbled out to the orchard. That's the last thing I remember about the beginning of the end of my innocence.

    I don't know how much time went by before I woke up. But when I opened my eyes again, the roles had been reversed. Now I was the dead bird, lying still, while my spirit whisked away, up beyond the apple trees and the pungent breath of that man as he ground away on top of me. *What is going on,* was my first thought. Nothing about it felt right, I knew I was in trouble. The fear that I'd been caught with my pants down made me numb. I had no idea how I'd gotten in this predicament. Overcome by shame I escaped into blackness and let my soul-less body sink into the dirt. With every effort I made to sober up, there was an equal and opposite force pulling me under, to unconscious-land. I'm not sure how much time lapsed while I blacked out, but I woke up when the roots of the tree began to grind my back. Instinct told me not to show any sort of physical response that could be misconstrued as enjoyment, so I lay there still as stone and waited for him to come. He must've been too drunk because eventually he just gave up, stood up, zipped up and walked away. I immediately sat up and looked for somewhere to hide. I didn't want to run into anyone, so I slipped into my underwear, adjusted my shirt, and climbed out of the dirt and into the braches of the apple tree. Shivering, terrified, and disgusted, I sat there for a half an hour, afraid to retrieve my cutoff jeans, crumpled on the grass below me.

    I was totally frigid by the time I was found by the guy throwing the party. He had stepped out to the orchard for a smoke and thought I was another trashed idiot. He told me to come down from the tree and put my shorts on; I dutifully obeyed and wandered back in the house to find Rebecca. She was nowhere to be seen, so I decided to find a safe place to sleep. During the search I moseyed through the kitchen, and zeroed in on the watermelon knife. Cutting was the perfect way to punish myself, and bring the pain to the surface where I could handle it. I forged lacerations in my forearm. The knife was sharp. It brought tiny specs of blood that bubbled up in a line and clotted before they had a chance to run. I stopped to admire my work, and was considering a few more slices, when some guy came by and saw what I had done. He told me it was time to call it a night. I agreed, and continued to search for a safe haven for sleep.

I headed upstairs to find a bed. This was not logical, considering what I'd been through, but I didn't think it would be cool to pass out in the living room. I remember a group of guys looking down on me from the top of the landing as I climbed the stairs. They looked like they knew what had happened, and that should have been a warning. Their smirking faces are a recurring image in the endless dreams I have about this night. I wonder if I should've known that moments later a second guy would walk into my space, and claim his share of my humiliation. It caught me by surprise, but this time, confusion and despair was replaced by anger. I knew what was going on, and I knew to tell him it was not o.k. I tried verbally and physically to defend myself, but with the strength of a dead bird and the blood alcohol of the comatose, I was no match for his determination.

When I woke up early the next morning, the monster was right next to me. We were lying face down and fully clothed in the middle of a wooden box—a waterless waterbed. I immediately wanted to get as far away from him as possible, so I slipped out of the bedroom in search of Rebecca. She was nowhere to be found, which was very bad news, considering she was my ride home. There were a few passed out people scattered throughout the house, but I knew none of them. With no one else to turn to, I swallowed the last of my dignity and asked the monster if he could drive me home. A little more mortification wouldn't kill me. I was already hollow and waiting for the taxidermist. I just wanted to go home, bury myself under the covers, and forget. The monster, appropriately named Richard, said one entire sentence to me during the drive. He told me he had a great time and wanted to get together again. "I have a boyfriend," I muttered, knowing he wouldn't take "no" for an answer. We spent the rest of the ride in silence. During that time I tried to bargain with God: my promise to never party again, if my only humiliation in this situation was personal castigation. I never prayed again.

I arrived home to discover my folks had found out from Rebecca's mother that we'd been to a keg party instead of a sleepover at her house. The first thing I faced as I walked in the door was Dad's wrath. "Bad girl, bad girl," is all I heard. Mom stood there looking disgusted, and for the first time I couldn't argue with her—I felt absolutely vile. They didn't ask why I could hardly stand up; they must've assumed it was the hangover. The penalization began when they clipped my wings, and took away my car keys, phone calls, and freedom for two weeks. But the punishment had just begun. Hangover in tow, I rode my bike five miles to work, standing up the entire way because I was too sore to sit down. I arrived to learn one of my co-workers had been at the party, and heard raunchy rumors about me and a college boy named Carl.

"Carl?" I asked with true confusion. I had no recollection of an encounter with Carl. Richard was the name of the guy I'd woken up with and he was the one I regretfully remembered. It wasn't until my co-worker brought up the name Carl that all the sordid details came back to me, and the realization brought me to my knees. Noting my abnormal response, Co-worker quit ribbing me, and I disappeared into the bathroom where I sobbed and puked for an hour.

Later that day I received a phone call from Mike. Before I had a chance to tell him what happened, he called me a whore. Apparently he'd heard about the event through the small town grapevine. Mike worked as a landscaper with

Carl, and first thing this morning Carl shared the one-sided details of our "tryst" with all his landscaper friends. Mike didn't defend my honor because he and I were a secret. He laughed with the rest of them and saved his fury for me. Dizzy with nausea, I tried to figure out my memory of our encounter. Meanwhile, no one had heard about Richard, and I wasn't about to bring it up. Richard had raped me, but I couldn't actually remember how my encounter with Carl began. I'd been unconsciousness during sex with him, and couldn't say if I'd refused or encouraged his advances.

All I knew was that I had no intention of sleeping with anyone except Mike that night. Promiscuity was not my style. I was a one-guy-at-a-time kind of girl. But being a slut was less embarrassing then being a victim, so I left it at that. Apologizing profusely to Mike, I simplified the story as much as possible. In the end, he thought I'd gotten really drunk and Carl had taken advantage of me. I decided to keep the Richard scandal to myself. At least I thought I could, until Rebecca called me at work towards the end of my shift. She was mad at me for abandoning her at the party. She said right before she left the party she found me in one of the upstairs bedrooms, lying naked next to a man she identified as the devil himself. In a tone that implied our friendship was over, she blurted out a story about her experience with Richard as a freshman. It happened at a party her brother had thrown at their home. "That asshole walked right into my room," she said, "and stole my virginity." My jaw dropped. She said she couldn't believe I would have sex with such an asshole. Then she called me a "backstabbing bitch" and hung up. The last call I received before I left was from Carl. He told me how much fun he'd had and then he asked if I'd like to go out some time. I wanted to scream and cry and throw the phone, then slide to the floor and die. But somehow I gathered what little pride I had left, and said, "You're definitely not my type."

That's the only thing that kept me from losing my mind that day. There were plenty of other parts I lost, the worst of which was my inhibition towards drugs. My prayers had been denied. I had every excuse to party harder than ever—and I was officially on a mission. During the two weeks I was grounded I tried acid for the first and second time. I locked myself in my room and left my family on the other side of the walls that were closing in on me. With plenty of time to sit around and think about what I'd done, and how I could have prevented it, I drew the conclusion that I'd be better off with a boyfriend. I didn't want to be independent after all; if I wanted to party like a wild banshee, I needed an escort. So I called on the one person I knew would be happy to act as my partner in crime: The townie named

Mike, who called me a whore when he heard I'd gotten screwed, was up to the challenge. By the end of the month I convinced him to dump his girlfriend and make me his main squeeze.

Unfortunately, Mike wasn't the kind of guy you take home to parents. He was a little rough around the edges, if you know what I mean. A landscaper by trade, he had regular work for two-thirds of the year and in the winter he moonlighted as a snow plow driver. Sporting a five o'clock shadow, he drove a truck that was guarded by a Rottweiler named "Neiko" (which meant "fight machine", if I remember correctly.) Mike loved Playboy, Schlitz, and watching the Patriots and Bruins games on his big screen TV. He also loved to tell the story about how he became an urban legend. The fifteen-inch scar that ran from his pelvis to his sternum authenticated his tale of the car wreck he'd endured back in high school. The accident happened when he tried to jump an old Buick with bald tires, across a wooden bridge during a rain storm. The chopper airlift to the hospital, which he referred to as "a wicked piss-a", was the only time he'd flown. It was an exciting-albeit painful-experience for him, and the six months he spent in recovery forced him to drop out of school. He couldn't catch up with his studies, and in his own words, "didn't wanna hafta do ova seenya yeahr." A G.E.D was the only proof Mike had of any reasonable intelligence; his diction often indicated otherwise.

Without a doubt, Mike was not the guy my parents envisioned for me. But I no longer qualified as someone who deserved better. I had always been the kind of girl a guy had to earn the right to be with, it was my claim to popular fame: the cheerleader who was party-girl adventurous, but not promiscuous. But after those tyrants spoiled me I was tainted and gave myself to Mike as damaged goods at a discount price. He wasn't the ideal boyfriend, but I thought, who am I to judge him? I was rotten to the core. The night Mike told me he dumped his girlfriend to be with me, he filled my gaping hole. It began with a six-pack of beer and moved on to another romp in the sack, during which I came, for the first time since my deflowering. When we were done, Mike propped himself up and starred at my nakedness, illuminated by the streetlight shining through the window shade. I was about to get up and close the blinds when he said, "Babe—you are one grade A piece of meat". I rolled over, snuggled up next to him, and let the tears spill out as he spooned me.

After Mike dumped his girlfriend and committed himself to me, I found the courage to tell him the real story about the night of the party. It was a test of his loyalty; I wanted to see if he'd offer to redeem me. He already knew

Carl had taken advantage of me while I was drunk, but when I filled him in on the whole scenario, and sucker punched him with the info about Richard, he went ballistic and threatened to kill them both. I started to worry that Mike would get arrested. But I became very distraught at the thought that everyone would find out what had happened to me. A slut was still cooler than a casualty, so I talked Mike out of retribution. After that I lived outside myself. No one could save me. I went back to seeing Mike as just a nice lay and an inexhaustible drinking partner, and started searching for grace at the bottom of the bottle instead.

"Whiskey drowns some troubles and floats a lot more." A dude named Robert C. Edwards said that. I wonder if he was a teenage alcoholic. I know I was. By the middle of senior year I couldn't get through the day without a drink. I'd often come home during "frees" to have a couple of them. I also snuck out of the house, three to four times a week in the middle of the night; Mike would pick me up, take me back to his place, and we'd get high, have sex, and sleep for a while, before I snuck back home to get ready for school. Miraculously, I was never caught. Maybe it's because I maintained an A average and played three varsity sports. Nothing seemed to be in disarray. A breathalyzer would have shown my brain was buoyed by booze, but aside from my ornery attitude towards my folks, there were no signs the ship was about to sink.

My cover came fairly close to being blown on several occasions though. One day I went to cheerleading practice while tripping on acid. Rebecca, who had given up on being pissed at me, and who missed her favorite party pal, offered me a chance to get high during third period and I accepted. A half-day Wednesday, we had one class to go, so we dropped the smiley-faced tabs at lunch. As captain of the cheerleaders, I was supposed to lead the crew in decorating the cafeteria that afternoon, in prep for the big game on Friday. Rebecca detested the other cheerleaders, but asked if she could tag along so she wouldn't spend the entire afternoon tripping alone. I knew acid wouldn't hinder her ability to blow up balloons, so I agreed. However, I failed to take into consideration how outrageously funny she would be. As a result, I was forced to let a few of my teammates in on the secret; there was no other way to explain my collapsing on the floor in epileptic laughter each time Rebecca let a balloon fly. "It's farting," she squealed, while I resisted temptation to pee myself.

I was still flying high when practice started. My role as captain required that I initiate the cheers; I'd solo the first verse and everyone joined in for the last three rounds. With my brain overcome by the sensation that my lips were moving independently from my mouth, I couldn't remember which verse we were on, and launched into a fifth every time. A few of my in-the-know teammates did not appreciate the hilarity of my psychedelic condition. Especially at the end of practice when the coach had us sign our contracts for the M.I.A.A rules. Massachusetts law declared that any kid who was busted for drinking or drugs would automatically be suspended from their team. Luckily, no one turned me in that day.

That's one example of how delicately I balanced on the fine line between success and disaster. On the outside I had it made: college bound, I was a triple varsity letterman, had a starring role in the big school play, and was voted "Big Woman on Campus" for the yearbook's "senior superlatives". Popularity was the only source I had for self-worth, I was secretly coming undone. Drinking had become my favorite past time and smoking pot was a close second. I cut on myself with great regularity. The razor blades relieved tension, and transported the torment to a superficial plane. I had no one to confide in; my only intimate relationship was based on sex and drugs. Mike said he'd never known a girl who was so pursuant of those things; that's what made us a perfect match, he said. Maybe that's why I felt our love had a weak and dangerous foundation, and refused to introduce him to anyone. After nine months of dating, Mike still felt like a scandalous secret. I loved him but didn't want anyone to know about him.

By the time graduation rolled around I'd pretty much disconnected from everyone. Rebecca and I drifted apart by the end of the school year. I'd relied on her to baby-sit me one too many times, and she told me she was fed up with that responsibility. Personally I think she had a hard enough time taking care of herself. She never spoke about her rape again, so I never had the chance to tell what went down between Richard and me. To this day she remains under the impression that I willfully had sex with the wretch who stole her virginity. Towards the end of the school year, our alliance was based on one common denominator—the desire to drink ourselves into oblivion whenever possible. Eventually my tendency towards blackouts, and subsequent inability to protect either one of us from harm, pushed Rebecca completely away from me.

On the morning of graduation I woke up feeling very sad that I didn't have a special crony to celebrate the day with, so I got drunk before the ceremony with some of my party pals instead. During the ceremony I put all my joy-filled expectation into the moment we would throw our caps into the air. I thought it would somehow bring an end to my suffering, or at least the reassurance that my time in this shitty small town was over. When the moment came and they announced "Congratulations, to the class of '91…" I stood up and chucked my cap as hard as I could into the atmosphere, hoping that upon its landing I'd find some promise in the future that lay ahead of me. It happened in slow motion: the cap soared and I looked around to try and spot a friend in the crowd. Big Woman on Campus was as alone as she'd ever been. The kids around me were like magnets as they embraced each other left and right. But spinning around to watch, I was repelled. All the years of climbing the social ladder were pointless. My existence was pointless, and the cuts I made with the blades that day underlined my temptation to end it all.

But I was too afraid to kill myself outright, so I spent my entire senior summer testing fate and antagonizing authority by breaking every rule. I begged to be busted—it's no wonder I got arrested twice. The first time I was sober, on the way to an enormous party. The cops set up a sting down the street to catch kids as they arrived. I had two cases of beer in the trunk when they nabbed us. Pissed about missing the party, I told the cop, "Do you realize how many murderers and rapists are roaming the streets right now? Why the fuck are you arresting me?"

"For possession of marijuana and transportation of beer," he said.

I countered: "Write down: possession of me by the devil, and transportation of my soul to hell." When he asked if I'd like to elaborate, I said, "NO," with great indignation. So he cuffed me. In the end I paid a twenty-five dollar fine and received a misdemeanor warning.

During my second run-in I was a good bit more cooperative, since I was tripping on mushrooms and didn't want them to suspect me. My friend and I got caught smoking a joint in a car that was parked in front of a party. The engine was running so we could use the lighter. We had no intention of driving, but had to convince them not to issue a D.U.I. My friend told the cops about the pot, and knowing about my recent confrontation with the law, told the officer it was his. Unfortunately, he'd grabbed the first thing he could find to stash the buds, which happened to be my old eyeglass case. Inside was a label with my name, address and home telephone number—clear-cut evidence of my connection to the crime. I didn't want to arouse suspicion and risk serious charges for a hallucinogenic, so I took the rap. This time I wound up in court, but amazingly, I got by without telling my parents. Mike bailed me out, and at eighteen I was old enough to face the judge by myself. I was also old enough to know I couldn't keep getting away with such behavior. When the judge let me off with a slap on the wrist in the form of community service, I was filled with disbelief. All the way home I wondered what it would take for me to end my self-destruction. I'd had too many close calls, and college promised many more.

Arriving home to an empty house, I plunked down on the couch. Conscience urged me to tell my parents the truth. Intuition told me if I did, things would never be the same again. I decided I didn't want them to be same again. So I mixed myself a cocktail and waited for my folks to get home. Two and a half drinks later they returned from work within fifteen minutes of each other. My mom was sitting with me when my dad came in, and the look on her face told him to prepare for something grim.

"Your daughter has something to say," she said.

"I got arrested." I told him.

"Are you on drugs?" he asked, exposing panic before anger.

"Yes." I said. They were knocked back by disappointment, and revelation.

"What kind?" Mom asked with trepidation.

"Marijuana, mushrooms, acid…and alcohol," I said. I disregarded my occasional overdose on aspirin.

"Well," she conceded, "I guess we need to get you some help".

"If you think we're sending you to school under these circumstances, you have another thing coming!" Dad's anger interrupted my Mom's gentle resolve.

"Dad," I hollered, regretting everything I'd said.

Then mother interjected, "The only discussion we should have right now is how to get you into rehab." With that, Dad backed down, and the three of us discussed the situation. One month later I entered the University of Colorado as a member of their freshman class, and a brand new constituent of A.A.

Tuesday, April 30

I thought I'd finish organizing my closet today, since I got swept away by history in the middle of that task yesterday. Alas, I've been derailed again, by poetry and memories. Now I feel the urgent need to tread the path of my failed relationships and discern right from wrong—once and for all—so I can find success in future unions. Thinking back to my college years I realize how confused I was when it came to choosing the right guy for me; the errors are clearly documented in two poems about the guys that popped into my life after Mike.

Halfway through my sophomore year I decided to end the strife with Mike, the alcoholic tag-a-long who followed me to college; a week later he took a hike and went back to Massachusetts with his pussy-whipped tail between his legs. I don't want to sound insensitive, but the guy tried to hitch a ride on my self-improvement. He moved all the way to Colorado to become a cook at a second rate burger place.

Working just enough to pay for the roof over his head and the Coors in his fridge, he focused his spare time on hanging out with me. Collegiate life seemed to open his eyes a bit, but there was nothing in that for me. When I finally realized I'd sailed to the New World with an anchor tied to my stern, I cut the cord, dropped all the dead weight, and flew solo for a while.

A year later I met Brad. He was the antithesis of Mike: smart, motivated and extremely fit and healthy, he seemed like the perfect guy. So I used my new tools of perspective to construct a boyfriend pedestal; built on the belief that hooking a man better than me would improve my self-esteem. Unfortunately, the ensuing inferiority drove me crazy. Here's the first stanza of my poem about Brad:

The Script

Take One

Girl hits her head against the wall.
"Why the fuck won't you say something?"
Girl bumps turntable, record skips.
"Tell me I can hurt you and you'd hate it if I left."
Girl lays her head gently on his chest.
"Tell me I'm good and you don't take me for granted."
Girl pushes herself away.
"Tell me that you love me...*please*."

We'd been sleeping together for six months when Brad told me he was still in love with his ex-girlfriend. In the shadows of his pedestal I told him it was over, but Brad wasn't one to accept rejection. He told me he'd do his best to forget her, and begged me to keep kissing his feet. The next stanza of the poem goes like this:

Take Two

>Girl tells boy that she loves him.
>Girl says, "Shhh, you don't have to say a thing."
>Girl takes his face in her hand and smiles.
>"It's okay that you're scared, I can wait."
>Girl backs away and sits on the bed.
>"There's no use in playing games."
>Girl looks boy right in the eye.
>"Come over here so I can touch you."

Right around our six-month mark, I met bachelor number two. The summer between my junior and senior year I focused on developing an irresistible physique—just one of the games I played to make Brad fall in love with me. While stretching at the gym one day, a guy approached me and said, "I'm with the stretching police, and you are under arrest."

Taken off guard, I abruptly lifted my chest off the ground and gazed though my endorphin haze at one very handsome man. My eyes scrambled up his six-foot frame, landing on a mane of shoulder length, shaggy blond hair. I squinted to catch a glimpse of his face, but it was lost in the glare of the halogen lights above him. I shaded my eyes and spotted an enormous smile, shining like a crescent moon atop his ruggedly square jaw. He had the cheeks of a Greek god; their hard angles, like exclamation points, sandwiched his pearly grin. I smiled cautiously back at him and snickered thinking, "*Hello, Velveeta cheese ball.*" Drawn to his physique and repelled by his technique, the scale tipped towards intrigue. I strained to come up with a snappy comeback, but cardio had made me brain dead. Squashing the pregnant pause he said, "You look great—keep up the good work." Then he turned to walk away, which was fine with me, since my commitment to monogamy meant I shouldn't take the teasing any further.

It was that one-guy-at-a-time mindset that kept me from extending myself when I ran into him a few weeks later in the basement of the theater building. I was about to head out and run an errand for the tech director of the Colorado Shakespeare Festival, also known as my boss, when Mr. Hottie came barreling down the stairs and swung around the corner. I was leaning over the water fountain, when I felt someone staring at my ass. I was wearing super cute, super short red shorts, and hours of cardio had made my butt look like a pair of cherries. When I turned around, he had a look on his face like he was trying to recall where he'd seen that ass before. Suddenly he announced with glee, "You're the girl from the rec center!"

"Hi," I said, with non-flirtatious nonchalance, darting my eyes to avoid his infectious gaze. He was so good looking. But I was "involved", so I shielded my eyes from the brilliance of his sun.

"What's your name?" He inquired, with unbridled excitement.

"Cleopatra," I revealed, stealing the pseudonym from a poster that hung behind him.

"So you're a snake-charmer, huh?"

His grin was spiked with poise and innuendo. I wanted to taste it but I already had a boyfriend, so I stammered, "Sorry, I can't talk. I'm late. But it's nice to see you again." I started to turn around but stalled as he said, "I'm Jim, by the way."

"Well have a good one Jim," I said with a wave. He looked like he was about to ask me on a date. So I rushed outside to hide my bright smile, and then unabashedly, and unintentionally, glanced at the noonday sun.

"See you soon," was all I heard as the door slipped closed behind me.

It would be two months before we bumped into each other again. By this time I had decided that Brad was a total commitment-phobe. I assumed it was because he was in

178

love with his ex, although he strongly denied it. The one thing I felt sure of was that he'd been in love before and had the potential to love again. So I continued to try and win his heart. By August I was clawing my way up to the top of the pedestal, and getting tired of it. We'd been shacking up for eight months, and always had a great time together, but Brad's heart was still not on the same page as mine. On Labor Day he got all wishy-washy and really pissed me off after he bailed out of our plans to go to the annual Kinetics race at the Boulder Reservoir. Attempting to give him a dose of his own insensitivity, I insisted that I was perfectly okay to spend the entire day without him. I headed to the reservoir with the sole intention of having a damn good time. Within twenty minutes of my arrival I ran into Jim.

"There you are," he said, as if he'd been expecting me. Then he took my hand, spun me around in a double pirouette, pulled me in and said, "If I told you, you have a beautiful body, would you hold it against me?"

"Ba-dump-bump." I said, imitating a drum roll.

We spent the whole day together and I had so much fun that I forgot about Brad. I didn't even second guess when Jim asked me for my number. I was very excited to see him again. That minor backstab to Brad made me feel like I was in the driver's seat, where I belonged. Jim was the real reason I headed home that afternoon, instead of back to Brad's to try and fix things. "I'm too tired," is all I said when Brad called to invite me to dinner. I guess that's where stanza three comes in:

Take Three

Girl walks on.
"Man you'll never know what you're missing."
Girl answers the phone, after the umpteenth ring.
"I have no idea how you feel, and frankly, I don't care."
Girl shrugs off his plea.
"When you're ready to take a stand, then we can talk."

My casual indifference must've worried him, since Brad offered me an apology and a bouquet the very next day. It was an act of chivalry that undeniably complicated things when the more romantic Jim graced me with his presence three days later. I suddenly knew Brad's pedestal wasn't built for two, and started to plan a sneak attack on his superiority in the form of a Trojan horse named Jim.

Even so, I was nervous when Jim called and asked me for my address. That tidbit of information would dramatically increase the possibility of Brad and Jim running into each other. But after my experience with Jim at the Kinetics race, I decided to keep my options open, so I told him where I lived. He showed up twenty minutes later with a blanket, a canvas, a pallet of watercolor, and an invitation to accompany him to Boulder creek for an afternoon of painting. I swooned as I stepped out onto the very thin ice of fidelity. Afternoon turned into night and Jim invited me on a moonlit excursion in the mountains, complete with campfire and an acoustic serenade. For the first and only time in my life I found myself completely torn between two men.

At this point I was extremely interested in taking things further with Jim, but I wasn't ready to break up with Brad. Brad may have been resistant to falling in love with me, but that didn't make him any less of a great guy. He was all-American cute, exceptionally smart, and the most naturally athletic person I've ever known. He was also an Alpha male in every sense of the word, and his aggressive masculinity was very sexy, especially in bed. Jim, on the other hand was rugby-player handsome; he was ultra self-confident, a Princeton grad, creative, artistic, and fueled by an absolutely contagious high energy. My desire for him meant my one-guy-at-a-time rule was close to breaking.

Over the course of few weeks I fell further into indecision. Brad, who could probably sense I was pulling away, was as affectionate as he'd ever been. Meanwhile, Jim chased after me with tenacity. I just couldn't bring myself to admit to him that I technically had a boyfriend. I wasn't actually cheating on Brad because I hadn't even kissed Jim.

We flirted like crazy, but I hid behind a good-girl façade and told him I needed to take things slowly. It's amazing what a man will do to woo you when you refuse to "put out." One day Jim visited me at the restaurant where I waited tables. He left me a huge tip and a poem scribbled on a paper napkin. It told the story of an intense love affair, as seen through the eyes of the man in the moon. It was a declaration of his devotion. And it frightened me.

It seemed unnatural for him to be so open about love when we hadn't even shared a first kiss. There was something weird about the fact that he liked me so much; he was too sweet, smart, talented, and attractive to be pursuing the likes of me. Groucho Marx once said, "I wouldn't want to be a member of the club that would accept me." In my limited experience, the loser guys were the only ones who devoted themselves to me, and the cool guys were the ones I had to chase. I began to have my doubts about Jim, and his love poem led to my speculation that he was a loser in disguise. Something told me that my affection for Jim would be fleeting and I didn't want to set myself up to fail again. After my shift at the restaurant I headed to Brad's place. We had just finished watching a movie when my poetic response erupted. I feigned a tummy ache then slinked into the bathroom to write:

What the Shooting Star said to the Moon

Pour me a glass of your moonshine darlin',
How much for a shot o' your wine?

The sky's the limit, as long as you're in it—
but you best not be wastin' my time.

My head hurts, my heart burns, my stomach's all knots,
a small price to pay for this high.

Yeah, it's our prime time, its high time we fly time,
before we must say our goodbyes.

Here comes the sun, I'll toast one last one.
The night'll be gone with a wink.

Outa sight, outa mind? That's bullshit, you'll find.
You'll always remember this drink.

Please one more taste? I'll get out of your face
and go back to my place in the stars.

Hell, let's get drunk. Let's get slam fucking skunked,
And stay juiced in this celestial bar.

Two days later Jim and I went out on our first dinner date. We kissed at the end of the night and it made me feel extremely guilty. I told him I didn't want to get involved with anyone at that time. I knew I had to cut my losses before someone got hurt. Unfortunately it wasn't quite as painless as I had planned. The final curtain fell when Jim showed up unannounced at my place the next night, just as Brad and I were leaving for dinner. I opened the door to find him strolling up the path. In an instant the juggling act was over. I introduced him to Brad as my buddy Jim. A slap in the face would have been less obvious. My heart sunk as he backed down the walkway toward the street. My heart shrunk as Brad fluffed his Alpha feathers up and said, "Looks like someone's barking up the wrong tree."

It took me three years to realize I'd been the one barking up the wrong tree. After graduation I hung around Boulder for a year waiting for Brad to graduate. By then I had moved in with him and assumed the natural progression would be for him to accompany me to LA so I could pursue my acting dreams while he applied to med schools. I wrote "The Script" at the end of our relationship. The inspiration for it came after Brad informed me that he would not going to LA with me, because he was headed to El Salvador instead, on a pre-med mission to fatten up his resume and work for Medicos Del Mundo. I was incredibly offended but knew nothing I could do would change his mind. With that, our three year, imbalanced love affair, faded to grey:

Take Four

Girl thinks to herself,
"God, you're a wuss!"
Girl shuts off the light.
"He's not a fucking mind-reader!"

Girl can't sleep,
"Why don't you pick up the phone and dial?"
Girl slips further under the duvet
"Shit, it's 2:30, maybe tomorrow."

Wednesday, May 1

When Brad told me he wanted to do the long-distance thing while he was away, I pulled the covers over my head and said okay. I was about to move to the big bad world of LA and figured lukewarm love would be enough to support my bravado as I crossed the Mojave into the land of incommunicado. The first month I was in LA, Brad and I talked every day on the phone. When his state-side training ended, he moved to a third world country, where mail arrived by donkey, and our static filled exchanges were reduced to bi-monthly. I was essentially on my own, which allowed me to spend all my time and energy creating a career in acting and making new friends. That's where Kelly comes in; she moved to LA two months ahead of me. Both of us wanted to pursue a career in film, but neither of us had any connections, so we became each other's number one confidante and connection. I don't know how I would've managed the transition without her.

In my second year here, I began to establish a plan for financial security. I knew waiting tables wouldn't cut it if I wanted to get ahead, so I took a second job as a spinning instructor and studied to become a fitness trainer. The few hours of spinning each week provided me with the cash I needed for acting class, headshots, and other audition expenses, like manicures and highlights. All these investments helped me book my first paid acting gigs: a TJ Maxx commercial and a starring role in a music video for the band Blues Traveler. This, in turn, paid for my first trip to Utah for the Sundance Film Festival. In exchange for a place to stay, I helped with the promotion of "Lap Dance", an independent festival of short films, and brain child of a couple of guys I knew from college. Matt and Trey, who had created a silly little cartoon show called South Park, wanted to make some waves and garner a bunch of attention at Sundance. It was a weekend filled with fun and inspiration; I returned to LA with a pocket full of business cards, a ton of respect for all the work that goes into marketing a film, and the attitude, "nothing's going to stop me now."

Unfortunately, I returned to find Kelly drifting to the other side. Fired on Friday, she'd decided to move back to Boston.

"What happened to the go-getter I left here on Thursday?" I squawked in disbelief.

"Her boss told her to 'go-getter' final check." Kelly had accidentally put Sweet and Low instead of Equal in her boss's coffee. That minor mistake prompted him to suggest she'd be better off shoveling shit at a slaughterhouse, where her half-assed effort wouldn't matter. Fighting back tears she told him where to shove his half-assed TV ideas. Then she twisted the old cliché and announced, "I will *never* work in this town again!" Despite the snappy retort, I didn't really believe that her mind was made. I knew she missed her family and friends, but I didn't expect her to split after hitting one little speed bump on the road to movie making utopia. I told her it was no big deal, but she didn't want to risk more rejection. By the end of the month she was safe and sound in our hometown again.

I missed Kelly a hell of a lot more than I missed Brad, which is relevant only because my relationship with him fizzled just one week after her departure. Back from El Salvador, and in the middle of his senior year, he had developed a crush on one of the underclassman he tutored in biology. Our connection was long gone anyway, so I thanked him for having the decency to break it off before he moved on to his next admirer. All the power to her, although he seemed most impressed with how impressed she was with him. It sounded way too familiar, and I'd finally had enough. She could have him. Of course, I secretly wished that she'd break his heart and knock him down a notch. My heartache for Brad was gone after a day or two and I set out to find a life in L.A, without my dearest comrade Kelly.

I immediately found a replacement roommate, but after six months of living with a guy who wanted to mooch everything from money and food to the phone numbers of all my girlfriends, I decided it was time to find my own place. I figured I could afford it with all the money I was preparing to make as a private trainer / actress. Unfortunately, there was a four-month lapse between the day I quit my restaurant job and the day I found my first client. Once again, I slipped into credit card debt. No longer able to afford my expenses, I was forced to take a break from investing in my career. That sabbatical from acting allowed me to grasp a more complete understanding of what was really important to me. With four hours of spin class each week I had plenty of time on my hands, so I set out to discover all that Southern California had to offer— outside the "Biz". Short on cash, I focused on activities I could do for free. Surprisingly, there were infinite options. The friends I found to replace Kelly were huge fans of the great outdoors, so camping, hiking, and biking became my life preserver, in the wake of extended unemployment. I spent the entire summer broke, but oddly satisfied. Those days of relying on a best friend or a boyfriend were gone, and I fell in love with independence. And that is why I can't understand how I fell for a man who clearly wanted to control me.

It happened in the middle of a wonderful weekend getaway to Joshua Tree National Park. I was relaxing after a long day of mountain biking, enjoying the campfire with three friends, when one of them giddily announced that the world renowned climber, Peter Solo, was camping right next to us. My buddy was a talented climber himself, so when I saw how goofy he got in the presence of this "superstar," I figured Peter might be an exciting person to know. Over the next three days in J-Tree, I found out that he was held in very high regard in the world of sports. By the time I left, I was smitten too.

> A hummingbird
> ~ wings ablaze ~
> Came honey-suckling on my breast,
> Then flew away.
> My petals fell,
> And wished me well.
> I couldn't help but cry that day.
>
> The moon caused tides to swell and sweat,
> Moan and melt,
> Such force I felt, it rocked my world.

Tongue twirled,
Toes curled,
Eyes crossed,
I'm hurled, into the wind.
I hope to find that friend again.

Until then: I revel in the chance I took,
To bait the hook,
Find fire in skin,
To fight and win,
Give in, give out,
And shout about my true desire.

My needs were dire, yet straightforward.
Now I move forward,
Find faith again,
That this is the way life's s'pposed to be;
Carefree,
Not risk free.

Safe and sound is not for me,
When love is in the air…

This is the precursor to the insanity that accompanied my fourth steady beau. I wrote this poem the day I returned from that wonderful weekend in Joshua Tree. It's dedicated to the only man who's ever swept me off my feet, during a tango on a mountain top, under the grand illumination of the blue moon. In J-Tree I fell crazy, madly, deeply in love; eight short months later I'd become crazy, mad, and deeply disturbed by a jealous freak that brought me to my knees and gave me the worst inferiority complex I've ever known.

Dr. Peter Solo was one of the most accomplished men I'd ever met. In addition to being a record setting rock climber, he was a neurosurgeon. Born Peter Solomon, he acquired an M.D. at 25, and was nicknamed "Dr. Solo" when Outdoor Magazine wrote an article about his legendary solo ascent up the Devils Thumb in Montana. When we met he was nearing fifty, but at six-foot and one hundred seventy-five pounds, he had the body of an Olympian. The only traits that indicated he was almost as old as my folks were his salt and pepper hair and pronounced laugh lines. Wrinkles and all, he had a beautiful tan face, angular features and deep-set, sea-blue eyes.

In addition to good looks, Peter had enough degrees and awards to fill an entire wall of his office at San Francisco's county hospital. Most of the certificates of recognition celebrated pro-bono accomplishments: from the removal of brain tumors in African children, to the operation separating Siamese twins who were joined at the head, Peter had a way of giving that got him in the news. Reporters loved him almost as much as he loved himself, and his world class essence kept all of us from recognizing a nutcase in disguise.

For the second relationship in a row, I felt like an underdog. Maybe it had to do with the fact that Peter called me "bitch" all the time; in bed it was his turn on, during tiffs it was his preferred nom, and in retrospect I can see how it made me sit up and beg for more respect. The magic began two weeks after J-Tree, when Peter flew me to San Francisco to stay with him. We had an almost perfect time together. Recently divorced, he shared a fantastic apartment in Sausalito with another forty-something bachelor. It was a weekend filled with dining, teasing, and tales of climbing. The only thing I had to cry about was the moment Peter chewed me out for flirting with his roommate.

"Do you think I'm an idiot?" He asked, after his roommate left the room.

"Of course not," I said with a confused smile.

"I saw the way you smiled at him. I can't believe you'd do that right in front of me."

"You mean, when I laughed at his joke?"

"Give me a break. It wasn't funny!" He snapped.

I stood there, not knowing what to say. Before I had the chance to reply he lay down the law. "I don't know how committed you've been to other boyfriends, but if we're going to make this work I need to know that I'm the only man in your life." I assumed he meant my dating life, and agreed. I told him that I believed in monogamy and he was the only guy I wanted to see. When I said "see" I meant to sleep with. When Pete said "see", he meant he didn't want me to look at another man. When I told him I was ready to commit, I meant it in terms of dedication. He thought I was signing up for imprisonment.

Due to the giant disparity in our definition of obligation, Peter had terrible jealous reactions every time we got together. I tried to concede to his regulations because I thought personal sacrifice was one of the keys to making a relationship work. So I sacrificed my dignity, especially when it came to activities in bed. I wouldn't be surprised if it was the first time Peter had been allowed to play out his fantasies. No self-respecting woman would let him say or do the things he said and did to me. Asking me to crawl naked on all fours on the floor and beg for sex, choking, slapping and biting me hard enough to bruise, calling me "Daddy's little bitch"; these are just a few examples of his deviancies. At first I thought it was fun to push the envelope and explore new areas of sexuality. But one night, after a particularly rough session, I had a dream that forewarned what would happen if I never learned to say 'no' to him. In it, Peter took me against my will, to a remote wedding chapel, deep in the Muir woods. After forcing me to say my vows, the scene cut to me running barefoot and bleeding through the woods, while Peter chased after me with an axe. I awoke in a cold sweat. Peter could see that I was terrified, but I refused to share the story with him. I didn't want to offend.

From that point on, I disagreed with him when he accused me of infidelity. This sparked major arguments, followed by his grandiose apologies. Somewhere between the two I would resort to cutting. Self-mutilation had a couple good uses. Whenever I punished myself, Pete became less intent on punishing me himself. Putting him in a mood of concern and sympathy allowed me to get my frustrated points across and self-mutilation was my way of screaming "I don't deserve your imputations!" Secretly, I felt I deserved them. I couldn't help but think that his nasty names for me rang true. I had been a liar, and a slut, and a worthless human being as a teen, and his ridicule hit me where I'd hurt back then. So in a state of confliction, I banged my head against the wall until he said, "I'm sorry." By the end of each fight I was distraught, not only from his violent outbursts, but from the self-abuse as well.

Peter said he hated having to yell at me. He also hated when I rode mountain bikes with my buddies, or when I causally smiled at his roommate, or when I accidentally locked eyes with those of a male passerby. His need for me to end all interaction with men was ridiculous. It drove me crazy, but I milked the fact that the crazier I acted, the bigger his apologies would be, when our fight was finished. And cutting always convinced him to recant his nasty accusations. Each time I hurt myself as a result of his verbal cruelty, he showed terrible remorse, and presented me with some sort of gift: flowers, a card, or sports gear. If he'd ever gone so far as to hit me during an explosion, I would've recognized it as a cycle of abuse. But even though his insults were painful, they weren't injurious; they weren't enough for me to leave him. Instead, I stayed on the defensive, lost my mind when my defense failed, and saw his gifts as proof that I was actually winning the argument.

The most impressive peace offer I ever received came after an enormously embarrassing outburst from Peter in my parents' presence. Even though I knew our relationship was rocky, I thought he had the potential to be a wonderful mate. He had many amazing qualities. So I asked him to come home with me at Thanksgiving to meet my folks. He was beginning to take us seriously and, ruled by insecurity, I thought if I played my cards right, a proposal might be possible. I figured that if my parents had reservations about our twenty-year age difference, they'd be too bedazzled by Peter's accomplishments to worry. Quite the contrary, my parents thought Peter was pompous, edgy, and mentally ill. Of course they didn't admit this until after he left—which happened sooner than expected.

Thanksgiving morning my mom and I were chatting in the kitchen as she rolled the crusts for an apple pie. She asked how my ex-boyfriend Brad was, and I told her that he'd recently called me out of the blue to wish me happy holidays. I explained there were no hard feelings between us and that it was nice to know we could still be friends. I'm not sure which of those comments sent Peter through the roof, but within minutes he was on the phone trying to book a flight to San Francisco. Bewildered by the conversation I overheard in the guest room, I went to see what was happening. The fury in his eyes told me there would be no talking him down this time. My mother came in when he started to yell at me and throw clothes into his suitcase. Scathing accusations like "untrustworthy," "lying," and "deceitful," were paired with expletives. My mother tried to defend my honor and calmly explained to him that I'd never do the things he accused me of doing. She approached him with kindness, indicating she wanted to help him, and then reassured him that neither one of us wanted to make him look like a fool. He didn't believe her. When my brother, father and grandfather arrived from the airport, they were greeted at the door by a rabid man as he threw his suitcase into the hallway and pushed past them on the way to hail a cab.

I spent the rest of the weekend crying over the humiliating end to a tumultuous relationship. Much to my parents' relief, I swore I'd never see him again. One week later, Peter sent me the first of many dozen long stemmed roses. Then he called my parents twice to apologize. I was beginning to think I should give him another chance when he outdid himself, and bought me a five thousand dollar bicycle in exchange for exoneration. It was an offer I refused to refuse.

Over the course of the next month Pete was on his best behavior. There was one incident where he opened my phone bill to find out if I'd been talking to Brad, but then he broke down and cried—said he was terrified of losing me. I saw that as a sign of true love, and forgave him again. When we spent three whole days together without a fight I told Pete that if he recognized he had a real problem with jealousy, things might work between us. My hope increased when he agreed to see a therapist after the New Year; he said if I stood by him, he'd make me the happiest woman alive. He added that the jealousy would be less intense if I proved my love and agreed to live with him. He wanted me to move to the Bay Area immediately. He said he'd found the perfect place for us, deep in the Muir woods, a little white house that reminded him of a chapel...

I told him I'd have to think about it. One week and three jealous allegations later, it was time to bail. After three days, Peter drove down from San Francisco, knocked out the window screen on my ground floor apartment, climbed inside, and swiped the bike. He left a note that said I didn't deserve his beautiful gifts. I was bummed about the bike but thought, "easy come, easy go". It certainly wasn't worth another heated discussion with him. Low and behold, a few weeks later I came home to find he'd used the same invasive technique to return the bike to me. A note that read "Sorry," was the last thing he ever said to me.

Thursday, May 2

I'm done reviewing my old love poems. Now I need to decide if I should sock them away, or burn them and rid myself of their memories forever. I've spent the last week mulling over this collection of twenty-nine: one for every year I've been alive, and at least one for every love I'd ever had—or so I thought. Then last night it dawned on me: I don't have a single poem about Max, although not for lack of creation. I wrote him a poem for Christmas this year; it spoke of how I wanted to have his children someday, and how I would stand by him with unconditional love and devotion, no matter what. Alas, I trashed the only copy of it after he asked me to move out; I couldn't contain the urge to destroy its pathetic documentation of misguided devotion. I'm having the exact same feeling about all the other love-sick lines. Perhaps I should use them to line the litter box; years of writing from the heart and I still don't know jack shit about love.

How could one person screw up love so many times in row? I've had boyfriends since the age of seven, and I can't seem to get it right. Worst of all, the story of Max and me is ludicrous in retrospect. I'm shocked and horrified to think I actually wanted to marry him, knowing that our relationship was built on a dream. It took me forty-eight hours to fall in love with him, and a year and half to crawl back out of the rabbit hole, and give up on the fairy tale. To be fair, I was due a storybook romance after the catastrophe with Peter.

During my rebound from Pete, all I could think about was finding another boyfriend. I needed someone to pick me up and dust the insecurity off, in the wake of verbal bashing I'd received. After I broke up with him I felt worse about myself than ever. Most of my poor esteem and remorse came from the self-abuse I exhibited during the most turbulent times with Peter. One incident in particular, where I spent the good part of an hour banging my head against the wall while Peter tried to talk some sense into me from the other side, solidified the sad assumption I had about my sanity. Peter's abuse drove me to act crazy, but so had all my relationships before him. So what did that say about me? I was damaged.

Damaged goods were all I had hoped to find in the search for affinity. My main objective was to find a man who could appreciate me and my malfunctions. No longer strong enough to focus on acting, or exercise, or self-improvement, I wanted to find someone who loved me for who I was, and possibly counterbalance my self-hatred. Surprise, surprise, boyfriend number five shared the same desire: seduction to combat ego reduction.

I fell in love with Max as soon as he confessed he was totally messed up. Max and I initially crossed paths at the gym where I worked as personal trainer. I'd been flirting daily with depression since the breakup with Pete. When Max's trainer asked me if I'd like to go out with him, I decided he'd be more fun to flirt with, and accepted her invitation to give him a chance. The matchmaker was the first indication of his shy and silent ways, and our first date was the first indication of his need to flee the tsunami of self-hate that cluttered his brain. "I've had a horrible week," was the first thing he said after he pulled up on his motorcycle that Friday afternoon.

"Nothing like a fast ride to cheer us up," I sung, as I swung my leg over his saddle and wrapped my arms around his waist.

"What time do you have to be back?" he asked.

"Monday," I said, as I slid my grip down towards his hips.

"You are my kind of woman," he quipped as he flipped the top of his helmet down.

His comment was as flattering as it was hard to believe. I never thought that 'little old me' would be good enough for the likes of Max. The part of his life that was supposedly a mess was hidden by his enormous career success. We met six months after he stepped down from his partnership at a Beverly Hills Law firm, to start his own business. He had also just ended a three-year relationship with the heiress to the Goodyear fortune, after she shredded his heart in a blender of infidelity. That admission was the most vulnerable he would ever be with me. It happened as we compared shrapnel scars from our latest breakups, during a conversation on the beach, right before our very first kiss, and momentarily preceding our first romp in the hay. Our relationship grew symbiotically and eventually brought us the kind of despair that's ever present in co-dependant love affairs.

What can I say? I was swept away by the whirlwind of adventure that defined our first 30 days together. In July of 2000, Max picked me up on his onyx black motorcycle and took me for a three hour tour of Malibu. Later we fine dined at The Grey Whale after a barefoot romp on the beach in bike leathers. All of which lead to us getting naked on a beanbag chair in his living room around midnight. I don't know if I fell in obsession with him at the Billy Idol concert on the second night, or the lobster picnic on the third, but I do know that when he asked me to go to St. Tropez with him, at breakfast on the fourth day, I was desperately ready to be his lady.

Maybe I should blame it all on St. Tropez. Besides being the most extravagant and exciting vacation I've ever enjoyed, the Cote D'Azur drew enough love out of Max to keep me afloat in the sea of mediocrity that followed. It was the first (and last) time he expressed an interest in marriage and children. It was also the first and only time I saw him indulge in three whole weeks of complete contentment. By the end of this amazing vacation I was utterly devoted to him. I didn't even balk when he tried to explain the severity of his mood swings to me on the plane ride home. I just stuck my thumb out and hitched a ride. In the weeks that followed I made several discoveries that should've changed my mind, but my introduction to Max's depression, addictions, and his questionable affiliations weren't enough to set me free. I was thrilled to be living in a dream. It was a lot better than living in sorrow.

Depression was indeed the biggest thing we had in common. I witnessed Max's first stint with it when he broke his elbow, one week after we returned from France. That moderate boo-boo became one giant "boo-hoo". It brought him down for the count; he spent the next four weeks lying prone on the couch; barely able to get up and go to work, let alone go on a date with me. So I hung around and nursed him back to mental health; did his dishes in the bathtub when his sink got clogged, mowed his overgrown lawn, fed the dogs, folded socks, anything to take the burden off him. It was the burden of being alive, a perspective I knew all too well. With my own experience of feeling bad in hand, I talked to him about how to handle it. I even made an appointment with a shrink—for me—in an effort to lead by example. I continued to see that therapist until just recently. I can't believe she didn't fire me when I told her I was moving in with him.

Six months after we returned from France, Max offered me the key to his new house. I was elated, in spite of the fact that I continued to uncover aspects of Max's life that disturbed me. The first scandalous practice I stumbled across was his secret affinity for cocaine. Next I found out about his dedication to O.J—a.k.a, the infamous Simpson. I found it extremely disconcerting that Max used connections to avoid 12 different subpoena's that called him to testify at the murder trial. You see, Max and O.J. coincidentally had lunch together on the day Nicole and Ron Goldman were killed. It was awful enough that he was friends with the guy, but the fact that he was unwilling to share his thoughts about O.J. with me, or the jury, told me he had something to hide. There was also a worrisome story about Max traveling to Europe to sell high-end art for a friend of his, who was in jail on multiple rape charges. Another case of misguided devotion, but who was I to talk? The story that morally compromised me the most was Max's experience with fraud. The fake marriage that earned this Brit a permanent stay in the states was a minor offense in comparison to the insurance fraud he pulled off, and was all too proud to recount. The most shocking tale I ever heard from Max involved the sabotage of his broken down boat. A little tinkering lead to its "accidental" sinking off the coast, and got him a settlement that paid for a brand new, more spectacular boat. These were a few of the facts from Max's past that indicated we had less in common than I originally thought.

Of course, there were plenty of other things about him I adored. For one, he loved to spend money on "getaways" whenever he felt down, and since he was depressed most of the time, we were always headed somewhere new: a ski trip to Utah, scuba diving in Mexico, a motorcycle ride up the California coast, and one time, a private flight on a Gulf Stream jet to Las Vegas for dinner. These excursions were typically accented with frivolous gifts: Max bought me a pearl necklace in Monterey, diving certification in La Paz, and custom leather pants at a boutique at the Hard Rock Hotel in Vegas. His gift giving reminded me of Pete's, except he offered them without the insults. As a matter of fact, there wasn't a jealous bone in Max's body, which probably had something to do with his lack of testosterone. Alas, the gifts and trips sort of made up for the lack of tits and ass we enjoyed.

The sad truth is: a few months after we moved in together Max became uncomfortable changing clothes in front of me, let alone making love. I thought it had to do with his depression. So did the shrink I convinced him to see, who diagnosed manic-depression and offered Max a lithium-based drug combination. Uneasy about the idea of popping so many pills, Max slugged them down with different combinations of cocktails, cocaine and cigarettes, until he found what he thought was a perfect balance of joy and oblivion. By this time, I was spending the majority of sessions with my shrink asking her for recommendations on how to deal with Max's problems. When Max's negative mood triggered a mood in me that lead to cutting, I discussed my own problems too. She said cutting was my way of asking for attention and trying to force Max to talk to me. Max always refused to talk, and since his shrink was on the verge of retirement, and couldn't be bothered with anything beyond a prescription, Max embraced therapy and said it was "working great." I might have believed him if it weren't for his perpetually limp dick. When two months of "therapy" passed without so much as a morning woody, I suggested he see a physician about his (little) problem.

"There's always Viagra," I said, with an unintentionally condescending smile.

"I'm thirty-three," he sighed. "That does not reassure me."

"Hey what's one more pill when you're popping nine a day?" I asked.

So he went to another doctor, who took a bunch of tests and discovered Max was missing testosterone—almost entirely. In a nutshell, his hormone count was lower than an average octogenarian. Max signed on for injections, and I signed on to wait. By October I was finally able to get a rise out of him, but something about the diagnosis didn't seem right. He had more good days than bad, but never went back to being the fun loving man I frolicked with in St. Tropez.

I thought solidarity was the key to a solid relationship, so I focused on Max's need, with help from all the King's doctors and all the King's horse pills to put him back together again. Feelings of hopelessness, joint pain, anger and fatigue were the complaints he expressed daily. As the severity of the symptoms increased he avoided me a little more each week, clamming up and retreating into himself. Unfortunately, the insecurity that accompanied my reflective depression kept me from leaving him. The misery I knew seemed safer than the misery I assumed would accompany a breakup. I didn't want to add another failed relationship to my long list of reasons to throw the towel in on life. As the holiday season approached, I clung to the screwy conclusion that the one thing that might get us back on track and happy again, would be an engagement. What better way to fix a disconnection, right?

While I waited to hear from Max about his thoughts on marriage, his nervous system was in the middle of a breakdown. We managed to share a pleasant holiday together: I created a sweet love poem, despite the lack of inspiration, and received a beautiful ring from him. Three weeks later he asked me to move out. He said he needed time alone to sort things out. But he promised we'd always be friends. We've hardly spoken since.

Last night when I realized I'd shredded my one and only poem to him I felt a tinge of regret, which quickly spun into a web of sorrow. As I contemplated Max's fucked up tomorrows, the notion to call him got the best of me. So I funk-dialed—and much to my trying surprise, his WIFE answered the phone. That's right—Max was married in Vegas last week. Through shaky vocalizations I congratulated him, then hung up, flung the phone, and cried like a baby. I feel a little crazy today from the news, like I really need to puke. It took Max four months to find his soul mate, a woman who's obviously better than me. Hope she knows what to expect when the honeymoon is done. I certainly won't feel sorry for him, or worry about him anytime soon. I really need to take time off from men for a while. If I can't understand this thing called love, I'm better off alone.

Sunday, May 5

I overslept and missed the Agape service this morning. After a complete analysis of my past relationships, I've decided the only way to deal with my inability to find a good man is to avoid temptation entirely. Now I need to figure out how to commit to this resistance while living in LA. I'm surrounded by great looking men every day. I don't know what to do. I'm not too keen about the idea of living in a convent; going to church once a week has been hard enough. Maybe if I become a regular, I'll find myself a kind-hearted church-going guy. Guess it makes sense to give that a try before I pursue utter celibacy. So I had every intention of getting up early to attend church this morning, but I went to bed late after experiencing my very first concert at the Hollywood Bowl last night. When Rick called with a last minute invite, he described the show as a special engagement. Online they listed it as a Night of Chamber Music.

"Isn't that what they play in institutions, to calm the crazies down?" I asked.

"Come on, it'll be fun. They're amazing seats."

"Well I haven't been…"

"…since when?" He prompted.

"Ever," I taunted.

"You've *never* been to the Bowl?" He cried.

"No."

"How can you call yourself an Angelino? I'll pick you up at six. Bring a jacket."

Two hours later a large picnic basket sits on my lap as we speed along the 101's lane number five in Rick's classic convertible Datsun. The 1970 1600 roadster is neon baby blue and barely big enough for two. Its' cartoon-ish charm is forever exaggerated by Rick's garish, button-down, polyester shirts. The one he wore last night was no exception.

"Nice shirt," I say with a smirk, as I glimpse at the red and white, KFC imagery, through wild strands of hair as they whip at my face.

"This is my favorite." He says with an excited smile. "But wait 'til you see the Colonel Sanders weathervane I bought on Ebay yesterday."

"Sounds like a winner." I guffawed.

"It's *an original*, from Kentucky. There's a bullet hole shot threw the colonel's heart—should be worth big bucks some day."

Rick's a collector. Most of his prized possessions are periodicals; he owns the complete volumes of numerous underground magazines from the beatnik years. He also has a strange fascination with old-school comedy routines. His VHS collection includes all of Buster Keaton's movies, extensive footage of Lenny Bruce, and his all-time favorite film, "It's a Mad, Mad, Mad, Mad World". Considering the ancient entertainment that Rick gravitates towards makes me wonder if we'll be surrounded by blue hairs at the show, but as we pull into parking, I spot plenty of peers. Taken aback by the tandem parking situation, I'm tempted to ask Rick how long it will take to exit this place after the show, when he steers towards valet parking. Thank god for snobs, I'd hate to be stuck in the lot with the rest of those fools. Rick hits the break, takes a second to teach the valet how not to stall his prehistoric transmission, and we enter what turns out to be a most magnificent arena.

Built in the 1920's into the hillside of Bolton Canyon, The Bowl is not the type of arena I expect to see in the middle of a city. Situated across the Freeway from Griffith Park, its 120 tree-filled acres face the entire range of Hollywood's rolling green hills. With seating for only

18,000 people, there are no bad seats. The first two sections are divided into boxes; each one contains a table set for four, and offers full service dining from the restaurant. Whether in a box or spread out along the bench seats, the majority of patrons garner picnic baskets and back packs filled with edibles and good libations. Apparently the open food and drink policy is one of The Bowls biggest attractions.

"Wait till you see our seats," Rick whispers, as the usher shuffles us across the stage. I maintain the blank face of a V.I.P as the usher guides us to a box that is just left of center in the very front row. After a brief introduction by the maître d', he excuses himself to fetch us some complimentary popcorn.

"*How* did you get these tickets?" I squeal.

"They're Michael's. He offers them whenever he's out of town."

"Who's Michael?" I pry.

"He's on the board of directors for my company. We were members of a dinner club for comedy writers years ago, and we've been friends ever since. I thought you met him once."

"I dunno."

"He's hard to forget—just shy of 4'11."

"Doesn't ring a bell."

"He was the supervising producer on *Cosby*, and co-created *Home Improvement*."

The arc of my brows exposes my actor's awe. "You don't say." I try to maintain a sense of maturity, but driven by shameless self-promotion I blurt out: "When are you going to introduce me?"

"He's a creative advisor for my show. You'll meet him soon enough."

Satisfied with his tease, I settle into my seat and take a peek at the Patina menu. One glimpse tells me we are in the chichi section: lobster salad, tuna tartare and filet mignon are a few of the selections. My mouth waters, I can't wait to delve into the forty-pound basket I've had to carry due to Rick's perpetually bad back. Lucky for me, our private table in the Pool Circle is a hop and a skip from the entrance. As I glance back at all the people behind us, I realize that with connections like this, Rick may actually be on to something. If Michael-with-the-Midas-touch is backing Rick's production, chances are the show will go far. It sounds like Rick's hit the lotto when it comes to creative connections. I'm about to cow tow and tell him how impressed I am, when the lights go dim, the music begins, and the two of us dig into the picnic basket.

I must admit the quartet doesn't really do it for me. My mind is drifting into space when suddenly Rick belches during a very subdued piece. The pint-sized flautist glares at us and Rick apologizes. He's had stomach problems all his life. Stinky cheese and red wine are not a proper pairing with his digestion. A moment later he excuses himself to the restroom, and I don't see him again until the start of the first intermission, a half an hour later.

"Good thing my date canceled on me, I don't feel so good."

"I'm second string?" I ask, with feigned indignation.

"Don't be silly, I called six other chicks before I called you."

"So this would've been your first date in what, ten years?"

"It's only been five years—since the day I sold the Jaguar."

Rick's admission reminds me of my latest conviction. I wave a white flag and say, "Call me anytime as an alternative. I won't be dating much, since I've sworn off sex."

"The fact that you would choose *not* to have sex makes me nuts, and don't even ask how my nuts feel about it." His response hints of irritation.

"After this last disaster I'm ready to give up on men." I whine.

Rick glares at me. "You know what your problem is? You fawn over screwed up guys. When you told me Max wouldn't have sex with you, I wanted to slap both of you upside the head."

"Max had a lot of problems, but I thought he was out of my league."

"You *are* the league," Rick screams.

I smile sheepishly. Then, in the shadows of his disgust, it hits me: I'm too insecure to find a guy I deserve, and until I believe I'm good enough for anyone, I'll fall short in my search for him.

So I guess it doesn't really matter that I missed the service this morning. If I did find myself a kind-hearted church-going guy I wouldn't know what to do with him. Guess I'm not quite ready for Mr. Right—which is why I got up and prayed this morning. Sitting up in bed, the cats curled around my feet, I kept it simple and sweet:

"What's up G? I'm really thankful for everything that's happened so far, but I could use your help from here on out." I was trying to decide what else to say when the phone rang.

"Hello," I said.

"Hey," Rick announced, on the other end of the line. "I dreamt last night that we both find love by the end of this year! I was so excited that I woke up right after I asked you to be my Best Man. So I didn't hear your response…"

"If I plan the bachelor party, do I get to jump out of the cake?" I asked.

"I wouldn't have it any other way," he replied.

Always a bridesmaid swam through my head. "I'd be honored," was all I said.

"What lies before us and what lies behind us are tiny matters compared to what lies with us."

~Ralph Waldo Emerson

Wednesday, May 8

9:30 PM: I should be in bed right now since I have four clients in a row tomorrow, starting a five am. But I can't sleep with everything that's on my mind. I just returned from Agape's Wednesday night service, and I'm excited to say that I actually heard every word that the preacher said this time. My focus wasn't stolen by daydreams or detours, and the G-word didn't give me heebie-jeebies. I think I'm ready to believe again.

I've skated across the surface of spirituality for the last few months, but Monday morning I decided to commit. First I meditated and prayed. Then I set out to face the day as if I were "a welcome mat for all that's happening in the universe". It was precisely that comment from tonight's sermon that struck a cord with me and convinced me to listen to everything else that was said. Which is funny, since the only reason I went tonight was to participate in the pre-service meditation. Agape's meditation has always intimidated me; 15 minutes sounds like eternity. But having focused on five-minute trials for the last few months, I knew it was time to delve deeper. Accepting that I might be overwhelmed by the effort to remain still for so long, I gave myself permission to go home as soon as the meditation was done, if I suddenly had the urge to do jumping jacks in the sanctuary. On the contrary—when the bell tolled at the end I was wrapped in a blanket of peace. Although fifteen minutes did feel like an hour, at no point was I tempted to return to my usual levels of brain activity. Instead, I nestled into the null and void and watched my thoughts float by like clouds in a breeze—it reminded me of counting sheep. By the time the sermon began, I was completely focused on the speaker and didn't even flinch when she mentioned the word God. For the first time since I started going to church, I totally jived with what the preacher said and I listened with an unpolluted mind.

I felt like a kid again; it seemed easier to concentrate on sermons when I was little. There weren't nearly as many distractions in the puritan sanctuary of my childhood as there are in the colorful halls of Agape. I was too short to see beyond the people who sat in front of me, which didn't really matter since there was virtually nothing to see. The white walls of our eighteenth century shrine were nearly barren, with the exception of the tapestry that hung behind the pulpit and displayed a flame that was the same color as my burnt umber Crayola. Unlike the vibrant lavender walls of Agape, The First Parish of my hometown had a monochromatic color scheme. Our minister wore a vibrant sash, but I can't recall anything else about her that was especially ornate. She presented her thoughts on God with the same reservation the sanctuary was decorated with on Christmas Eve. I suppose the sprigs of spruce on the pews, tight red bows on the wreaths, and fancy candelabras were all the "Hallelujah" my fellow Unitarians could muster. The minister's words seemed equally evasive: "Believe what you want to believe," was the message I received. Left to my own device, my version of God was intertwined with my beliefs about conscience. I thought God was somewhere inside of me, in the same place my morals were stashed. I believed that God's job was to point me in the direction of good intention, and keep me out of trouble. That belief worked fine for me, until I became a teenage alcoholic.

After I graduated high school, AA gave me a different take on the role that God should play. The folks at rehab said I was afflicted with a disease called addiction. It told me I was powerless, and needed to rely on something outside of myself if I wanted to survive the harsh realities of life. Since my spirit was broken by the time I found AA, the idea of God as a crutch made sense to me. So at the age of eighteen I prayed to my "higher power" and quit believing that any aspect of me was divine. During college I spent a lot of time acknowledging my imperfections and taking 12 steps to erect a better self. Finally, after three years of devoted AA membership, I realized it was insecurity that had broken me, and alcoholism was just a side effect of serious teenage strife. With that conclusion I cut the cord with my higher power, dropped out of "the program", and started to search for strength from within again.

Graduation from college coincided with the end of my relationship with AA. After that, self-confidence came in waves. A healthy combination of self-doubt and dignity accompanied the role of supporting my self financially. When it came to emotional support, boyfriend Brad cheered me through everything I set out to do, but he didn't adore me with the kind of reckless abandon I wanted in a relationship. Once again, the gym became my sanctuary in the search for self-assurance. Unfortunately, there wasn't enough energy in my cells, or hours in the day, to pursue physical reinforcement with endless vigor. So I decided to flex my intellect in an attempt to create the most confident version of my self I'd ever known. After ten years of needing it, I signed up for therapy.

Psychiatry became my new religion. Rather than pray and wait, I learned to ask for help in a more efficient way: I paid a shrink to listen to my complaints, and followed her instructions on how to relate. She told me I was a victim of circumstance. The Prozac she prescribed confirmed that I was a slave to chemical influence. This was my church of thought, but despite the thousands of dollars I spent, and hundreds of pills I popped on the path to self-sufficiency, God continued to infiltrate my thoughts.

Even though I'd wrapped myself in the cloak of an infidel, there have been lapses in my agnostic leanings. Usually it occurred as a result of being awestruck by the beauty of my surroundings. When environment becomes ethereal I become acutely aware of a divine presence. It happened one time when I was twenty-two. I was driving across the Colorado plains after a lightning storm. As my wiper blades flung that last remnants of hail off my windshield, the clouds cleared and the rays of the sun streamed down towards the ground. In the middle of the prairie sat a white barn that was partially shaded by an enormous oak tree. As I drove along the bend in the road my perspective changed, and the barn became immersed in a two-tier rainbow as it touched down on both horizons.

Blown away by its magnificence, I was forced to pull to the side of the road because I could no longer see through my tears. I felt surrounded by goodness—there was no denying my connection to the universe that day.

During the sermon at Agape tonight, I tapped into that same sense of connection. The message was simple: God is love. The speaker asked us to think of love as a molecule—like the building block of everything, and the glue that binds us together. That was easier for me to grasp than any other image of God I'd ever heard; a spiritual perspective that has nothing to do with hierarchy, and can't be defined as a link or a separation. Sounds like a relationship I can live with, that is until I find my next religion. Thank God—you've been a long time coming.

Saturday, May 11

I think I made a mistake in choosing a roommate. The more time I spend trying to relate to Amy, the more I realize she's not the kind of person I should be aligning myself with these days. But when she invited me to join her and four of her closest friends for drinks last night, it seemed like a great opportunity to expand my gaggle of girlfriends. I'm amazed by how many friends she has. Every week Amy goes out with a different person for what sounds like an incredibly good time. It should come as no surprise; she's a bonafide lush, talk-show outgoing, and has the body of a swimsuit model. Amy reminds me of a model in many ways: she has gorgeous hair, long legs, dresses like a fashion queen, and prefers cocaine over calories any day. That appears to be a formula for success when it comes to socializing in this city. The few times Amy and I have partied together, I've had a fantastic time—so I was really looking forward to this Girl's Night Out.

When I told Rick about my plans during our Friday morning run, he said it seemed like a great opportunity—for both of us—and begged me to let him attend. "You're the perfect wingman!" he exclaimed.

"I'm not a matchmaker, Rick."

"That's because you don't know any women."

"So, neither do you."

"So, I better take advantage of your camaraderie while I can."

"Girls night out is not about meeting men." I say.

"Bullshit. I bet five bucks one of you will get laid."

"I told you, I'm not looking for a man right now."

"What goes around comes around; I'll help you find a man whenever you're ready." With that, he had me. Rick would help me find love if he could, it was only fair that I do the same for him. Although hooking up after a night at a bar isn't about finding true love. Considering Rick's long-term abstinence, a little lovin' would be a huge improvement. I asked Amy if he could tag along.

"He'll have to meet us at the bar," she said.

"Why?" I asked.

"Don't you know the advantage of going out with all women? You don't have to stand in line, or pay for lines", she said with a wink.

Removal from the carpool didn't deter Rick; he joined us at The Joint at 10 pm. We'd been there for an hour already, and I'd spent the entire time trying to contribute to a conversation about shopping. By the time I spotted Rick near the bar, I needed a break from the girl talk, and another drink. So I sashayed over to greet him. By the time I got through the hive of buzzing people, he asked me what I wanted.

"What are you're having?" I asked.

"An erection," he said, as he looked at my friends. "But I ordered a Cape Cod."

"Vodka / cranberry it is," I concurred.

"My treat," he offered sweetly, as he gazed across the room like a dog waiting for a bone. "So how bad does my hair look?" he asked, with a nervous swipe to the right, in an attempt to fix his wind coiffed 'do. Rick's brother is completely bald, and gay. A famous brow boy at one of New York's trendiest salons, he has the fashion sense of a hoity toity flamer, and routinely ridicules Rick for wearing Hawaiians. He says Rick dresses like a clown, to which younger-brother Rick replies, "Least my big top isn't BALD!"

"Your hair looks fine," I said with a grin, masking my thoughts about his thinning mop. "Cheers," I added, toasting his glass. Then we pushed our way towards Amy and her harem.

A half an hour later I spotted the pretty red head from our clan brush her hand through Rick's hair. He looked like he was in heaven, until she leaned forward and threw up on his shoe. Amy sneered and announced it was time to go. As the seven of us coordinated the carpool and exchanged directions to a party in Brentwood, Rick offered to take the sick girl home, "killing two birds with one stone", mumbled Amy.

"Bringing a sick girl to a party is almost as bad as bringing a guy." She said after we climbed inside her car. "They deserve each other."

"He's trying to be nice." I interjected.

"Nice is when a guy buys a round of drinks, not when he offers to take the drunk girl home. He just wants to get laid. That girl's a slut, but she's not drunk enough to have sex with him."

"Yeah, he's a dork," Amy's friend piped in; they laughed and I sat there tongue-tied.

I didn't know if I should defend myself—or Rick—or what. I wanted to call him and tell him to drop the bitch off on the next street corner where she belonged, but I thought that might cause me to wind up on the next corner too. After all, the little slut was their friend. So I rode along, then ran off to get high the minute we arrived at the party. The hunt for pot was easy. Since the four of us tripled the number of women, men swarmed and offered us almost anything we wanted. There was no blow though, so Amy sniffed out choice number two and wound up hanging with the pot smokers. She softened a bit around the edges as the THC set in—by midnight we were chatting, laughing, and having a generally good time. That is, until the conversation turned to sports.

Suddenly I felt very tired. Luckily, without the help of amphetamines, Amy was on the same page. She stood up at half past one, thanked the host and said, "Time to go". There was a collective sigh as the guys realized the last of the ladies were leaving.

Heading home I felt relieved to have made it through the night without a fight. Maybe I was being too sensitive and protective; maybe Rick could use some pointers on how to be a better man. I was about to tell Amy there were a few things she could teach me about making friends, when she asked me to grab her phone from her purse. At the bottom of her Prada bag was an enormous bag of pot.

"I didn't know you had weed." I said.

"What d'ya mean?" She asked, with faux confusion.

"Where'd you get this giant sack," I asked, exposing the ounce of green.

"Oh no, I must've snaked it by mistake!"

I inventoried her bad behavior: she'd trashed Rick, called her good friend a slut, and stolen the stash from the host of the party. I wanted to call her on it, but decided to play her game instead. "So you're going to share the wealth, right?" She eyed me with contempt, knowing her snatch should look like a happy accident.

"Yeah...sure...I mean, I feel bad, but what am I supposed to do?" She asked.

"Keep it." I said. "You deserve that pot after all you did for that party."

"I like the way you think," she said. Then she handed me one little bud.

I called Rick first thing this morning to find out how the night had gone for him. He told me he was disappointed in himself because he balked and didn't ask for a kiss after he walked the red head to the door; he said he didn't want to take advantage. Kind of gross that he wanted to kiss the sick girl, but aside from being a little needy, he's far from being a geek. He needs no social adjustment. I told him he was a good man, and somewhere out there is a good woman looking for him. I promised to point her in the right direction if I happened to meet her first. Clearly that's not going to happen if I continue to rub elbows with the likes of Amy. Guess I need to be more selective in my search for friends. Looks like I may have to move again.

Sunday, May 12

I went to the eleven a.m. service at Agape today and came away with a new perspective on mothering. It is Mother's Day, after all. The reverend, a dread locked, gray-haired, African American man, began the sermon by saying "Word from your mother: you're better than this." Then he asked the congregation to think back on all the times we'd heard this message from our mothers, and remember how it made us feel.

As a kid, whenever I did something to disappoint my mother she sent that message to me via the silent treatment. I prefer the clarity of verbal communication. Mom's acerbic silence filled me with guilt because I wasn't able to defend myself. My father, on the other hand, told me exactly how he felt about my bad behavior. I didn't exactly enjoy being yelled at by Dad, but at least the earth shattering arguments in the aftermath gave me a chance to state my case.

My mother had no interest is discussing my mistakes. She simply insisted that I go to my room to "think about it." Think about what? I wanted to ask. How much fun it was to skip class and smoke grass in the parking lot? Or how rebellious it felt as an eight year old, to ride my bike to the candy store, when I was supposed to be confined to our dead end street? Or how empowered I felt at five, when I charged the neighbor boy ten cents and then pulled down my pants for a three-second glance? Whatever I thought about during lock downs in my room, it had nothing to do with regret. I felt guilt, but never repentance. Rules were meant to be broken, and I wasn't going to end my naughtiness just because Mom told me to think about it.

This morning's sermon shed a whole new light on the message Mom had tried to send me. A mother's reprimand, the reverend said, isn't about telling a kid they're bad, it's about telling them they could do better. He explained that when a mother says, "You're better than that," it's an encouragement to stop messing with behavior that's beneath you. It made me realize what Mom had wanted me to think about all those years. I called her as soon as I got home.

"Happy Mother's Day" I said, when she answered the phone.

"Thanks," she said, "and thanks for the gift! I love it."

"No more excuses." I said, lovingly.

My mother has expressed her desire to get back in shape for years. This year I convinced her to hire a personal trainer. She bought ten sessions along with a gym membership six months ago, but decided the trainer was too expensive and resolved to work out on her own. Her motivation has waned ever since. I recently suggested that she join a class, to provide her with a scheduled commitment. The plum colored mat and embroidered top I sent are meant to be an impetus.

"Purple's my favorite color," she gushed.

"I really think you'll like Yoga." I said.

"Thanks for your encouragement."

"What comes around goes around."

"I hope I encouraged you," she said, unsure. "I always tried. I promised myself I'd never be as negative with you as my mother was with me."

Grandma passed away last year. In addition to Mother's Day, today is her ninetieth birthday; a double whammy in the grief department. So I was a little surprised to hear my mother speak of her negatively. "I don't remember grandma being negative." I said in her defense.

"Well," Mom said, "she rarely had anything nice to say, and when she got mad, she had a way of making me feel bad without uttering a word."

"Maybe that was the only way she knew how to do it." I said. It suddenly occurred to me that guilt tripping was the only version of punishment Mom had ever known—and she'd tried to do things different. Opting to share some of the insight I received from this morning's sermon, I told her that Grandma's pessimism was probably passed down to her, and silent criticism was the only way Grandma knew how to tell my mom that she could do better. Casting a rosier light on Grandma allowed Mom to switch gears and share some of the wonderful aspects of her mother she missed. Among other things, we talked about Grandma's garden, her delicious fried fish, and her miserly recycling of Christmas wrap—a tradition I have now adopted. After twenty minutes of reminiscing, Mom asked me how my life was going.

"I think I may have to move again." I said.

"Why?" She asked.

The question was accompanied by her tone of second-guessing that puts me on the defensive. I didn't want to get into the chain-smoking, line-snorting, money-hungry details about Amy, so I simplified the situation. "My roommate's uninspiring. I want to live by myself."

"You know the only regret I have, about getting married right out of college?" She asked.

I assumed she was about to launch into a negative rant about brash decisions, so I mumbled, "what?" and waited for the axe to fall.

To my surprise she tried something new. "I never experienced the independence of living alone," she said, "and I definitely want that for you."

"You do?"

"Yep, I do."

"I thought you were going to ask me how I can afford to move again."

"So how can you afford to move again?"

"I'm not sure," I confessed. "I used up all of my savings when I moved out of Max's."

"Well let us know how much you need—we just want you to be happy."

"Thanks for your support."

"It's nice to know I'm a little better, than my mom was, at giving it," she noted.

After we said our good byes, I hung up the phone and gazed through my dining room window at the planters of Pansy's outside. Contemplating the struggle and troubles, my mom and her mom had faced before me, I wondered: can I ever do better? To avoid the anxiety of such a daunting task, I focused on the present. Calling the cats, I interrupted their sleep and offered them a handful of crab flavored treats; then I shuffled them outside for a romp in the sun. When we lived at Max's, the cats had a large grassy yard to explore, a koi pond that teased their hunting instincts, and a low traffic neighborhood they could wander around at their leisure. Now they're confined to the apartment because it's located on a busy street, so I accompany them a few times a week on minor excursions around this less than perfect cement playpen. Today we'd been outside for twenty minutes when the manager came by to inform me that cats aren't allowed in the courtyard.

"I thought pets were allowed here." I said.

"They are," she said, "but only *inside* your apartment".

"But I'm standing right here, watching them."

"Sorry, house rules—take 'em or leave 'em."

"I'll leave them." I conceded, and sprinkled catnip at her feet. "Consider this my thirty-day notice."

She walked away in a huff and the reality of my brash decision sunk in: moving sucks, I thought to myself. Doing my best to maintain a positive attitude, I addressed the cats: "Hey kids, we're moving again!" Pebbles brushed against my leg and Sandy stared up with his big pumpkin eyes. "But this time, I'm going to find us a place where you can roam—like the good old days." Sandy meowed and Pebbles flopped down in the catnip. "I just want you to be happy," I said with good cheer. Then I gave each of them a pat on the head, and reveled in what it meant to learn to love like a mother.

Wednesday, May 15

4:20: I just pulled the last three hits off a roach I had left from the weekend, now I'm settled in for the night to write. The ritual of writing is fourth on my list of efforts to inspire a cease-fire in my busy mind. Number one on the list is a vow to tell myself 'I love you,' every time I look in the mirror. Lately I've been praying twice a day, so that comes in as a close second. Meditation is third. I want to meditate every morning, but I continue to find it difficult to stay still, so I blow it off more often than not. These weekly writing reflections are tied to my meditation, that's why they only happen a few times a week. Currently in fifth place are trips to Agape, which are as insightful as they are infrequent. Going to church twice a month is enough, since the sum of these five endeavors is all I need to feel a hundred percent better than I did when I started to compose this story four months ago.

I feel so damn good these days. After a long bout with confusion about what I was supposed to be doing here on earth, my soul feels suitably satisfied. I celebrated this fresh perspective when I bought Rick lunch at the Literati Café today. I told him to consider it a "thank you" for encouraging me to see myself as an artist again. He promptly informed me of an even greater cause for celebration: a Friday morning meeting at NBC. My excitement grew as he reminded me to pay my dues and renew my membership with the guild, so I'll be good to go when it's time to shoot the first episode. I promised to put it on my list of things to do, and made a mental note to him seriously. Every actor, writer, director in this town has something to say about the next big thing they're working on, but Rick falls under the category of folks who aren't completely full of shit. He has a real office, a board of directors, and so far he's scored meetings at the all the major networks. He even has a couple of investors who gave him a fat check on the stipulation he'd have a show on the air by the beginning of the year, a.k.a "pilot season," in television terms. Worried about his shrinking bank account, the fear of liquidation gives him the courage to call on his executive connections and book as many meetings as he can before the studios' summer hiatus begins.

After suffering seven years without a paycheck and having his sitcom riches erode, it looks like Rick's time has finally come. I told him that this afternoon, but reminded him that whatever deal he finagles isn't going to make him a more accomplished artist, it will simply allow him to afford fancy stuff again. In a defensive tone, he asked what was wrong with wanting recognition for his work. I reminded him what he told me a few months back, when I asked him if the poems and journals I'd kept to my self all my life qualified me as a real writer.

"If you write, then you're a writer", he'd said.

"I want to write a book, but I don't know who to write it for. Should I keep these incessant thoughts to myself?"

"Artists must create the same way they must breathe, eat, and sleep," he said. "You're an artist even if you keep your art to yourself. Don't make "sharing it" the motivation to follow through, just write whatever you want and see where it takes you."

Buoyed by his wisdom, Rick smiled to expose a ruffled piece of lettuce in his teeth and said, "If a story's been stuck in your head for long, it's probably time to share it."

"I've been tripping on this tale for 20 years." I admitted.

"Then quit tuckin' it—and wag it!"

"I started to, four months ago, and I can see where it's taking me."

We finished our lunch on that note. I wanted to write some more as soon as I walked in the door, but decided to call my dad first, since it's his birthday. The gift I sent arrived on Saturday, but he dutifully waited until today to open it. For his 57th birthday I inscribed a poem on top of a watercolor I painted, and had it framed. Called *"The Apple of my Eye,"* the poem detailed our similarities and thanked him for how he raised me. "Your gift made me proud," he said, which didn't surprise me, since it was an entire page filled with praise. Rather than discuss the compliments I paid him, he talked about its artistic quality instead: the woodsy hues of the apple tree, the sponged green leaves, and the poetic line that defined "integrity". He was impressed and pleased, which are the same emotions he exudes whenever he talks about his own artsy endeavors these days.

My father, the mathematician, has become an award-winning photographer over the last few years. "Street photography" is now his second full-time job; he pursues it with vigor whenever he has time off from work as a computer programmer. According to mom, his relentless dedication to photography partially contributed to my parents need for a marriage counselor. I must admit, his never-ending comments about the search for the perfect shot can be annoying. Don't get me wrong, I love that Dad is an artist—it helps me relate to him. Ever since they started therapy, my mother continues to tell me how much I remind her of my father. Under the circumstance, it seems a tad insulting. Most of my life I've struggled to get along with my dad. I never understood the computer-programmed version of him, but now that he's a photographer, I can see our similarity. Come to think of it, our shared "let's talk about me," mentality is documented by my need to write this book.

Right on cue, when Dad was through analyzing my work he immediately launched into a discussion about his: "Did you check out the new shots I posted on my website?" He asked.

"Yeah; as usual, I like the still life's best."

"I appreciate the critique," He said. "It means a lot to me."

"Let's do an exchange," I suggested. "I'll send my comments, and you can send me a few of your prints to frame."

"Sounds great," He said, "That should justify some of my 'wasted days' to your mom."

"Don't' listen to her," I said, "she's wrong. You're not wasting time; your pictures capture time, for the rest of us to see."

"I didn't know you even cared about my photography."

I didn't agree or disagree, I just thought about how shocked he seemed to get encouragement from me—a sign I fall not far from my mother's tree too.

After I hung up the phone I decided to work on painting some more bumper stickers for a poem I wrote, called Bumper Sticker Lingo. During one of our recent runs I mentioned the term "word painting" to Rick, in reference to poetry. He asked me if I'd ever tried painting any of them. I don't consider myself a painter, but it seemed like a cool idea. The bumper stickers I've completed so far add a whole new dimension to that poem. They also spawned the decision to paint for Dad's birthday. I'm not nearly as slick with a brush as I am with words, but painting is a ton of fun.

Holy cow, I've spent the last three hours as an artist, a nice counterbalance to the three hours I spent working as a personal trainer this morning. It's been a day filled with great conversation too. If only I could spend all my days in such a memorable way. I suppose I should finish it off with an attempt at meditation. So goodnight, I'm done fighting the good fight; time to silence my mind and hit the hay.

Tuesday, June 11

So much for my weekly writing commitment, although I do have an excuse for this month of literary neglect—I moved! I'd barely started looking for a place when I found a single, right up the street from where I was living, for the exact same rent I paid to live with Amy. "Single" isn't exactly right, it's a "bachelor," which means no kitchen. The entire unit, including the bathroom, is the size of my bedroom at the last place, but what my new apartment lacks in space, it makes up for in charm. The art deco complex, built in 1920, is one of the oldest buildings in West L.A. My favorite amenity is the claw footed bathtub, so deep I can practically swim in it. My make-shift kitchen consists of a dorm-sized fridge, a microwave and a hot plate. Right now I have to eat on my bed, but that will change once I buy a little table.

All in all, I adore it. The cats really like it too. Since we're far enough away from the busy street, I can let them come and go as they please. Pebbles has already gotten in trouble with a few of the neighbors: for pooping in the rose bushes and boxing with a neighbor's cat through their cat door, are just two of her latest offenses. Yesterday she was MIA all day until my neighbor came home to find her asleep in the laundry basket inside her closet. Luckily, that neighbor is a cat lover and thought Ms. Pebs was so cute she didn't care about the hair on her freshly washed clothes. Sandy's less interested in such sophisticated exploration, he spends his time soaking in the sun and chasing butterflies that frequent the honeysuckle right outside my window. I did receive one complaint about Sandy from the lady downstairs, who worried he might catch one of the doves that hover around the courtyard. That problem was easily resolved with a couple of 99-cent bird bells. Hung on their collars, the bells produce a lovely little jingle that announces their return and cues me to open the door for them.

With this new place comes the unadulterated feeling that life couldn't be more perfect. I have everything I need inside this two hundred square foot space without a roommate. Six months ago I lived in a home that was palatial by comparison, but I was plagued by the sense that something was missing. Turns out it was love that was missing. As Max and I lost affection for our selves, it became impossible for us to love each other. The self respect I've gained, combined with the unconditional love I get from "Sweet P" and "Mr. Sandman," is all I need to feel complete. I do realize there are certain things that are missing from my life, a point that was made clear when I had to bungee five bags of groceries to my motorcycle yesterday. I'd gotten carried away shopping and forgot that I don't own a car. Instead of getting upset by the absurdity of the situation, I laughed along with several onlookers. The fact that I made it home with nary a broken egg made me realize how lucky I am to have transportation in the first place. What if I had to walk the five miles from Trader Joes? It's all about perspective.

That attitude was reinforced when I spoke to Adriana last week. It was the first time we've talked since her baby died two months ago. Rather than discuss the tragedy, and the trauma she's faced since, we focused on the leaps and bounds her surviving twin has made during his interminable stay in the N.I.C.U. Baby David now weighs a whopping two pounds, fourteen ounces—more than twice his initial birth weight. Adriana must wear sterile surgical gear from head to toe when she holds him, and most of the time her touch is limited to the glove-like apparatus that inserts into his incubator. She did share with me the sad news that he's almost blind, a situation that's exacerbated by the fact that her four year old dog spontaneously lost its vision three weeks ago. She actually laughed as she explained the lesson she learned after she rearranged the furniture to vacuum. The poor pup ran head first into the coffee table. She said she was glad it was her dog, and not her son, who taught her the importance of spatial continuity when it comes to visual impairment.

    She also mentioned her recent dream about a panic attack set off by the thought of having to take the SAT's again. In high school, Adriana took the SAT three times before she got respectable enough scores to get into college. She woke up in a cold sweat from the dream, but admitted it was a nice break from the recurring nightmare she's had about Gregory's death. There's an interesting connection between those stressful scenarios. Adriana has ADD, a condition that brought her much suffering when it came to making the grade—there were many days she thought she couldn't survive the pressure of high school. The last two months have been filled with much greater anxiety, days where it took all of her strength to drag herself out of her bed at the Ronald McDonald house, and head to the hospital. Knowing that her surviving son and her husband need her has been the main influence that's kept her from losing her mind. I silently cried as I told her that if she survives this, she can survive anything. We've been friends for 14 years, and I told her I loved her for the first time. I also told her to let me know if there is anything I can do to help. "Keep us in your prayers," she said. So I prayed for the third time today when I got off the phone.

Life isn't fair, but I can finally see it's not supposed to be. I'm also beginning to realize that balance does not mean monotony. I'm beginning to accept the bi-polarity of life, the yin and yang of the universe. I cannot fight the tipping of the scales from time to time, and shouldn't rely on pot, or Prozac, as a way to find equilibrium. The real trick is learning how to get through the tough times without all the drama. Finding God is not the answer, although I'm the first one to admit my outlook on life has improved greatly since I started to pray. I do believe that love is the tour de force when it comes to getting through life without unnecessary strife. When I hear about Adriana's struggle, I'm completely humbled. Especially when I think about all the times I wanted to die, because I didn't want to face another difficult day. Shame on me—whoops, I'm not supposed to say that anymore. Well then, I can pretty much guarantee I'll never consider killing myself again. Thank God I've had the insight to quit crying over spilt milk. I used to think I'd eventually figure out how to make everything go smoothly, and live happily ever after. Boy was I way off on that mark, but at least I know how to feel happy most of the time.

I just heard a little bell toll. One of the kitties must be ready to come in, it's nice to know they miss me after an hour or so; that's all the reason I need to get out of bed in the morning. Affection is definitely one thing that makes life worth living. This miniature apartment doesn't bother me at all—it's a shoebox full of love.

Wednesday, June 26

I'm dating again, or I should say, I'm available to accept dates. I'm finally feeling good enough to meet a good man, and this is my announcement to the universe to send one my way. Actually, the initial announcement went out yesterday on Match.com. I went on the website to check it out and wound up submitting myself—sort of. I posted my personal bio, and opened myself up to the thousands of male members who will be blown away by what I have to say, but I didn't join, because I don't want to have to pay for membership; I'm a little mortified to admit I'm considering an online service. I also didn't post a picture, because for one: I want to remain incognito, and two: I was curious to know if anyone would respond without seeing what I look like. So far I've received three emails from interested parties, all of whom demand that I send along a photo. All three attached pictures of themselves, and low and behold, none of them are cute enough to respond—goes to show I'm as shallow as the next guy.

It shouldn't surprise me they want all the details they can get before they agree to a date. That's the enticement of an online dating; I can sit in my pj's drinking tea while I gather all the info I need about a guy, info that might take months to decode if I outright dated him. The bachelors on Match.com have personal statements, boxes checked for those who want kids, ways to indicate their tax bracket, and a list of their hopes and dreams. Kind of creepy, but it skips the formality of the first dinner date, where you spend most of the time trying to subtly gather what you can, while sniffing their pheromones, and ignoring the piece of meat stuck in their teeth. The online comments I get to read make for a quicker elimination process; at the age of 29, it's all about efficiency.

Posting my bio forced me to think about what I want in a man, and forced me to take a look at myself; where I'm at on the scale of availability. Some of the details I checked off included info about my height: just shy of midget-y, my education: University, and my cup size: 34, barely B. Just kidding; I didn't describe my boobs, but I suppose I should include them in any picture I send. My personal statement was fun to sum up; I wrote that I want to be: spiritual and free, hopeful and strong, caring, daring, married and calm, and courageous enough to live a long and hearty life. I also wrote that I'm a trustworthy, confident, loyal and loving, writer-actor-trainer / bumper sticker maker. Using adjectives to describe myself helped me consider the description of the guy I hope to find. There was no specific space to list what I want in a guy—I can see how that might seem crass, but I did create a secret list for myself. It helped me see I'm ready to find the man of my dreams. I finally have a clear-cut idea of him.

First things first, I'm searching for a "soul mate." I want to find a man who's active, attractive, emotional and fun. I want a guy who's going places; a young one who's mature for his age. I want someone creative. I want someone who'll be great in bed, and loves sex. I want a guy who has his own life, his own opinion, and who can argue with me without pushing my buttons. I want someone who will back me up when he knows I'm right and will teach me about my weaknesses, with kindness. I want someone who will offer me unconditional love. These are bare necessities. I trust this miracle man will have more to offer than I can even imagine.

I've already enumerated the negative traits of my past relationships, now it's time to take a look at the good lessons I learned from all the loves of my life. Let's see: Alex taught me to be shameless when it comes to expressing love, Mike taught me birds of a feather flock together. Brad taught me the importance of family. My relationship with Pete taught me that age does matter. Max taught me that no one can love you completely, if you don't love yourself, and money doesn't buy happiness.

So what's with the sudden change of heart when it comes to dating? I know it's time to try when I gawk at every handsome guy that walks by and my libido, kicked into a high gear, leads to a lot of eye contact with random males. As a matter of fact, my flirtatious gaze got me a first date proposal last week. Out on the town with Rick, Tina (my party pal), and her roommate, the four of us convened at Swinger's for a late night feast, after dancing in Hollyweird. The minute we walked through the diner door I noticed one of the waiter's ogling me. I stared right back at him with an inviting eye and so he traded tables with our waiter so he could introduce himself to me. I know this because he unabashedly admitted it when he arrived to take our order seconds later. I was a tad embarrassed, but flattered nonetheless. He went on to tell the entire table that I was the sexiest creature he'd ever seen; a statement that contained more compliments then Max paid me the entire time we were together. When he returned to our table for the last time, he called me gorgeous and asked for my number. Tina ribbed me, Rick gave a nod, and I obliged.

The Waiter called Sunday night to say he'll be in Vancouver this week but will call me as soon as he gets back. I'm excited, but want to maintain zero expectations. He appears to be very adept at love pampering, but during our fifteen minute phone call I gathered some information about his fast-talking persona. He's a Yale-trained actor, and I think he may have a little "method" up his sleeve. Despite his overt admiration, I think he just wants to sleep with me. There's nothing wrong with that, I could use an orgasm or three, but I get the idea his intentions end there. My female intuition says this guy wants a screw and nothing more. I'm not saying I won't screw him, but I need to recognize that's all he's after so I'm not surprised when he quits calling.

I have the exact opposite instinct about my neighbor downstairs who's recently showed some interest. My little apartment doesn't come with a parking spot, so the week I moved in I asked the guy with the widest spot in the carport if I could squeeze my motorcycle into the corner next to his car. He agreed, and I left a card of thanks on his windshield, which provoked him to ask me out to lunch the next day. He's driven me to Trader Joes twice since then, and yesterday he asked if I'd like to go to a movie sometime. Neighbor Guy is kind and cute, but he's forty-three—not exactly what I have in mind when it comes to a boyfriend. He's also divorced with an eleven-year old daughter, which seals the deal when it comes to disinterest. Of course, an orgasm wouldn't hurt, and Neighbor Guy and I do have chemistry. The booty call convenience of sex with The Neighbor is enticing, I just have to make sure he knows where I'm coming from the same way I understand The Waiter. Any guy I get involved with will know exactly who I am and what I want.

This round of dating is not a dress rehearsal. I'm no longer scrambling around blindly in my search for love. I may find a few more "friends with benefits," before I find The One, but the bottom line is: I want a man who wants to share my life. I want a partner and won't settle for less. That doesn't mean I'm searching for perfection, I have no intention of chasing anyone or placing any man ahead of myself. There are no pedestals higher than mine. I'm in no rush to find a guy. I'll recognize him when I see him. Fully in charge of the direction my life is heading, I must remember to make *choice* choices. Who knows, maybe I'll enjoy some innocent orgasms in the meantime.

Friday, July 5

My original Fourth of July intention was to hang out on the beach all day with Tina, but an hour into our sun soak this afternoon, some hot guys from a big group beckoned us to join them. We sashayed over to play two rounds of volleyball, and a few pints of microbrew later we left the beach to caravan with our friends to a party in Pacific Palisades. We wound up at the house of a guy by the name of North, whose famous father composed music for such classics as A Streetcar Named Desire, Cleopatra, and Ghost. I discovered this during the accidental tour we took in search of a bathroom. While Tina took her time to primp, I stood in the living room and absorbed the incredible view of the Pacific as it surged a thousand feet below the hillside mansion. Outside, the afternoon sun blazed down on the burgundy bougainvillea that draped along the balcony and made for a vivid backdrop to the Gustav Klimt-clad living room. In addition to colorful fine art, there were film posters everywhere. A box frame displayed tickets from fifteen Academy Award Shows. Upon closer investigation I realized they were all tickets for a nominated guest. When the host found me wandering around the room, I asked him outright if his father had won an Oscar.

"Yep, and then some—he won the Academy's Lifetime Achievement Award."

"Can I see it?" I asked, brazenly.

"Sorry, he took it with him when he left."

I assumed the worst, in this world of divorce. "At least he left the posters," I said sarcastically.

"Yeah, lucky us, they wouldn't fit in his casket."

I opened my mouth, inserted my foot, and prayed for Tina to save me.

Amazingly, Junior didn't hold my tactlessness against me. Perhaps it was the concerted effort I made to make funny, cool, and politically correct comments from that point on that allowed him to forgive me. By the time the fireworks began to explode over the coast below, sparks were sizzling between us too. Shortly after the sun went down, the party moved to the hillside deck and Jacuzzi. From that vantage point we had full view of every show that illuminated the sky from the Palisades to Palos Verdes. Faint displays exploded in the inland distance, while three different local shows burned brightly above the city lights that line the curved coast, otherwise known as the "Queen's necklace", With seven people in the hot tub, there was hardly room for hanky panky, but we slipped a couple of kisses in as the moon rose over the horizon.

Junior's mountain biker body was HOT; it matched perfectly with his Ranch style home. I wanted to holler, giddy-up, when he nuzzled up next to me. In the heat of the moment romance got the best of me and I pictured us riding into the galaxy; the glow of the Milky Way guiding us far away from the loves we've lost. I was wooed by the assumption that the two of us had come a long way from heartache: he with his dad; and me with Max. My heart pumped full of fairy tales that fed my head, but I managed to stay focused on the small talk.

"So what do you do?" I asked flirtatiously.

"Mountain bike…hike…hang out with my friends." He said.

"I mean, for work." I clarified.

"Oh, I don't work." He said.

"Are you in between jobs?" I pried.

"No. When my Dad died I decided to enjoy life as much as possible. So I quit school and moved in with Mom."

"So this is your mother's house?"

"Yep; Dad bought it before they met, but she inherited it."

"I'm so sorry about your Dad—how long has it been?"

"Twelve years," he said. Then he cracked another beer. "But it feels like yesterday."

That's because you've been at recess ever since, I thought to myself. After that, I saw the night for what it was—a flash in the pan connection that would be gone with a wink. I did enjoy the goodnight kiss we shared before my departure, but knew it would be our last. I had a great time today, but a trust fund babe is not my type. Safe to say, the dating game is underway; score one for good common sense.

Saturday, July 6

Neighbor Guy lives in the apartment below me, and two doors down. We went to see a movie last week; the date was okay, but I wasn't as attracted to him as I was when we first met. Something about the way he looked all goofy-eyed at me made him seem too eager to please. When he admitted he dyes his hair to hide the gray, I started to drift away from the conversation. I tuned out completely when he confessed that he's unemployed. "Men at Work" was a popular music group when I was a kid. Men-NOT-at-work is the group I keep hearing about these days. Needless to say, an unemployed divorcee is not high on my list of potential boyfriends. Even though there's a fat chance for romance with him, I haven't ruled out getting to know him; I have a feeling Neighbor Guy's got something to offer me.

Maybe that's why he's been hanging out on his patio all week. It seems strategic, like he's waiting for us to cross paths. I have to walk right above his place to get to mine, so I can't pretend I don't see him when he's outside. So far his lounge chair has led to numerous, not so random, run-ins. This morning I left before seven to train someone and he was outside reading.

"Hi there," I said, with half-assed early morning cheer.

"Hey!" He exclaimed.

"Good book?" I asked.

He nodded and held it up to show me. "Conversations with God," it read.

"I've had a bunch of those lately," I offered candidly.

"You should read this book." He said. Then he dove back in it, for emphasis.

I returned home at noon to find a brand new copy of the book and a card propped up on my doorstep. Inside the privacy of my apartment, I opened the envelope and read: "It's been great getting to know you. Take a look at this book; we'll have a lot to talk about during rendezvous number two."

Only if your commentary's more original than this, I thought. Fatigued from the early morning personal training, I plunked down on my bed and read a bit. I got through two chapters before my low blood sugar announced it was time for lunch. I dined on quiche, the only item I can squeeze into the freezer of my little fridge, and chewed on my thoughts about the opening chapter. As I perused the pages of this gift from God and the Neighbor Guy, I drew a conclusion: maybe I should attempt a second excursion with him. It may be a coffee date, or a walk around the block, but some kind of meeting of the minds. I'm pretty sure I'm not looking to flirt with him again, but I'm dying to find a spiritual connection outside of Agape. As long as I'm open and honest, and don't lead him on, the universe will clarify why we've been brought together. Until then, a second arrangement is necessary—more to be revealed.

Sunday, July 7

Lucky for me, Neighbor Guy was inside his apartment this morning when I tip-toed upstairs doing "the walk of shame." It's been a long time since I returned home in the a.m., wearing bed head and dancing duds. If I'd known I was going to wind up with The Waiter last night, I'd have brought along a change of clothes, but my Saturday night plans didn't involve The Waiter until I discovered my out-on-the-town gal pals had dropped ecstasy without me. Much to my dismay, Tina and her roommate, Misty, were already "rolling" when we hit the strip. Turned away from the first club, which was filled to capacity, the fast tripping duo couldn't wait to get their groove on, so we rushed back to the car and sped off towards Hollywood and Vine. As Tina accelerated into the first turn, I knew I didn't want to be in the backseat of a drug-addled driver. I must admit I also felt a little miffed they hadn't included me in their debauchery, so I asked them to drop me off at my bike. As we turned off Melrose onto their street, my cell phone rang; perfect timing. It was The Waiter, wondering where I was. I told him I was headed to his place, partly because I didn't want the night to end early, and partly because I wanted Tina and Misty to know I had other places to go and people to see.

The minute I arrived, The Waiter offered me Merlot, and we settled on the couch for some get-to-know-you gab. Actually, he did most of the gabbing; I sat there getting drunk and staring at his wiry, muscled frame, his blue-green eyes, and the lump in his pants that grew as he told me about an audition he had in Vancouver last week. His monologue included the announcement that he too, is now unemployed. He was fired from the restaurant where we met, when he abruptly left town for an audition, all in the name of the actor's chase. I appreciate the fact that he's hungry and goal oriented, but behind the façade he's just another unemployed actor. By midnight he had talked my ear off and I knew there wouldn't be a second date for us, but the wine was gone and I was horny. The Waiter/Actor's soliloquy had gotten old and I was tired of listening to him rattle off his resume; time for him to shut up and perform for me.

The sex was good, but not quite long enough to hold me until breakfast; I left at the crack of dawn. The

Waiter/Actor said he'd call me, but I could honestly care less. My only concern was that I would run into Neighbor Guy as I snuck back into to my apartment. I plan to be open and honest with him about us, but I would like to keep my other trysts to myself. So all in all, this was a very productive weekend. Three bachelors down, 8 million or so to go, it's a big job. Thank god I've got a week to recuperate.

Friday, July 26

Sorry I've been so incommunicado! I had to squeeze six work days into three, to make up for the spontaneous vacation I took last week. I work about twelve hours a week, so normally no big deal to steal away for a few days. Except from the perspective of my five a.m. "type A" client, who thinks her physique will disintegrate if we miss a day. But between the added expense of my recent move and the cost of traveling to the motorcycle races in Monterey, I couldn't afford to skip a single session this time.

Happy Friday—the work weeks done. Now it's time to reflect on my trip, which was well worth the strain of the juggle. Monday evening I returned from a ride that completely changed my way of thinking. Cruising on my bike for hours on end, with nothing but the sound of the wind in my helmet, inflates the good thoughts and whisks away the bad. Similar to meditation, my motorcycle mind gets clearer throughout the course of a trip. This time, the switchbacks of Big Sur redefined my quest for love. As I negotiated the twists and turns of Highway One, at an average speed of forty, I realized the fast route is not always the best route. And riding with a crew of lesbians made me realize that just because love is in the air, that doesn't mean it's meant for me. I may be ready to find a man, but he might not be ready to find me, so I need to sit back, relax, and enjoy the limitless possibilities.

You never know what could happen; I certainly didn't expect to run into my long lost friend Karen last month, but lately it seems that I connect with all sorts of people in the most unusual places. Three weeks ago, Rick and I took the subway downtown for Sushi—it was the first time I ever used the train in LA. We climbed on board in Hollywood, and sat right smack down behind Karen and her girlfriend.

Karen and I met in 1997, during the AIDS Ride; we were two of the 3,000 bicyclists who rode from San Francisco to LA to raise funds for research. After a nice conversation in line at the porta potty on the third day, we rode together for the rest of the week. Unfortunately, our friendship evaporated back at home. Mostly because she lives in Silver Lake, the far side of the moon when it comes to traffic, but there was also a minor incident where I balked when she tried to kiss me after a night of dancing at a gay club in West Hollywood. I had accepted her invitation to rave at Rage, because I wanted her to know I have no problem with gays. I guess she misinterpreted my liberalism for closeted Lesbian love. She groped, and I flinched, citing mistaken identity. She apologized—said she thought I would be an easy convert. "No harm, no foul," I said with a smile, but I had the sense she was insulted. Within weeks she faded away.

When I tapped her on the shoulder on the Subway, she was genuinely pleased to see me. During the ten-minute trip downtown, I learned that she, too, had bought a motorcycle. We exchanged numbers at the end of the ride. Karen called the next day to say that she and her girlfriend were accompanying their friend, Nancy, to Laguna Seca for the Honda Super Bike races. She invited me to join them. "Twist my rubber arm," I said.

We left Thursday. Karen rode her Suzuki, with girlfriend Miranda on the back. I rode my BMW dual sport, and Nancy, who teaches race school at Willow Springs, rode a Ducati Monster—her favorite of the four different bikes she owns. She and I hit it off immediately, which helped distract me from the continual display of affection between Karen and Miranda. Gay or straight, couples that constantly lock lips in public annoy me. Luckily, the make out sessions were easy to ignore as I zoned in on the plethora of riding information Nancy offered.

After a lesson-filled lunch break in Solvang, I started to think about how great it would be if I found myself a guy who loves motorcycles. That idea filled my brain for about ten seconds before a more powerful notion took over: *stop trying to define him.* Throughout the next two hours, I took in the sights and sounds of the ocean, while waves of enlightenment lapped at the shoreline of my psyche. *I need to have an open mind,* I thought. *You can't steer towards destiny.* "No rush," I whispered, as I downshifted into another 180-degree turn.

That evening, the four of us dined on fish and chips at The Pismo Beach Whaler then headed to The Cue, where we played pool until they closed. Back to the hotel, Nancy and I volunteered to leave the lovebirds alone so they could fool around. It didn't bother me, I was wide-awake, and there is nothing I love more then a hot tub after three beers, and as many hours of riding. The outdoor spa closed at ten, so we had to scale the fence and crawl across prickly bushes with bare feet. The hot water stung, but the bubbles felt good bouncing off my tired derriere. Nancy and I talked for fifteen minutes before she suddenly cozy'd up to me and slipped her hand under my thigh. "Does this bother you?" She asked.

"Um…no," I said, awkwardly.

"You're hot." She purred, and my head started to spin—I didn't know what to say. I felt like the shortest kid had just asked me to dance and I didn't want to insult him, or her.

"Can I kiss you?" She asked.

I'm not into girls, I said silently, defending the urge to control my world.

"Ummm…" I hummed, stalling. Suddenly, I heard God say the same thing my mother used to say at the dinner table. *Try it. If you don't like it, you don't have to finish.*

"Ummm…" she said, mocking me.

"Sure," I said.

She placed her lips on mine. *Where do I put my hands?* I wondered. The kiss didn't bother me, I couldn't tell the difference between hers and a man smooch. The hard part was the lack of hard parts. Her face was delicate and petite, her hair long, legs soft and squishy, and the breasts? They were completely off limits. I had no interest. So I held my arms rigidly at my sides. The longer we kissed, the more I felt like I had been forced to dance with the smallest boy in the class. I've never been attracted to a guy I thought I could beat up, and I felt the same way about Nancy. Our kiss ended when I reached that conclusion.

"Not doing it for ya, huh." She asked, like an accusation.

I apologized. "You're cool; I'm just not into it."

"Funny, I had you pegged as the perfect convert."

I am a convert! But these stimulating conversations with God have got to stop!

"You can call me straight, but not narrow." I said with a shrug.

"Well you can call me horny, but not desperate. I'm going to go tell the bitches it's time for bed," she said. That was the last time she hit on me.

The next morning was a tad uncomfortable. It was obvious Nancy told Karen about our kiss, since Karen woke me up with, "Helloooo, you little Lesbo". At half past six, the five of us stumbled into the dawn light to prepare for the grand finale that would get us to Laguna Seca a few hours before the first race. "Ride your own ride," was the last thing I heard as I merged onto PCH. The section between Pismo and Monterey on HWY 1 is a motorcyclist's Mecca. Never-ending twisties rise two thousand feet above the sea, weave around the tall pines of Big Sur and Carmel, then spit you out in Monterey Bay. Time stood still, and flew by; we reached the inland Highway to Laguna Seca in the wink of an eye.

When we arrived at the racetrack we each paid for a standard two-day pass, then snaked our way down to Ducati Island in the center of the infield, where Nancy knew one of the pit crews. Even with her racing connections and my feminine wiles, an hour went by before we were cleared to steer our bikes towards the pits. Three sets of sexy girls got in before us, using their ultra femininity to woo security. I tried to flirt with the guys the minute we got there, but Nancy interrupted by introducing me as the newest member of their pussy posse. Despite her attempt at sabotage, I managed to abuse the rules and feign enough interest to get us to the head of the line. I couldn't believe the audacity of this girl gang when they called me a slut because I got them into the pits quicker then Nancy could.

That was the first time I felt isolated by them because of my sexuality, but it wasn't the last. I thought going to the races with a bunch of chicks would make for a memorable female bonding experience, but Midway through Saturday I couldn't see the difference between hanging out with the Posse, and hanging out with guys.

"I love the smell of race fuel in the morning," Nancy said, when we first arrived.

"Check out the tits on that one," Karen added, in reference to a young woman strutting around in a mini skirt and shirt that advertised Pennzoil.

"Do you have to be so obnoxious?" Miranda whined. I tried to relate to her lipstick lesbian sensibilities and invited her to roam the clothing tents while Karen and Nancy studied the "machines". "I'm not leaving Karen with all these Lolita's strutting around", She said.

"I'm going shopping," I announced. None of them batted an eye.

The word "lesbian," was beginning to sound like "let's be men," to me.

Maybe I wanted to compensate for my lapse in sexual judgment the night before, or perhaps I was turned on by the testosterone in the air, but I flirted with half a dozen guys as I meandered across the infield. Laguna Seca was much more fun then I thought it would be. I assumed the racetrack atmosphere would be full of dirt and greasy guys, I was pleasantly surprised. Lined along the grassy infield were row upon row of colorful tents that offered everything from discount tires to lawyers for hire. One attorney specialized in settlements for bikers who'd been hit by commercial vehicles. He handed out mini bumper stickers that read: Kill a Biker, Go to Jail. He also had a plaque that listed the names of fifty deceased riders. "Clients of yours?" I asked.

"No. That's the list of guys who have died on the way to the races. I've been coming here for thirty years, and every year we lose another one. This morning there was a collision between two bikes, one guy died at the scene and the other ones in critical condition. Rumor has it that they were riding pretty aggressive, so, unfortunately, there won't be any restitution for their families." Memory of an ambulance whizzing past us earlier flooded my brain.

"Keep up the good work," I said.

"And you keep the rubber side down," he retorted.

Next, I made my way to the BMW tent where I admired the latest models and high-end riding gear. Motorcycle manufacturers surrounded the grassy knoll: Aprillia, Triumph, Kawasaki and Norton were the few I perused. I finished my exploration at the Ducati museum, where display bikes dated back to the early twentieth century. When I had my fill of gawking, I followed the scent of funnel cakes to the food court.

Sitting down to sip a raspberry Slurpee, I took in the sights and sounds of all the happy families milling around. Opening my eyes after a painful brain freeze, I couldn't help but notice a young stud staring at me from behind the counter of the Hot Sausage tent. No longer seeking a soul mate, I had the freedom to flirt with any guy that enticed me. I spent fifteen minutes talking to the cute kid behind the counter, who appreciated the way I devoured my wiener. When he asked the name of my hotel, I asked him his age. To his dismay, eighteen was too young for me. That's the excuse I used to keep our immature interaction short and sweet.

Next, I headed towards the line of tents that had apparel for sale. After collecting two t-shirts and a pair of leather pants, I was ready to return to the pits. The first race was announced as I wiggled past security to reunite with my friends. I arrived to find Miranda sulking in the corner, while Nancy and Karen peered over the shoulder of the mechanic who prepared the bike for Number 22. Distracted by steamy, sweaty flesh, I zoomed in on a guy who'd been disqualified, as he peeled off the top of his leather suit to expose a hairless, meaty torso. He looked like a banana, and I wanted to take a bite. I expressed my hunger to Miranda instead. "There are a million gorgeous guys here."

"What'd you buy?" she asked, ignoring my score.

"Perforated White leathers," I said.

"Model them for us," Nancy suggested. I ducked into the corner of the tent to undress, since there was virtually no difference between pulling my pants down in front them, and men.

"Great ass!" Karen cheered.

"Let me know if you need help getting those off," Nancy added.

"You can look, but don't touch," I retorted.

Annoyed by their boyish vulgarity, I opted to wander again. Heading towards the racetrack I heard catcalls from Karen as a busty young woman rode by on a Honda. As far as I could tell, "show ho's" were in charge of riding the race bikes from the pits to the tracks and back. Seemed like a fun job. The most scantily clad girls stood around to hand out promotional stickers and take pictures with passersby. There were two dozen male racers, each squeezed into brightly colored leathers with black pucks on their knees, designed to absorb the scrapes from the ground as they bore down around the corners. The pit we lay claim to was stationed inside turn number three, at the end of a long stretch where riders hit their highest speeds. I stood right behind the fence, next to the tripod of a photographer who had a massive telephoto lens. It was an awesome location. There were at least a hundred folks on the other side of the track, all straining to catch a glimpse of the pack of riders. Even from my vantage point, it was difficult to focus on them as they whizzed by, and curiosity got the best of me. I asked the official with a radar gun how fast he had clocked them. "185," he said.

Meandering back to base camp, I spent the rest of the day drooling over race dudes, while my comrades drooled over the tools. Nancy's interest in me waned as I reclaimed my status as heterosexual. There were no hard feelings though. Later on the five of us enjoyed a long night of drinking and darts at a bar on Cannery Row, before settling in for another short night of snoozing.

Sunday was almost exactly the same as Saturday, except I had less money to spend. When the last race ended, we hit the road and knocked a hundred miles off the return trip. We settled in San Simeon, ordered a pizza from our motel room, and went to bed early. During breakfast on Monday morning, I picked Nancy's brain again, on how to take the turns efficiently. "Keep the rubber side down", was the last thing she said to me; it reminded me of the guy who was fighting for his life. I asked God to watch over both of us.

The last two hundred miles of riding brought tremendous clarity. When it came to the turns, Nancy said I should maintain as much contact with the road as possible. She told me that staying grounded is the most important aspect of avoiding a "low side", where lack of traction forces the bike to slip and slide. This made me think of my last two boyfriends. I laughed at the fact that I'd discussed marriage with each of them weeks before our relationship ended. Staying grounded seemed like a good rule of thumb.

As the day wore on, I noticed that most of the rules of riding could be applied to the rules of love. Nancy told me to keep my eyes on the road and use peripheral vision to scan my surroundings. Wide eyes seem like a great tool in the search for a soul mate as well. She also told me to look as far into the turns as I could. "Don't worry about the bumps right in front of you." She said. "Peripheral vision guides you past them; just pick a trajectory, trust the direction, and accelerate into the corners. "If you get into trouble," she added, "hit the throttle, lean hard, press on the outside foot peg, and breathe."

Her message was simple: second-guess yourself and you will crash and burn. Makes sense in terms of boyfriends too, since I'm the only one who knows what's best for me. Of course, it's my duty to communicate what's best for me before I get hurt, an analogy that rings true for riding too. The last lesson Nancy shared had to do with splitting lanes. "It's your job to let other drivers know where you are," she said, "and the quickest way to state your location is to make some noise." She reminded me that the engine gets louder when it revs in lower gears. "When in doubt," she said, "honk, shout, do whatever it takes to make them hear you." Perhaps this is sound advice for dealing with men then too?

One thing's for sure—motorcycling is a dangerous sport, but practice and protection reduce the risks. The scariest thing Nancy said is there are two kinds of riders: those who have crashed and those who will. I hope I land softly when it happens to me. I've had plenty of wipeouts when it comes to love. Luckily, I've been able to avoid permanent damage. Falling down hurts, but it's not the end of the world. The real trick is to not be afraid of falling. Fear is no longer an option. I've got too much love to give.

Tuesday, August 20

Dating sucks; in the last three weeks I've gone out with a narcissist, a priss, and a man I never should have kissed. The latter happens to be Neighbor Guy, who won't leave me alone since we locked lips. I know I promised to have an open mind, and I don't want to be unkind, but I've got to get rid of this guy pronto.

The problem began when we drank some wine and hormones got the best of me. It only took a few minutes for me to realize I wasn't interested in going further. In an attempt to avoid an insult I told him I didn't want to date him because he lives below me. He said he'd move. I laughed. It was the same laugh I offer the Special Olympics gymnasts that I coach, when they tell me a joke—it translates as: very funny, now let's get back to the task at hand. In the case of Neighbor Guy, the task was to make him understand that friendship is all I want from him. I thought he understood what that meant, until he invited me to his cousin's wedding in Santa Barbara. At first I declined, afraid that infatuation had made him blind to my disinterest. "No strings attached," he said, claiming his only motive was to have a non-familial dance partner at the reception. I agreed to go.

    The trip from LA to Santa Barbara clued me in to his ulterior motives. This forty-three year old dude acted like we were in grade school, and insisted on holding my hand the entire ride. It wouldn't have been nearly as strange if his daughter weren't in the back seat, getting her first impression of me. She seemed cool, as far as ten year-olds go, so I didn't want her to know I thought her dad was a geek. I tried to act as friendly and uninterested as I could, with his and my fingers intertwined the whole time.

    Upon our arrival at Hotel Andalucia, the décor of the outdoor patio told me I was underdressed. It felt like a blessing in disguise. I'd chosen the perfect dress to leave a bland impression; a full length, full sleeved, crushed brown velvet culottes-gown, it was non-traditional enough to be a poor choice for a fancy wedding. Its non-easy-access style screamed, "Don't you dare try to touch me." I decided that even if Neighbor Guy continued to woo me, his family would persuade him otherwise. As we meandered around the garden during cocktail hour, the implication of our connection became suspect. Neighbor Guy went from holding my hand on one side and his daughter's on the other, to drawing me into a one armed embrace. He also omitted the word "friend" during every introduction. Then Aunt Sue came right out and asked me if I'd ever been married, and acted a little too excited when I said no.

Throughout the reception I saw numerous relatives wink or pat him on the back as if to say congrats. Doing my best to act depressed, I couldn't get him to leave me alone. I refused to dance, didn't talk to anyone, and sat there sulking the entire time. When he dove across the dance floor to catch the garter, and smiled gleefully at me, I knew we were on different pages. The level of my discomfort increased as the night wore on, and peaked when I met his grandmother. The fact that I lack childbearing hips, she said, made me the perfect candidate for step mom. At that point I requested, in a disgusted monotone, that Neighbor Guy take me home. He declined, citing the night was early and he was too drunk to drive. I wound up sleeping on the couch at his parents house because I refused to share a room with him and his daughter. By the time we returned to Brentwood I was no longer interested in being his friend.

That leaves me with one less platonic option when it comes to finding a date for all the weddings I've been invited to recently. A couple that I train just invited me to Cabo for their wedding in November; guess I'll go alone.

Next month my cousin's getting married in Pasadena; so much for non-familial dance partners. Last night I got a phone call from one of my best friends from college, who's engaged to the woman he dated when we were in school. After ten years of pursuing separate adventures and sowing their oats, they reconnected, and decided their long lost love was destined to be a holy matrimony. My immediate response was "holy jealousy," why can't I go back in time to find My Man?

One thing's for sure: I can't go back to my most recent relationship because the man I thought I wanted to marry six months ago got married in Vegas last May. Considering his recent M.S. diagnosis, I never guessed he'd be searching for a girlfriend, let alone a wife. He told me he needed time to get his life together; it took him two and a half months to find a woman who is more qualified than me to get him through his tough times. I hate to admit I'm insulted. I'm not even sure why. I don't love Max anymore. He drew out the worst in me, but I can't stand the fact that he rejected me on the premise that we were both messed up and then turned around and found the love of his life. All I've found is my self, and most of the time that's enough, but not when I have to go stag to everyone else's love fantasy. I've tried to decode the messages the universe is sending me, so what's up with all the freaking weddings?

Marriage, shmarriage, these lovers are making me sick. It's no secret I want to get hitched, but I'm trying not to focus on that goal while I search for a mate. Unfortunately, I can't seem to dodge the barrage of wedding invitations. Is this a test? Am I supposed to prove I can celebrate everyone else's amorous success—while I search high and wide for my own? I'm trying to be a good sport about this, but Dear God can't you throw me a bone?

Wednesday, September 11

"What a beautiful day!" I said, as Rick and I started our morning run.

"Bah hum bug", he retorted. There was a deflated spring in his step.

"You got the 9-11 blues?" I presumed.

"No, I woke up with God's boot on my head."

"What's the matter?" I asked.

"I don't want to talk." He slowed to a crawl.

"Then don't talk…and don't walk," I said. "Run."

We set off in silence, each of us taking in the sun, and the clouds, respectively.

Finally, I got tired of listening to him sigh, and interrupted his lack of enthusiasm with a dose of my blossoming optimism. "I'm ready to pursue acting again, and I'm not going to quit this time." I joyfully declared my pursuit of happiness in the form of artistic endeavor. As we cruised around the golf course at less than an aggressive pace, Rick became privy to my new philosophy: "Muffling the artist in me is no longer an option," I said. "So I reestablished my membership with S.A.G."

"Did they welcome you back with open arms?" He asked.

"No, I made up a tragic story about my parents getting divorced and my lover being diagnosed with a terminal illness, so I wouldn't have to pay late fees on top of the belated dues."

"How imaginative of you," he smirked.

"I may not care about making money as an actress, but I'll be damned if my fine acting skills can't keep me from being fined by the Guild."

"Congratulations," he said, with little fanfare.

"Speaking of my fine acting, what's happening with your show? How'd the meeting go at NBC?"

"Looks like we're left with one last pitch at the WB," his head hung down. "The networks all love the concept of the show, but they can't understand the concept of convergence. Last night my partner told me if our final meeting falls flat too, he'll have to accept a job offer in Tampa."

My heart went out to Rick. For the last few months he's filled me in on the details of his project. I'm sworn to secrecy, but the basic idea is a reality TV show that propels the audience to an internet search engine. The show poses as a documentary, and gives the audience an intimate peek at the inhabitants of a small community. Each episode will subliminally convince the audience to log on to the website, to discover more about these people. Through the website the audience will be able to interact with the community and buy everything they see or hear about on the show.

 Rick has reinvented the wheel when it comes to TV. His show will be financially fueled by revenues from the website, instead of commercials. Without the influence of advertisers he'll have a lot more creative freedom than the average sitcom does. The concept is genius and his pitch received a standing ovation at Disney, but as soon as he started to explain the website, the execs said, 'forget the internet, let's just add some commercials and call it a deal.' Rick won't budge. He insists it's a matter of time before the execs see the light. Unfortunately, with his partner threatening to move to Florida, time is of the essence. As Rick and I jogged today, I asked him what he planned to do. "Move," he said, defiantly.

 "Closer to the ocean," I hoped.

 "Yeah, the Atlantic," he replied.

 "What do you mean?" I asked, surprised.

 "I don't want to live here anymore."

I was floored. My closest friend, my confidante, my creative inspiration, was about to walk out the door. I suddenly saw the towers crumble down again.

"But all your connections are out here," I implored.

Affirmative thoughts rapid fired from my brain. I knew it was selfish to ask him to stay for me, so I focused on him instead. First I told him that with his talent it'd be a shame to walk away from the entertainment industry. "New York has TV too," he responded. I pointed out that the struggles he's faced in LA have made him resilient. He said his "thick skin," will protect him from the New York winters. Finally, I reminded him that a positive perspective is the key, and he shouldn't let rejection destroy his destiny. He said his destiny includes having a family someday, and he'd never raise kids in LA. "You don't even have a girlfriend!!" I said, with a tad too much conviction.

"Thanks for the insight."

"What about me?" I whined.

"It's not about you", he sighed.

"You want to brainstorm reasons to stay?" I pleaded.

"No. I gotta go." He screeched to a halt and said his back hurt, his head hurt, and he really didn't feel like running. After an abrupt goodbye, he headed home and left me to shuffle my sorry ass around the golf course alone.

Back at my pad I flipped on the tube and chugged down a glass of tea. National memorials for the one year anniversary of 9-11 were in full swing. Sitting in the comfort and safety of my home, I watched the sadness unveil on TV. I may be far away from the heart of the tragedy, but every speech seemed to be aimed at me. "Adversity makes us stronger," they said. "Life goes on." *Yeah,* unless you're one of the men and women who died in the towers, or one of their wives, husbands, parents, children, or friends, who are forced to face endless days without them. Rick thinks he'll find happiness in New York? The tears that fall there suggest otherwise.

Who the hell am I to preach optimism? Over the last fifteen years I thought suicide was a viable way to end a reasonably bad day. When the shock of 9-11 wore off last year, I realized it was time to quit crying about dying, and live up to the life I'd been given. I'm not the only one whose eyes were opened on that fateful day. After the terrorists struck, priorities shifted for people all over the country. Tom Brokaw announced on the news last night that a baby boom has begun as a result of people getting together in the months after the towers fell.

Forget propagation; a year ago I was an incomplete person. I wasn't living up to my potential, spiritually or emotionally, and I consistently focused on what was wrong with my life. It got to the point where minor glitches in my Grand Plan made me think life wasn't worth living. Luckily, my new and improved perspective has brought a cease-fire to my mind. The glass is fuller than it used to be, but there's still room for improvement. Obviously, if I were truly open to whatever the universe is sending me, I'd embrace Rick's decision to leave. After all, it's not about me. I'm sure going to miss him though.

Come to think of it, if the people who faced death in the rubble of the fallen towers have the strength to go on, they're more qualified than me to teach Rick about faith and optimism. I guess I should wish him well, and on his way. He knows what's best for him, and I trust we'll both be taken care of, even if it happens on opposite sides of the country. Until then, I must admit, I'm not ready to let him go just yet. I know what's best for me, and Rick has a few more things to teach me before he goes.

"After they had explored all the suns in the universe and all the planets in each sun they realized they were alone, and they were glad, because they now knew they would have to become all of the things they had hoped to find."

~ Lanford Wilson

Sunday, October 20

"You are not alone," was the opening statement of the Reverend's sermon at Agape this morning. Oh yeah? I thought to myself. My best friend wants to move to New York, I haven't had a good date in the last eight, and my cats have become my primary confidantes. I glared at the Reverend on his pedestal and sent him a silent retort. Easy for you to say, you've got a chunk of humanity sitting in your sanctuary, eager to hear you speak. I, on the other hand, must rustle up the company of my cats when I want an audience for my rant. The fact that I spent the entire weekend ALONE, might be why I was put off by the topic, but I sat there with open ears anyway.

The sermon wove in and out of ideas I could grasp, and those I might choke on if I swallowed too fast. When the Rev. said something about quantum physics I disengaged, only to gaze out at fifteen hundred other folks who seemed to comprehend his cryptic concept. After fifteen minutes of gawking at the congregation I was able to follow one tangent he pursued. "Everything is made up of molecules," he said. I'm no science buff, but I do recall the basic rules. Any fool can believe in a molecule, and my comprehension bred a sense of connection. I suddenly felt part of an enormous entity. When the Reverend said, "Love is surrounding me," I knew what he meant. I could feel it.

As the hour wore on, I started to understand the "Science of Mind" doctrine that promotes "God" as love. I can't say I believe in God completely yet, but by the end of the Reverend's homily I was inspired to do what I need to do to elude this encroaching loneliness. I even went so far as to sign up for one of the "Sweet Sixteen" parties that are being sponsored around town next month by members of the congregation, in celebration of Agape's 16th anniversary. Maybe I'll meet a spiritual, happy and healthy man there. At the very least I hope to extend my circle of friends.

Until then, I'll have to find solace and joy in solitude. It's not that bad spending time alone, now that I can stand myself. Living without cable has strengthened my communion with me. Rather than spending every evening with TV, I've had to rely on reading and writing as my primary source of entertainment. The highlights of my nights are the kitty shenanigans: Pebbles and Sandy love to chase each other across every inch of my two hundred square foot apartment. When the three of us are low energy, we lie on the bed and listen to the audio version of the book, "Autobiography of a Yogi."

I never thought I'd say this, but Yoga is now my favorite exercise. Not for the physical challenge it presents, but because it calms my mind and helps me appreciate quiet time. I've spent years whipping myself into shape through aggressive and heart pounding workouts, while I allowed my emotional life to spin out of control. My "no pain, no gain" approach to life fostered a notion that big, bad, bold emotions are the only way to go. Yoga has taught me to pay attention to the minor moments that make up each day, because they can be as memorable as, say, crossing the finish line. I used to think that bringing melodrama to my life would keep me from getting bored. What better way to spice up a day than to cry, or get high, or cut on myself, to get a rise out of a guy. I realize now that concocted drama is a waste of energy. Deep breathing can provide the same release as a tantrum, and no on gets hurt.

Breathing brought an epiphany today. After I got home from the service I felt antsy about spending another afternoon solo, so I decided to relax by doing yoga on my bed. I started with the ujayii breath and let the sound of the ocean roll out of my head. Closing my eyes I began to free my mind from the need for company. Just be, I commanded. Heavy breath escaped my chest and I noticed that every once in a while one would be bigger than the others, like a rogue rave interrupting the rhythm of the sea. I was trying to regulate my breathing when a string of words sang their song to me.

> *Rogue wave capsizes a yacht,*
> *And imagines itself as larger than the lives aboard.*
> *Then the news is announced*
> *And the wave is reduced*
> *To a hiccup in a grandiose sea.*

The words ended, and I breathed in slow and deep. Wanting to cling to the silence, I crossed my legs, lay my forearms on them, and held my thumb and middle fingers together, in the classic meditation pose. A good bit of time went by before I felt a tiny wet nose bump against my knee. With my lids squeezed tight I fought to hold focus on the nothingness. The silence was serene and I didn't want to lose the peace, but Pebbles wasn't in on the plan. She went from sniffing my leg, to curling up in my lap, and that was the end of that. The meditation was done, along with the sense of isolation. How could I feel desolate in the middle of all this love? God, in the form of a purring fur ball, works for me. So kudos to you, Pebs, I am not alone.

Wednesday, October 30

Oh God, what have I done? How could I be so *dumb*? I deserve what's happening. I earned this pain, I should be maimed. I want to slice an X across my chest, carve "stupid" across my forehead. I hate myself. What have I done?

I'm a horrible person, a cigarette-smoking boozehound, that couldn't wait for a drink, couldn't wait for a stinking cigarette. I'm such an idiot. I want to cut myself so bad, the resistance hurts more than the razor will. I can't control it. I hate myself. I have to bleed. No willpower. I'm worthless. I *need* to bleed. I hate myself, how could I do this? I *deserve* this agony. I should feel ten times more pain than I'm feeling now. I have no right to be happy.

My unconditional love sucks. I'm not fit for love. I'll never be a good mother. My needs get in the way; when I want wine and cigarettes, nothing else matters. Now that I've smoked half the pack and the bottle is gone, I've started to resemble Pebbles, as she stiffens into a cold and lonely death. Sandy won't come out of the bathroom. He knows it's my fault she got run over. He probably wants to hurt me. I know I do.

 I spent all of ten minutes calling their names before I justified leaving. I'll be home before dark, I thought. What's another twenty minutes? It turns out, twenty minutes is enough time for dusk to introduce a shade of darkness that sheds an ugly light on my priorities. I'M A TERRIBLE MOTHER, too selfish for love. Oh, Pebs. What have I done?

Sunday, November 3

This is the first day this week that I've felt like a human being. I've been living like a cretin, stashed away in a cave, with vodka, pot, butts and a razor blade to take me to oblivion. So far, I've relinquished resistance to everything but the blade, although I keep it near and dear in case I get out of hand again. I feel like I need to be punished: for letting Pebs run free, for drinking away misery, for dropping her off like a sack of trash at the Vet, because I couldn't afford a proper cremation. Wrapped in gingham and nestled with a mish mash of flowers, I bungeed her cardboard box to the back of my bike and drove her to her final resting place. Once there, I had a few more moments to apologize before I paid a thirty-dollar fee to guarantee her a spot in the mass incineration oven.

"For three hundred and fifty she could be cremated alone, and returned in an urn," the sympathetic vet offered as an initial option.

"Wow. That's expensive," I remarked, feeling more and more worthless by the minute. I'm a heartless creep. I prefer to spare expense when it comes to dead pets. To exaggerate my role as a lame-o, I paid for the version of cremation I could afford and spent the rest of the day, high as a kite, debating if I should use a steak knife to carve my pain away. I must've traced "I'm sorry" along my thigh a hundred times with the blunt edge, but something kept me from going to the flip side. I may be messed in the head, but my body remains free from damage. The same force that kept me from cutting helped me realize I shouldn't continue down this path of self-destruction.

That's the main reason I went to church this morning. As I sat in the service at Agape, desperate for salvation, guilt and sorrow drowned my soul, and told me I didn't belong there. At the end of the sermon the Reverend announced names from the prayer box. I was ashamed that I'd been afraid to add my name to the box—worried someone would call me out for being at fault. As the Rev. drew attention to the folks who deserved prayer, I sunk down in my chair and hid my tears. When the service was over I was itching to head home and get shnockered, until I caught a glimpse of some relevant information on the back of the program. There was an announcement for a pet bereavement group that meets every other Sunday. Today was the day.

The post-service gathering helped me feel alive again. Watching three strangers sob about their dead pets, helped me see I'm not a fool for feeling distraught. The only regret I had was that I didn't bring a picture of Pebbles to show them. The only image I presented was of me as a horrible person. Thankfully, the facilitator pointed out that since I clearly loved my kitten and she obviously loved me, she said I'd be better off focusing on her memory, than the mystery behind how and why she died. At the end of the bereavement service, the woman who lost her thirty-eight year old parrot suggested I build a shrine to memorialize Pebs, and forget about the blame and shame game.

So that's what I chose to focus on when I got home. First I placed Pebbles blue ceramic bowl in the center of a stool and filled it to the brim with crab cake treats—her favorites. Next, I plucked gardenias from the courtyard, bound them together with her collar, and set the flowers in a crystal vase beside the bowl. Then I taped my favorite photos of her to the wall behind the shrine. One picture showed her soaked from head to toe, after a misguided attempt to swim with the fish in the Koi pond at Max's. It captured her adventurous spirit perfectly. I propped it behind the collection of toy mice that lined the front of the shrine. Tea lights completed the scene. They offered a flickering light to illuminate happy memories.

Staring at the shrine, an image came to mind of Pebbles welcoming me home last week. No matter where she was, she always came running to greet me when she heard my motorcycle enter the driveway. Last week, she beat me to the punch. In her excitement, she stood up on her hind legs and hopped alongside me as I drove by, waving her paws in jubilation. I laughed out loud as I got off my bike. Then I scooped her up and placed her on my shoulder pad, where she sat, like a sass, while the slower half of the welcoming committee—a.k.a. Sandy—strutted behind.

After twenty minutes of reminiscing, I squeezed my eyes tight, stored my recollection deep inside, and blew out the candles with a breath of fresh air. I lifted my lids to find Sandy sniffing the bag of crab cakes. I tossed him a slew of them. He gobbled them up, and then jumped on the bed. For the first time since Wednesday, he looked directly at me. I could see his misery. Using words he'd recognize, I verbalized our sorrow, "Pebs was a *good* girl."

"Mrrr-ow," he said. I rubbed his head.

"It's just you and me kid." He lay there as I stroked him from head to tail. "I love you, bud." He rolled over and offered me his belly. "Do you forgive me?" I asked. My voice cracked. He didn't respond, so I whispered for both of us, "yes."

I leaned down and lay my head on his chest, to show how much I love him. I smelled and listened to him breathe. His heart rate raced. "We're going to be okay." I said, petting again. Then, as a gesture of my faith, I stood up, delicately grabbed the folded tissue from my desk, and went downstairs to the dumpster, to throw that stupid blade away.

Sunday, November 10

What a difference a week makes—I feel so much better than I did last Sunday. In fact, the last few days have been filled with enough healing and mourning that I actually disassembled the shrine today. I still have all the pictures on the wall, but I no longer cry for fifteen minutes a day. I suppose that has to do with the closure I received yesterday at my memorial service for Pebbles.

I got the idea for the memorial a few days ago, when the same neighbor who informed me she was dead, stopped by to see how I was doing. This woman, whose name happens to be "Kat," had a good sense of what I'm going through, since she lost her feline a year ago. She recently adopted two others. When she heard tires screech Wednesday night she worried it was one of them lying in the street below her apartment; and ran downstairs immediately. During her initial glimpse out the window, Kat saw a young male driver slow down, realize what he'd done, and flee. The woman behind him stopped, graciously, and by the time Kat got outside, the woman had started to direct traffic around the accident. She immediately told Kat to grab a blanket from the trunk of her car, and transport my lifeless sweet P to the sidewalk. There was nothing they could do. Kat thanked the woman for her generosity and set out to find me. Discovering I was gone, she wrapped Pebs tight in the blanket to spare me the gore, and placed her in a cardboard box with flowers from the courtyard.

When I arrived moments later, Sandy was wandering aimlessly around the courtyard. His tail twitched nervously. I went over to pet him as Kat rushed around the corner. "I've been looking all over for you." Her tone made me sick.

"What's the matter?" I asked.

"Sandygotrunover," she stammered breathlessly.

"He's right here," I pointed, relieved.

"Oh honey, I'm so sorry. It was the little one then."

My hair stood on end. "What do you mean?"

"Pebble's is dead." After that, nothing she said even mattered.

I was very appreciative when she came by to see how I was doing the other day, and expressed heartfelt thanks for her kindness. She said it was the least she could do—since it could've just as easily happened to her cat too. That one little comment helped rectify some skewed ideas that were messing with my head. Most importantly, it helped me realize it wasn't my fault Pebbles died. It also made me aware that it wasn't fair to keep Sandy eternally confined to my tiny, non-air conditioned apartment. When I shared my fear of letting him roam around again, Kat agreed it was the right thing to do. She admitted that she worries about her cats all the time, especially since she's seen seven different pets come to unfortunate ends under the wheels of cars during the thirty-three years that she's lived here. Oddly enough, it hasn't kept her from letting her cats run free.

"After years of worrying that my last cat would die, my worst fear was realized." She confessed.

"How'd it happen?" I asked tenderly.

"In his sleep—at age twenty."

"Did anything ease your pain?"

"Yeah, I had a memorial service for him."

A memorial for a cat sounded corny, but I decided it was worth a try. Later that day I posted a sign near the mailboxes:

For those who knew and loved her…Pebbles passed away under the wheel of a car last week. Please join her brother Sandy and I, for a memorial service to celebrate her life and spunk. There will be an informal gathering from 2-4 pm on Saturday in the courtyard. No gifts please, just well wishes, to send her on her way.

In the hours before the service yesterday I started to feel nervous about being labeled as the weird cat lady. Luckily, when I told Rick about the cup cakes, he agreed to get there promptly at two. Then, like a true best friend, he showed up early to help organize. Covering the plastic picnic table with an antique embroidered tablecloth, I transferred the items from the shrine downstairs. Rick lit the candles and I poured the juice. At 2:15 we sat down to wait and see who'd be looney enough to join us. Thirty minutes later, no one had shown. I started to feel stupid and asked Rick if he thought we should wrap it up early. He told me to wait. After another ten minutes of idle chitchat I was beginning to feel really insecure, when one of my downstairs neighbors arrived. I didn't know his name but I knew from casual conversation that he and his girlfriend work as sushi chefs at a nearby Japanese restaurant. He started by saying that his girlfriend was sorry she couldn't get away from work. Then he handed me a handmade Salmon roll she'd sent along as a gift. I thanked him and offered him a seat. He said he only had a thirty minute break and didn't have time to stay, but he wanted to express his condolences and share a funny story with me.

Apparently Pebbles frequented their apartment, and constantly tried to play with their cat. He said their cat was shy and invariably ran away from Pebs. The last time she came by their apartment, he said, Pebbles tried to stir things up by running out the cat door with their cat's favorite toy. Much to their surprise, she waltzed back in the next day to return the prize. His story was short and sweet, as was his visit. I thanked him, and sent him back to the sushi bar with a plateful of cup cakes.

Shortly after he left, another neighbor came along. I'd only spoken to this woman once. She re-introduced herself, handed me a sympathy card and told me how much she missed Pebbles. She went on to say that her cat had been run over on the same corner last year, and she didn't have the heart to get another one. Instead, she welcomed Pebs as a timeshare pet, and routinely invited her in to cuddle on the couch during Oprah. I was enjoying the image of Ms. Pebs as a whorish love bug, when Neighbor Guy came walking by. I don't know if he's hurt by my rejection, or had somewhere to go, but he said a quick hello, handed me a card, and then hurried home. Before I had a chance to open it, the other neighbor told me she'd seen him with a garden hose washing the blood off the street after the accident, to spare me from seeing it. That was the most heartwarming story I heard all day. At a quarter to four, Rick and I began to clear the table. That's when Kat arrived. She handed me a card along with a book about mourning, and told me to call if I ever needed anything. I thanked her again. She left, and Rick said, "You sure have a lot of friends here."

"Actually," I confessed, "Pebs had a lot of friends. I'm just blessed by the affiliation."

Gazing up at the little room that had become my home, I spotted Sandy sitting in the window. The thought of letting him wander made my heart ache, but I knew it was time to let go and give him space. So I went upstairs, opened the door, and sing-songed his name. He was apprehensive, which didn't surprise me. Kat said Sandy witnessed the tragedy, and stood on the sidewalk watching as they wrapped up Pebs and carried her away. Curious to see if he'd learned a horrible lesson, I scooped him up and carried him towards the street. When we got within fifty feet he scratched me, scrambled down, and ran frantically back upstairs.

"Sandy'll be fine," Rick said from behind. "He'll be chasing tail again in no time."

"I'd feel better if he never went outside."

"I'd feel better if I won the lottery, married Natalie Portman, and woke up with biceps and a bubble butt."

"Very funny," I said.

"*Yes I am.*" He retorted.

"I miss Pebs." I said, with a sigh.

"She's probably stealing toys in kitty heaven," he concurred, as if to reassure me. Then, after a memorial-sized moment of silence, he broke into an off-key rendition of "Memories," from the musical "Cats." And for the first time in eleven days, I laughed.

Sunday, November 17

I have to stop trying to plan my life. I spent a half an hour in the shower yesterday making grandiose statements about what I wanted from the Agape Sweet Sixteen Party I was headed to later in the afternoon: I want to talk to as many people as I can, I want to fully believe I don't need a man, I want five new friends, and I want unconditional love. Only one of these statements came true yesterday, and I had a fantastic time at the party. I may have the power to make great things happen, but sometimes better things happen, in spite of me. I guess it's best to sit back and relax, and let the universe decide what to send me. All I can say is: Thank God I was not in charge yesterday.

As I rode to the beach on my motorcycle at dusk I made a conscious effort not to speed. Under normal social circumstance showing up late wouldn't matter—but this was a church party. It was scheduled to kick off at 4:30, with a sunset ceremony. I really wanted to be there from the start, but I had a client until then. Lucky for me, finding a place to park was a cinch, since I can squeeze my bike into the tiniest spot between two cars. I quickly swung my leg over the bike and took off towards the beach. The group had just gathered around the bonfire when I arrived. I slipped quietly out of my backpack and jacket, and shimmied into the circle of friends I hadn't met yet.

The agenda behind this celebration was to recognize the sixteen-year anniversary of the Agape, and raise funds for a permanent sanctuary. My own agenda was to align myself with spiritually minded young people. Sweet Sixteen celebrations were happening all over town, I chose the beach party at Playa because the bonfire and acoustic music combo sounded like a place to find some cool thirty-something's. When I scanned the crowd to establish the median age range, I knew I was on the money. The first person I laid eyes on was an incredibly hot surfer dude, who stood directly across the pit from me. His magnetic smile sent a message that he was thrilled to see me. As I continued to glance around the ring, I spotted a large number of retro hippies, some eccentric artist types, a handful of lesbians, and a gaggle of yoga geeks—the kind that take veganism a tad too seriously. Mixed in with the people I considered potential friends, were a couple of handsome men. My circuitous gaze wound up back on the extremely cute surfer dude, and to my pleasant surprise he continued to beam at me.

I shined a grin back at him and the hostess announced the beginning of the ceremony. She welcomed us and introduced herself as Mimi. Then she announced her personal intention for this evening: to bring a group of wonderful people together to witness the initiation of change in each other's lives. She hoped we all would leave with an amazing outlook for our future. She walked around the ring as she spoke handing out small pieces of white paper to everyone, and half a dozen pens.

"Write down something you want to rid from your life," she instructed. As people passed around the pens, Mimi stepped towards the fire and announced with thorough resignation, "I'm throwing away APPREHENSION!" She tossed her paper in the flames, and then snagged a kernel of corn from a wooden bowl next to the fire.

"Is popcorn part of our amazing future?" An obvious friend of hers hollered.

"Throw away BAD JOKES," she said, "and I'll give you all the popcorn you can eat,"

"No way," he said, "I won't survive without my sense of humor. But I *will* survive without my wife, so I throw away my FEARS ABOUT DIVORCE."

People cheered as he playfully tossed the paper ball into the air, like a three point shot into the inferno. Mimi told him to grab a kernel and hold onto it, until everyone had a chance to incinerate their worries. One by one, people stepped forward to announce what they wanted to burn. Surfer dude went early on, and threw away DEBT. Someone else threw away ADDICTION. When it came to me I knew exactly what to do. "I throw away SADNESS", I declared, in defiance of Pebbles death. After a self-conscious toss I grabbed a kernel and blended back into my spot. Surfer dude smiled at me again. After the last person had gone, Mimi informed us that the second half of the ceremony was based on a Native American ritual that involves planting a seed. She told us to head towards the shore so we could toss our kernels in the ocean.

"This time," she emphasized, "keep your intentions to yourself. The secret in the seed is between you and the universe—so say it silently."

The group neared the hard packed sand, and one by one we walked to the edge of the water. Each person took a moment to make a wish, hurl the kernel, and step aside to give way to let the next person go. I hung back for a bit, so by the time it was my turn, I knew exactly what I wanted. As an ode to the thing I miss most about Pebs, I wished for unconditional love. Then I threw the kernel, as hard as I could, and watched it kerplunk into the sea. I turned around to find surfer guy walking towards me.

"Hi." He said, with ultra confidence.

"Hi." I answered.

"My name's Steve. What's yours?" I don't know if he detected a sliver of an accent when I said my name, but the next question contained a hint of suspicion. "Where are you from?"

"Boston." I exclaimed with east coast pride.

"NO WAY!" he said, "where?"

"Sudbury."

"NO WAY!!" He exclaimed, "I'm from MARLBORO."

"Really," I asked, taken back by the fact that he'd grown up nearly next door to me.

"That's crazy." He said. "So what do you do out here?"

"I'm a personal trainer."

"NO WAY!!" He said. "I'm a trainer too!"

"Wow, that's cool." I offered nonchalance to contrast his response. "Hey," I added, "You know where I can stash my jacket?"

"What's with the enormous jacket?" He asked.

"I rode my motorcycle here. I don't own a car."

"NO WAY!!!" He bellowed, "I DON'T OWN A CAR EITHER!!"

Steve thought this was another strange coincidence, but the first thought that came to my mind was, "that sucks." I quickly realized that as a sign of sneaking expectation, so I decided to chill and go with the flow.

"I love motorcycles," he continued. "I grew up with them."

"You want to see it?" I proposed.

"Sure," he said. He carried my backpack as we made our way to the street. As soon as we came around the corner of the house, Steve spotted my steel blue Beemer.

"AWESOME!!" He exclaimed, gawking at me, and my bike, alternately. This *is* awesome, I thought to myself, matching his unbridled enthusiasm. I let Steve salivate for ten minutes before I offered him the chance to ride it. He declined—said he didn't have a license. I assumed he meant motorcycle license, and figured he didn't know how to ride, so I let it slide.

When we returned to the bonfire, the party was in full swing. My eyes adjusted as the last hue of purple light turned to night. Wispy charcoal-colored clouds spotted the sky and hid the stars, but the bulging ellipse of an almost full moon rose swiftly above the horizon. Its subtle brilliance let me inconspicuously study Steve's face for the first time. He had happy eyes, and a smile that flashed the world, "Welcome." His broad frame stood at least a foot taller than mine, and I couldn't help but notice that his bare feet were as narrow as they were long enough to surf on. I also spotted a U.S. Marine Corps tattoo on his upper arm; it was the only detail that didn't lend cause for celebration. His sun-bleached hair gave him a beach vibe; the salty curls that wove around his head reminded me less of a Marine and more of a male Medusa. Shadows cast by the moon made his cheekbones seem high, his shoulders wide, and his butt seem "shelf" enough to support a glass of wine. As homage to his derriere, I jokingly threatened to leave my empty glass on his behind, if he refused to refill it for me.

"What would you like?" He asked.

"Whatever you're having." I said.

"Water," he replied, "I don't drink."

"Then I'll have a glass of wine," I said, aware of one similarity I didn't want to discuss at the time. 'I used to be in A.A.' isn't a great statement to make when asking a recovering alcoholic to pour me a drink.

As soon as Steve returned with my beverage, I started to play the name game with him. When further investigation proved we'd grown up less than ten miles from each other, we focused on overlaps in our experience, to figure out if we'd met before. We immediately established that Steve is the same age as my only brother, and I am the same age as one of his five sisters. Even though he's only two years younger than me, we have zero acquaintances in common because we went to school in different districts. We did discover that his family and mine dined numerous times at the same Irish Pub called Kennedy's. We also found that, at age fourteen, Steve worked at a Burger King right next to the ice rink where I took skating lessons. Strangest of all was the realization that I'd taken my driver's test at the DMV, situated around the corner from where he lived. Chances are I drove past his house on the day I became licensed to drive. It was precisely that tidbit that allowed me to rib him about the fact that he was a motorcycle enthusiast, without a license to ride.

"When are you going to get your motorcycle license?" I asked him.

"I lost my license because of a D.U.I." He replied with zero hesitation, and a dash of remorse. Then he clarified, "Actually, it was two D.U.I.'s."

Cow-a-bonga! Steve was the *perfect* bad boy for me: rehabilitated! "How long you been sober?" I dared to ask.

"Two and a half years," he said. "I get my license back in six months," he added. Then instead of going off on his own tawdry tangent, he listened to my tale, which started off with, but was not limited to, details about the death of my cat. He heard my ordeal, offered just the right amount of belated condolence, and then convinced me to switch gears.

"I saw you throw SADNESS in the fire. So…say something happy." He prodded.

"I'm almost done with my book," I offered.

"What are you reading?"

"Actually, I'm writing it," I said. Then I smirked at my own pretension.

"What's it about?"

"It's a tale of search for love and enlightenment."

"Here's to a happy ending." Without missing a beat he leaned over to kiss me. It was a fairly insignificant peck on the cheek, but it felt like fire and ice on my face, and made me crave another. As luck would have it, I waited many hours for smooch number two. In the meantime, Steve and I huddled together in front of the bonfire as I sang along with the guitar player, whose acoustic music eventually charmed the stars into revealing themselves.

After my second glass of wine, Steve and I spent a half an hour jumping on the trampoline inside a blow up castle in the sand. My heart inflated with every bounce. I don't know if it was because of this sense of security, or in spite of it, but something told me I should resist the temptation to sleep with him, if and when he invited me to see his apartment that was down the street. By the time midnight rolled around, Steve and I were attached at the hip, and I knew without a doubt I would see him again. As the party wound down, we lay side by side on a futon, listened to the sound of the sea and took in whiffs of wind, filled with the scent of burning embers. When Steve invited me to check out his place, I refused, for the sake of doing things differently. I knew he was going to be my next boyfriend, and didn't want to give it up on our first date. Don't get me wrong, I was totally excited by him, but I owe it to myself to take things slow. Of course, I didn't want to leave the party empty handed, so I took advantage of one last nuzzle to get a feel for his anatomy—a taste of what was to come, eventually. I leaned forward, ran my hand along his thigh and stopped when I arrived at his button fly. The next time he kissed me, I swiped him. Low and behold I got exactly what I wanted: indication that this boy was blessed. A few kisses later I clearly declared that I didn't want to go any further. Then I prayed I'd see him again soon.

Apparently "tonight" wasn't soon enough, since Steve called this morning to thank me for an incredible time, which would've been really unoriginal if we'd gone all the way. Since we didn't, it was sweet. I agreed to meet him again, for dinner tonight. When I headed to his place at three, I had every intention of holding on to my celibacy. Fortunately—depending on how you look at it—I realized that twelve hours of abstinence had already set him apart from the rest. So when Steve opened the door, drew me inside, flashed his spectacular grin and kissed me, I opted to let the universe decide. The universe told me to let my guard down. So I obeyed, and got laid before dinner. For heaven's sake, I think I found myself another boyfriend! Let's hope this one's for good.

Sunday, February 2, 2003

Twelve days until Valentine's Day and I couldn't be more confused about love. Most of the other aspects of my life are sizzling right now; I just landed two new clients, I'm auditioning again, and I'm training for my first triathlon. Unfortunately, every relationship I developed last year has fizzled or completely disappeared. The pause in the conversation with God is my fault. The "end of the run" with Rick is not—he's moving—but it makes me feel lame all the same. As for the demise of a relationship with Steve, I'm not sure who to blame.

That's why I ended a three month hiatus and went back to Agape this morning. I knew my return to the sanctuary wouldn't alter Rick's plan to abandon me, but I thought it might strengthen the fledgling bond I have with God, and clarify the situation with Steve. The first thing I asked as I began to pray was: why can't all my relationships be as solid as the one I have with me? Lately the self-sufficient zone

I'm in has provided me with so much unconditional love, I no longer feel like I need a guy, or a deity.

Who am I kidding? When it comes to Steve I need him to need me. So far, our interaction has been even-keeled, to say the least. I don't know what it means. The slow and steady pace has thrown me for a loop; I usually fall in love quick, but that hasn't been the case with him. I can't decide. In many ways, he's the perfect mate: super friendly, positive, athletic, and hard working, he has huge heart, and a knack for not pushing my buttons. The problem is: he doesn't push my buttons—I don't have the same roller coaster sense of excitement or frantic anticipation that typically escorts my new man.

Maybe it's because we haven't been on any fancy dates yet. I discovered early on that Steve's finances are pretty tight, which is understandable for a guy who's only been here for a year. And while he did take me out to a nice restaurant on our first date, I've pretty much had to cover most of our outings since. We seem to have a great time no matter what we do, but a typical date consists of luscious sex and a trip to Blockbuster, not always in that order. My all time favorite excursion happened when we borrowed a couple of beach cruisers from a neighbor, and biked to Marina Del Rey. Like a couple of teenagers, we peddled around the docks, and flirted for hours. Steve's currency deficiencies stood out to me as we peddled past Max's boat slip, but I quickly squashed that bitter bug and focused on his trillion dollar smile instead. With all the fun we had just cruising around, his new-to-LA-poverty didn't bother me. Steve's east coast whit and thick Boston accent, reminded me of my childhood; the nostalgia made me want to pop a wheelie, and squeal, "I love you, Stevie Wonderboy!!

That would've been weird though, since we haven't even hinted at the "L word" yet. It seriously worries me. With Valentine's Day around the corner, it's time to commit or quit. The countdown began when Steve borrowed my new car for a job interview on Tuesday, but rudely refused my invitation to stay. He had a boot camp class to teach on the beach the next day and didn't want to bother me for an early ride. Unfortunately, it rained, which meant no work for the poor guy. In an attempt to distract him from lack-of-funds frustration, I stopped by his place later in the day, to offer him a rainy day romp in the sack. To my horror, he wasn't in the mood. Our first uncomfortable moment, and I did not handle it well. Personal experience with Max's M.S. driven impotence intensified the situation. It made me wonder if Steve also had some kind of *real* problem. Steve made it out to be nothing. He said the only *problem* was that he needed find more work, but he promised to make it up to me.

I had high hopes for our Friday night, and the first couple hours were pure romance. In the midst of bachelor squalor, Steve stirred up a delicious Italian dinner. Then we spooned and watched "Sex and Lucia". Halfway through the movie, we were about to make out, when a rat-a-tat-tat interrupted us. Without hesitation, Steve opened the door to a sniveling acquaintance. The guy had just left his live-in girlfriend, and needed a place to stay, so Steve, with his penchant for generosity, turned off the tube and invited him in. I slept in my own bed that night.

The straw that broke the camels back happened yesterday. In a failed attempt to make it up to me, Steve called early in the evening to invite me to join him and his friends at a strip club, a "bon voyage" for a Marine buddy of his, who ships off to Iraq tonight. I had no interest in toasting the war, or the naked dancing girls, so I curtly refused the invitation. As soon as I hung up the phone, misgivings flooded my brain. I decided to share some of them with Steve, in an email:

Dear Steve:

You appreciate a stripper's tease, but for some reason sex doesn't always appeal to you. I'm beginning to believe I'm not your type. Don't worry—I'm sure there's someone out there who has big boobs, and a car you can borrow.

That's the best explanation I have for not answering the phone tomorrow. Sorry it didn't work out.

I hit send and exhaled the rush of fear and frustration that hounded me all week. Then a thunderous thought hit me: I just broke up with a guy via *email*. And it was easy. No cutting, no crying, no crucifying. Guess he's not the man for me. A hundred percent sure of that conviction, I faded into slumber.

My assurance slipped to seventy percent by the time I woke up at dawn. I lay there and ruminated for an hour on how and when Steve would respond, and how long I should wait to check my inbox. Obsession prevailed over logic; I logged on five times before I gave up and went to the early service at Agape. When I walked into the sanctuary, my confidence about calling it off was at fifty-fifty and falling fast. My head was so congested with doubt the Rev. couldn't get a word in edgewise. I don't recall a single word he said.

I do, however, remember the benediction. Since I've been away, certain improvements have been made to Agape's auditorium to accommodate the expanding congregation. The speaker's image is now projected onto two giant screens, so people can see no matter where they sit. I appreciated this addition, not because it helped me listen, but because it gave me the confidence to sing and pray along with the telecast lyrics. The visual aide was the only thing that held my attention long enough to distract me from the ominous sense of destruction that wrapped itself around my prayer-deprived head.

At the end of the sermon, the benediction flashed across the screen. I read the words voraciously. When I rushed through the exit to check my messages after the service, one particular stanza stayed with me; "I am one with the infinite rhythm of life. It flows through me in love, and harmony, and peace. There's no fear, no doubt, and no uncertainty in my mind." *No doubt*, I repeated, as my cell phone announced, "One new message." *No fear*, I whispered, as the voice mail said, "Message left Sunday, at, nine forty-five."

"Hi, it's Steve." The recording began. "I don't know what to make of your email— I guess you don't like strip clubs. Fine with me, I'm not into them either. Anyway, give me a call when you get this. I'll talk to you then."

"No uncertainty," I said, as I wrestled with the temptation to call him back. What's the matter with this guy? Doesn't he know I broke up with him? What more can I say, besides I want my helmet back. Then, like lightning, another spontaneous thought struck: I *should* head over to Steve's, which *is* right down the street, to explain my irritation in person, and confiscate the spare helmet I loaned him, before he damages it in retaliation. I scrolled threw my quick dials to find "Steve", and punched "send".

"Hello," he said.

"Hey it's me. I'm right up the street. I want to come by and grab my things."

"What things?" He asked.

"My helmet, and my toiletries."

"Okay. I'm home. Come on by." He sounded confused.

"Fine," I said, with an angry sigh.

Steve had just stepped out of the shower and wore only a towel when he opened the door. I glared at him. "You washed off the smut, I see."

"What?" he said.

"Where's my stuff?" I asked.

"I'll tell you where your stuff is, if you tell me where your head is at."

"I'm not ready for a serious relationship." I said.

"Then lighten up."

"I need to know where we stand."

"I'm standing right here, naked. I thought that was enough for you."

"Is that what this is, in your mind, a good time?"

"I've had a great time," he said wholeheartedly.

"I need more. I want a commitment."

"I'm not ready for that", he said defensively. That was all I needed to hear before I gathered up my gear and fled. Years of tears welled up as I said goodbye.

That was four hours ago. I've been trying to figure out where I went wrong ever since. The more I think about it, the guiltier I feel. I think I made the wrong decision. I broke up with Steve because *I'm* afraid of commitment. I'm terrified I won't get as much love as I give. I'm afraid to invest because relationships end, and last time I was left with less than I brought. Or was I?

The pain I felt at the end with Max brought all sorts of amazing change. Why should I complain about it? The end of that affair was the start of a new perspective, one that's supposed to be about zero expectations and infinite love. I've been perusing the rules of my philosophy and think I finally understand the root of today's catastrophe: I tried to manipulate Steve, but the only person I can control is me. And last night's tantrum tells me, I still have a way to go when it comes to self-restraint.

In an attempt to focus on the positive, I made a list of personal abundance that included everything I have infinite access to, and control over, these days. Love, money, and orgasms were at the top of the list. As I began to see the incredible levels of self-sufficiency I've achieved in the last year, it made me wonder: why should I worry about Steve's ability to provide for me? I have everything I really need.

So the real question is: do I love Steve?

I figured God would probably ignore me after my less than attentive engagement at church, so I turned to Rick for some answers. "I need to talk." I declared with urgency.

"I need coffee," he said.

"You sound stressed."

"My place is a mess and I'm tired of packing."

"Packing what?" I asked suspiciously.

"I'm getting ready to move."

"I thought you were undecided."

"It's time." He sighed. "I've been here fifteen years, and LA's been slamming me lately. New York is where my investors are, my advisors, my family…"

"You're leaving, and you don't have the decency to tell me face to face?" I pointed one finger at him, and three at me—for dumping Steve in an email.

"Would you accept a honey-spiced latte, as an apology?" He asked.

"Meet me at the Literati in ten." I said, with reticent acceptance of his lousy news.

I served him my bad news as soon as he got there. "I broke up with Steve yesterday."

"What!?" He exclaimed.

"I don't think he's the man for me."

"Are you crazy? He's totally in love with you."

Yes I am, I thought. "No he's not." I said.

"How do you explain your birthday?" Rick asked, as a reminder of the wonderful time Steve had shown me on my thirtieth. I'm not one to exaggerate birthdays, but this year, after everything I'd been through, I developed high hopes for the "Big 3-0". Much to my surprise, Steve arranged for me to receive a 90-minute massage right before the tattoo I had scheduled in the afternoon. He then escorted me to the ink parlor, and held my hand when the pain made me wince. I told Steve that the tat on my back symbolized my last name, which means "dragonfly" in Czech. I did not tell him the significance of getting that particular tattoo on my thirtieth birthday. It represents my belief that I'll relinquish my maiden name at some point during the next decade. To mention the word marriage to Steve seemed strange, since we hadn't even broached the L-word yet. So I didn't admit the secret meaning, but the fact that he was there meant more to me then he could ever know. Later that evening, Steve accompanied me and six of my friends to my favorite Italian restaurant, where he generously paid for our portion of the bill. I was extremely touched by his extraordinary efforts, and told him so.

"That *was* a special occasion," I said, as I chastised myself for forgetting it. To nail his point, Rick continued. "What about when I saw the two of you standing outside that yoga class?"

"What about it?" I asked.

"Remember when I told you I honked and waved, but you guys didn't see me?"

"Vaguely."

"You were so into each other, I couldn't get a honk in edgewise."

"Sorry." I said.

"Apologize to Steve, not me. What'd he do that was so offensive anyway?"

"He invited me to a strip club."

"Did you go?"

"*No.*"

"Oh—you prefer men who care less about sex", he said, in reference to my biggest complaint about my ex.

"No."

"Then what's the problem?"

"I'm tired of guessing." I said. "I want to know where my love life is headed."

"Then date a psychic!" He yelled.

Suddenly, I knew what I needed to do. "I should give him another chance."

"Yeah, like I should "let" Pam Anderson in my pants."

"You really put things in perspective, Rick. I'm gonna miss your sophomoric humor."

"And I'm going to miss your masochistic ideas of a good time." He said.

"You still don't like running, huh?"

"Running is fine. It's your self-analysis that drives me crazy. Do me a favor—call your boyfriend and tell him I said he can take it from here."

"I still get you till the end of the month though, right?"

"Sure, come on by and help me pack whenever you want." He said, with a devilish grin. Then he crumpled his napkin in his cup, a sign it was time to leave. Standing on the sidewalk at Wilshire and Bundy I couldn't help but think about the countless times Rick and I had parted here, two blocks north of his place, and one block south of mine. It felt so much harder this time.

"I can't believe you're leaving." I whined.

"I can't believe I'm breathing, after all the times I've had the wind knocked out of me in the last six months. But hey, life goes on, whether we like it or not." We kissed each other's cheek, and hugged goodbye. I started to cry.

"Hey," he said, forcing me to lookup at him. Then he plucked a bulb from the Rhododendron bush beside us and placed it in my palm. "This bud's for you."

That was the last thing he said before he headed home to finish boxing up his stuff, and I headed home to box my own ears, as punishment for bad behavior. Slapping myself upside the head, qualifies as self-abuse—and I'm not allowed to do that anymore. So here I sit, feeling like shit, and missing Rick and Steve. I can't believe I'm going to be alone again. The anniversary of my miserable move from Max's is right around the corner; looks like I'll be sad and single this Valentine's Day too.

That kind of thinking is bad; better distract myself with a list of the reasons why Steve is the ideal man for me. In addition to his Greek god good looks, his happy outlook on life, and all the things we have in common, there are many reasons I should believe Steve's money trouble is temporary. He gets up at the crack of dawn to train his clients, who pay him a fraction of the fee I charge, because he'll do whatever it takes to make his personal training business a reality. He also works a second job that he despises, to supplement his income while he searches for more clients. More notable than his current lack of funds is his confidence, and his ability to make light of his situation.

Case in point: a few weeks ago I arrived at Steve's place on a Saturday afternoon and told him I was "starving." I wanted to head to the nearest deli, but Steve told me to kick back and relax while he made me a sandwich. I reluctantly agreed, knowing he always had to scrape together his last pennies for food. When he proudly displayed the peanut butter and jelly sandwich I realized he wasn't even remotely ashamed about his lack of money—which made him seem smart, and sexy.

There's also the loving way he talks about his family. Steve's parents, like mine, have been married 36 years, and he adores that fact. He and his five sisters get along magically. Family is the only thing he misses about Massachusetts—one more thing we have in common. It's kind of hard to fathom how much we have in common, and I can't get past the virtual guarantee that everyone who's important to me will adore Steve, when and if they have the chance to meet him. What's not to adore? He's funny, sincere, sober and clear, outgoing, friendly, honest, and how can I forget energetic? I'm pathetic! What have I done? He *is* the one! Am I blind, or just out of my mind? Steve is what I've been fighting to find. This break up was a test! So now the final question is: am I ready to trust in love again?

Saturday, February 15

Valentines Day is done, and love is in the air! Hard to believe, when you consider where my head was at a week ago. Last Saturday, I still wasn't sure what to do about Steve. I didn't know if I owed him a phone call, an ear full, an apology, or all of the above. I wanted to be mature, yet demure, in my attempt at reconciliation. But as I struggled to find the perfect words, all I came up with were phrases of frustration. I continued to worry about Steve's income, and the thought that he might leave me love lost and forlorn. By the time Saturday arrived, I'd marooned myself on an island of self-pity, created a shield of hostility, and was surviving on crap TV and cigarettes. I was lying in bed with the shades drawn, watching Sleepless in Seattle when Steve phoned at 4pm.

"Hey it's me." He said.

"Hi," I replied—a little too cool.

"Listen," he said, without the dance. "I don't know what happened last week, but I think we should give it another chance."

"You do?" I asked, with a timbre of trepidation. After my incendiary and insulting email, I knew one false step could easily change his mind, so I combined arousal with restraint and said, "I think so too."

"Come over," he commanded.

"Don't you think we should talk about it?" I asked.

"Only if we do it face to face, I want to see you."

He opened his heart to me when I least deserved it, and all I could say was, "I think we should take it slow. After everything we said last week…."

"'We', didn't say anything," he corrected. "You got pissed and said some things you shouldn't have said. But I'm used to irrational females—I have five sisters."

"Are you calling me irrational?" I inquired.

"No. I'm calling you to ask you to quit acting crazy, and come over and play with me."

"I don't think we should rush back into things."

"I haven't heard from you in a week! I'm tired of idling. A man has needs, you know." Steve's communication skills seemed obviously influenced by sisters; I've never known a man who was so in touch with his feelings. This muscle-bound former-marine was turning out to be a big ol' ball of sensitivity, it made me want to race to his place, to make up, and make out with him. Two more minutes of conversation and I was sold; I hung up the phone and rushed out the door. Steve opened his front door as soon as I placed my foot on the top stair, as if he'd been watching for me through the peephole.

"Sorry about the email." I said, sincerely.

"No problem," he replied. Then he leaned down and engaged me in a long and luscious kiss. That was the end of our lover's spat, and a new beginning for my love affair with Steve.

I was so sure Valentines Day would inspire us to say 'I love you'. When I saw how Steve handled my obnoxious email, and realized he doesn't have the capacity or the drive to push my buttons, I knew he should be the first recipient of my truest love. The time has come for me to try it—I've successfully offered true love to myself, and my cats, but I haven't experimented with other human beings yet. I had high hopes for our Valentine's date, but I'm also hyper aware of not rushing things with Steve. I don't want to repeat my history of falling madly in love within the first week, only to discover I have no idea what I'm getting into. This time I promised not to say it first. I definitely have those feelings, but I want to marinate in them for awhile, until I'm sure they're real. So I was prepared to say 'I love you' last night, but needed Steve to initiate. And I'm happy to say, I'm perfectly okay with the fact that it didn't happen. It was an incredible evening anyway.

My bachelor apartment without a kitchen didn't keep me from cooking a romantic meal. Steve and I enjoyed a dinner of crab legs, stuffed artichoke hearts, wild rice, and fruit parfaits, all assembled in the borrowed apartment of my neighbor Kat, who gave me permission to use her kitchen while she's out of town on a cruise. Steve, who hasn't had a drink in several years, brought me a lovely bottle of Chardonnay as his gourmet contribution. After dinner he announced he had a surprise for me. Then he disappeared down the hall to my apartment, changed clothes and his character, and returned as "David", my personal masseuse. He spread a flannel sheet across Kat's dinning room table, put a CD of loves songs in the boom box he snaked from my place, cracked open a bottle of ylang-ylang massage oil, and proceeded to give me an hour-long body rub. One thing led to another and I'm embarrassed to admit, we made love on top of Kat's dining room table.

All in all, it was an amorous day for me. At the end of the night, as I stood alone in my bathroom brushing my teeth, I took the opportunity to whisper "I love you" in the mirror. I didn't miss hearing it from Steve because I felt surrounded by it. Love radiated through the room as I smiled at myself in the mirror, when Steve wrapped his arms around me as we fell asleep, and when Sandy curled himself in a fuzzy ball at our feet. It was the same love that hovered above me last week, when I was depressed and stressed about being alone. But last week I wasn't looking for love, I was looking for pity; opening my eyes to the abundance of love has made all the difference.

After all, true love is not defined by words, but action. Steve hasn't said it yet, but he clearly expressed it, when he accepted my apology without asking why I said the wretched things I said. If he'd asked for an explanation, I would've been forced to admit it had nothing to do with him. My worry about his money trouble has to do with my own financial struggles. Likewise, my concern about Steve going to the strip club had to do with my notion that strippers have big boobs (an area where I'm lacking) and Steve's desire to see them must mean he's dissatisfied with me. Even my desire to hear him to say 'I love you' has to do with my fear that I may not be loveable. Lately I've received a clear message from Steve, that I am loveable. More importantly, he loves me for who I am, foibles included. So I've decided to make Steve my guinea pig for receiving unconditional love from me. I hope he's ready.

"If a person has never encountered love toward himself or herself from any quarter, it is very sad. But if that person can meet even one person who will show unconditional love—simply acceptance and compassion—it is bound to have an impact. Because there is a seed in himself, this act of love will start to ripen that seed."   ~ Dalai Lama

Friday, August 26, 2005

Time flies when you're having fun. My last entry was in 2003! I can't believe how far Steve and I have come. Now I can laugh about how worried I was back then, that we hadn't said 'I love you' yet. These days we say it so much I take it for granted. It's easy to say it several times a day, since we live together.

A year and a half ago, I said goodbye to my single and moved into a one-bedroom apartment with Steve and Sandy. Three months later, on Valentine's Day we adopted a kitty from the pound and named her Lucy. The love affair in our house has been a relative breeze ever since. Lucy has a bad habit of hissing at Sandy, but she seems to be mellowing out as she learns how much power love can have over anger. As far as Steve and me, we have arguments too, but I've never had an easier time getting along with another human being. Steve offers me the best example of how to love I've ever had. His affection is perfection on the worst days. On the best days it brightens our fun so much that I have to wear shades.

Just kidding—the shades I wear indoors protect my eyes from the flashy accoutrements I inherited from Rick when he left. On the first day of our cohabitation, Steve expressed out-right distaste for the electric orange items that dot the landscape of our living room. I kindly reminded him that Rick's generosity allowed us to furnish our apartment, for the rock bottom price of free, and until we have the money for a color-correct upgrade, we should be grateful we don't sit on the floor to watch TV. As far as I'm concerned, the orange décor is a bright and beautiful contribution to the ever-improving quality of life I'm living these days. Of course, the most extravagant aspect of my living situation is that I'm consistently reminded how much Steve loves me, which helps me love myself, which in turn, helps me love Steve—like a circle of supportive continuity.

I've never felt so much support from another person, other than my parents. Speaking of my parents, I can't believe how much assistance I've received from them lately.

I suppose my positive perspective helps me see all the loving things they do for me, but then again, the proof is in the pudding. In January this year, my parents unequivocally blessed, and offered to pay for, our upcoming wedding.

On our second anniversary Steve got down on one knee, and asked, "Will you marry me?"

"Of course I will!" was my auto-response. If we follow in our parent's footsteps, our marriage will go the distance; his folks, and mine, celebrate their 38th anniversaries this year. I expect to celebrate ours on October 14th, 2043. Living as husband and wife for thirty-eight years must be worth the strife. It requires the same drive you need to survive to a ripe old age, the only difference is that marriage is made up of a team, and as long as we continue to love each other (and both live a long time), we won't have to go it alone.

So far we've been a great team when it comes to planning the wedding. My parent's generous offer to foot the bill took the money worries out of matrimony, although Steve and I still find cause to argue about how much we spend on groceries each week. The only other conflicts we've faced, as of late, are due to the monster I'll call Groomzilla. Steve has preconceived this wedding more than I have; the flowers, invitations, decorations, he wants to have a say in all of it. I get a kick out of his interest in the details, but sometimes I wish he'd relax and let me handle it. Last week I told him I was going to a crafts store to buy clay for the place cards I want to make. Exasperated by my attempt to exclude him, Steve requested that I *please* wait for him to get home from work, so he could join me. Then he insisted on assisting with the place card assembly, every step of the way. Wow, I thought, I wish he'd just leave this stuff to me. Sometimes, being part of team is more annoying than it is helpful. I recently assigned a couple major tasks to Steve; maybe I'll get lucky and overwhelm him enough that he'll leave my tasks alone.

Yesterday a friend asked about engagement photos, a detail that's somehow slipped my mind when it comes to the endless number of appointments we have to make. I asked Steve if he thought we should bother, and told him I didn't really care. "What do you mean, you don't CARE?" He asked incredulously. The conversation ended abruptly when I told him, if he cares SO MUCH, he can take charge and call the photographer. Despite the minor power struggle that's developed between us, I find Steve's excitement about the wedding to be sweet, if not a little neurotic. After that short and somewhat heated discussion about the engagement photos, I considered the alternative. How would I feel if Steve took the average guy's passive approach to wedding planning? Steve's desire to help me is one of his greatest traits. So I told him I love him, and I'm happy to have my picture taken with him even if it *is* a setup shot in a posed embrace on the beach. I think he's sufficiently overwhelmed with other projects at this point; we'll probably do without the extra photo shoot.

As with any couple in a long-term relationship, I occasionally question whether Steve is the perfect mate for me. It happens on rare occasions, when his neuroses don't jive with mine. There are many more moments when I know that Steve is the closet thing I could ever find to a perfect match. We shared a special moment like that two and a half years ago, on his twenty-eighth birthday. Steve's not one to celebrate birthdays, so we kept it low key. As contribution to the small party his roommate threw him, I brought homemade cupcakes (concocted in the borrowed kitchen of my neighbor Kat—who coincidentally has no clue about the debauchery that went on the last time she gave me her keys). In addition to sugary birthday fare, I brought Steve a crayon-drawn card, and a cool T-shirt.

When I arrived at his place, he was getting ready for the party. I interrupted the careful application of his hair gel (another example of what happens to a guy who's raised with five sisters) to ask if we could take a walk down to the beach and watch the sunset. One last coif and he agreed. He held my hand as we strolled two blocks to the beach, landing in the exact spot where we'd met, six months earlier. We plunked down in the cool, evening sand, and I handed him the card. It read: "Here's a list of the things I promise to do for you on your birthday each year: Make you a homemade cake, tell you how great you are, remind you how thankful I am that fate brought us together, and love you like nobody else can."

He made reference to the very last line, "Is this true?"

Refusing to say it first, I denied his inquisition, "You're not supposed to ask me that."

"Well do you?" he asked, ignoring my imploring.

"Yes! But I want you to say it first!" I felt like I was in grade school.

"I love you too." He said.

"THEN WHY DID IT TAKE US SO LONG TO SAY IT?"

He paused to consider the answer. Then, in a perfect Boston accent, he replied, "Nerds of a featha flawk togetha." I nearly died and went to heaven. It was classic: Steve, ribbing me, as I tried to take life seriously. He has a wonderful knack for lightening me up, if you know what I mean. But his comment made me have to pee.

"You're pretty funny," I gushed, as we rushed back to his apartment.

"You're pretty awesome," he replied.

So who cares if it took us six months to say 'I love you'? That's twenty-five times longer than average for me. I'd like to think our relationship will last twenty-five times longer than the two-year affairs that I'm used to. We're at two and a half years and counting; counting the days until our marriage, that is. One of the greatest lessons I've learned from our engagement is that life is never perfect, even when you're in the midst of planning a happy ending. Thank God for the minor mayhem of life—if it weren't for the imperfections of my day-to-day experience, I might feel pressure to try and get everything right. To prove I can embrace that I'm not perfect, I got drunk last night while we watched "Spinal Tap". After three cocktails and a bunch of bong hits, I started to say some inappropriate, and sexually explicit, things to Steve. He loved every minute of it. What can I say? Sometimes I wish he would judge me more. It might help me get my shit together in a couple of ways. For instance, I'd really like to quit smoking pot every day; remember to pray every day; increase the amount of community service I do; decrease the amount of lip service I give Steve; and learn to appreciate how lucky I am, to have a loving, creative, strong and committed, generally above-average Me to fall back on, when I just can't seem to be perfect. More than anything, I want to dream big, walk tall, and learn to love the small and somewhat insignificant achievements I make each day. So here's to completing 120 place card settings for the wedding with Steve this week. And cheers, to many years of homeland security.

It's the end of an arduous war.

Acknowledgements

To Wonder Woman, from Super Girl, thanks for your early encouragement. To the Genius, e.b., you are the sweetest muse a girl could ask for. To soul sista Myanna, you are Lightning's first fan, and my eternal friend. To the entire supporting cast, thank you for shaping me. And to my Big Love, Stevo, you are the sun that sustains my universe; you brighten my days and lighten my life. I'll always remember that kernel.

Made in the USA
Charleston, SC
28 August 2011